MYSTERIES
& MARVELS
OF
NATURE

PART 1

MYSTERIES & MARVELS
OF
OCEAN
LIFE

Rick Morris

Consultant Dr David Billet
Institute of Oceanographic Sciences

Designed by Anne Sharples
and Lesley Davey

Illustrated by Ian Jackson,
David Quinn, Chris Shields (Wilcock Riley)
and Nigel Frey

Cartoons by John Shackell

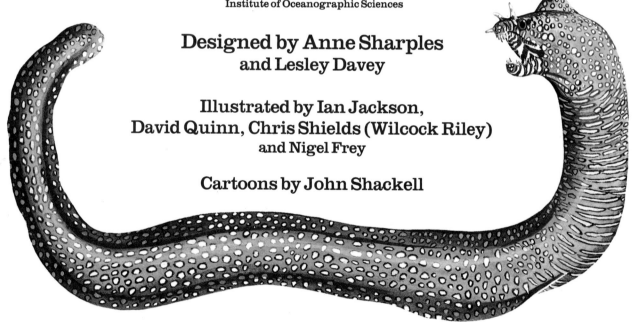

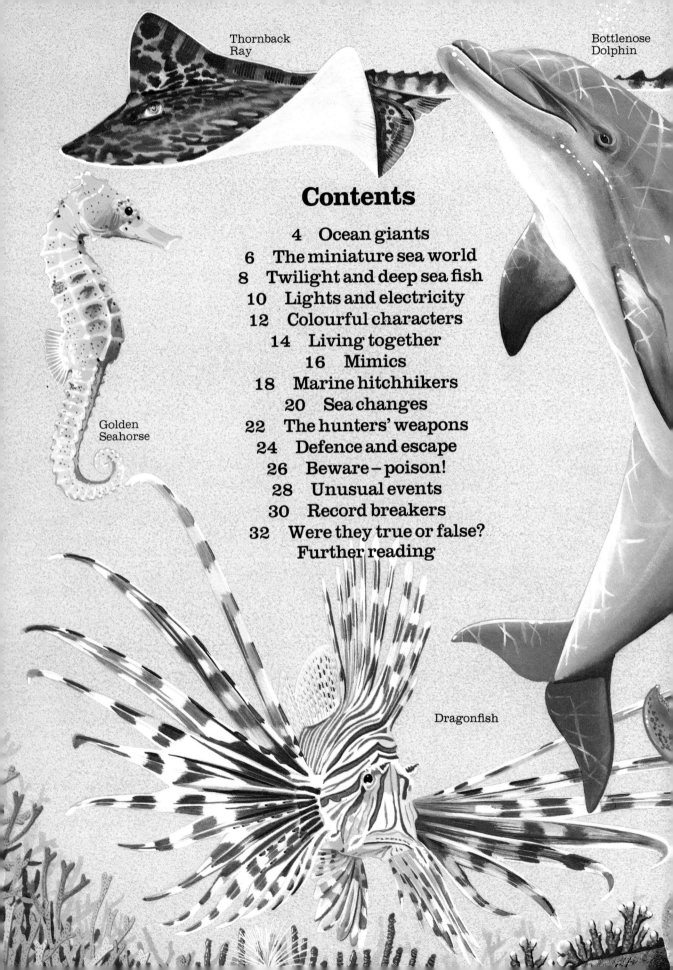

Thornback
Ray

Bottlenose
Dolphin

Contents

Golden
Seahorse

Dragonfish

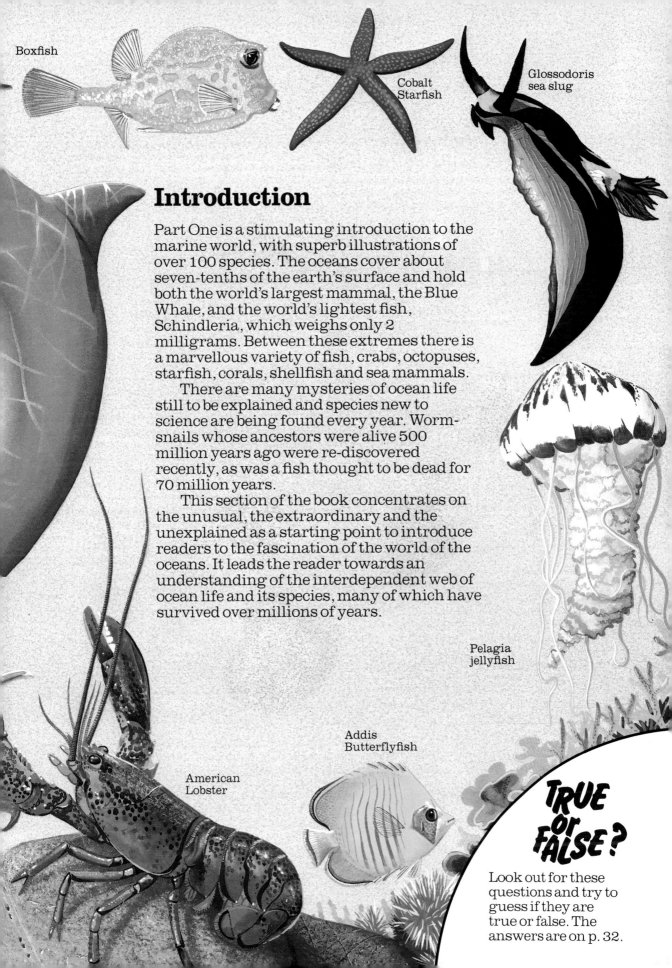

Boxfish

Cobalt
Starfish

Glossodoris
sea slug

Introduction

Part One is a stimulating introduction to the
marine world, with superb illustrations of
over 100 species. The oceans cover about
seven-tenths of the earth's surface and hold
both the world's largest mammal, the Blue
Whale, and the world's lightest fish,
Schindleria, which weighs only 2
milligrams. Between these extremes there is
a marvellous variety of fish, crabs, octopuses,
starfish, corals, shellfish and sea mammals.

There are many mysteries of ocean life
still to be explained and species new to
science are being found every year. Worm-
snails whose ancestors were alive 500
million years ago were re-discovered
recently, as was a fish thought to be dead for
70 million years.

This section of the book concentrates on
the unusual, the extraordinary and the
unexplained as a starting point to introduce
readers to the fascination of the world of the
oceans. It leads the reader towards an
understanding of the interdependent web of
ocean life and its species, many of which have
survived over millions of years.

Pelagia
jellyfish

Addis
Butterflyfish

American
Lobster

TRUE
or
FALSE?

Look out for these
questions and try to
guess if they are
true or false. The
answers are on p. 32.

Ocean giants

The largest creatures in the world live in the sea. The biggest of them – the whales – must rise to the surface to breathe air but fish can breathe underwater.

The enormous Blue Whale ▶

The female Blue Whale is the largest animal alive today. She grows to over 30 metres long and weighs about 160 tonnes. This is about 25 times heavier than the world's largest land animal, the male African Elephant.

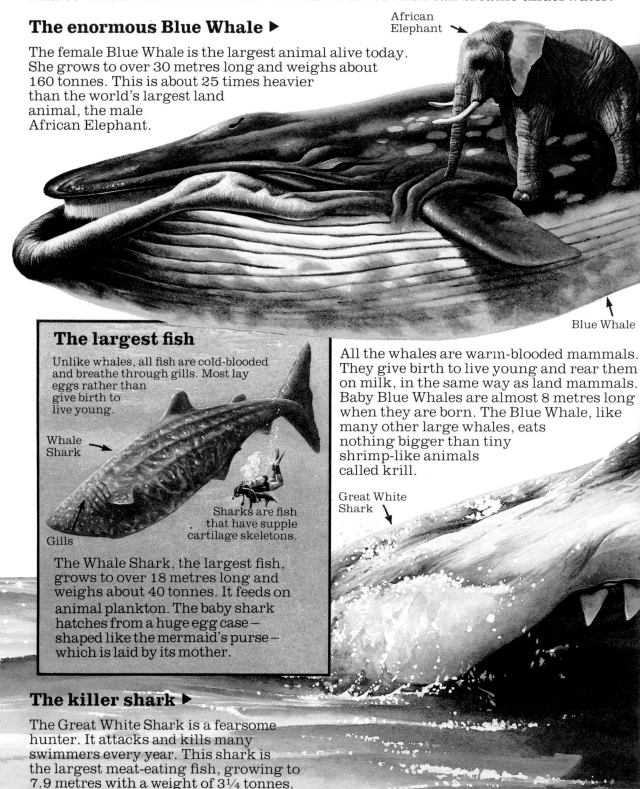

African Elephant ↘

Blue Whale

The largest fish

Unlike whales, all fish are cold-blooded and breathe through gills. Most lay eggs rather than give birth to live young.

Whale Shark →

Gills

Sharks are fish that have supple cartilage skeletons.

The Whale Shark, the largest fish, grows to over 18 metres long and weighs about 40 tonnes. It feeds on animal plankton. The baby shark hatches from a huge egg case – shaped like the mermaid's purse – which is laid by its mother.

All the whales are warm-blooded mammals. They give birth to live young and rear them on milk, in the same way as land mammals. Baby Blue Whales are almost 8 metres long when they are born. The Blue Whale, like many other large whales, eats nothing bigger than tiny shrimp-like animals called krill.

Great White Shark ↘

The killer shark ▶

The Great White Shark is a fearsome hunter. It attacks and kills many swimmers every year. This shark is the largest meat-eating fish, growing to 7.9 metres with a weight of 3¼ tonnes.

Supersaurus, an extinct dinosaur, was larger than the Blue Whale.

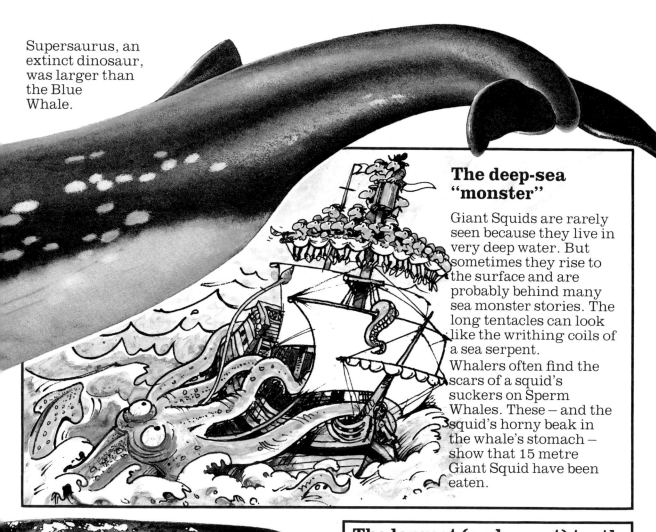

The deep-sea "monster"

Giant Squids are rarely seen because they live in very deep water. But sometimes they rise to the surface and are probably behind many sea monster stories. The long tentacles can look like the writhing coils of a sea serpent.

Whalers often find the scars of a squid's suckers on Sperm Whales. These — and the squid's horny beak in the whale's stomach — show that 15 metre Giant Squid have been eaten.

The largest (and rarest) turtle

Pacific Leatherback Turtle

The Pacific Leatherback Turtle is the largest reptile in the sea, growing to a length of 2.13 metres and a weight of 453 kilos. The female crawls ashore at night to lay her eggs in a deep hole which she digs in the sand.

TRUE or FALSE?

Big turtles cry.

The miniature sea world

The oceans are full of plankton – tiny plants and animals which drift in the sea. Most plankton is too small to be seen without a microscope, so the background to these pages shows magnified views. Each type of plankton has a distinct shape, often a startling geometric pattern. The young of sea slugs, crabs, starfish, barnacles and many fish start life as plankton, swimming in the surface waters and feeding on each other and the plentiful plant plankton. Ocean currents sweep them to new areas that the adults have not colonised.

Phytoplankton

The grass of the sea ▶

Microscopic ocean plants – phytoplankton – are known as "the grass of the sea" because they form a rich "pasture" on which animal plankton feed. Over 2 million million tonnes of new phytoplankton grows every year, mainly in Spring.

Krill – the food of whales

Krill is a large animal plankton – like a small shrimp – which eats phytoplankton. Many of the huge whales live only on krill, sieving it from the water. A Blue Whale – the largest whale – eats about 4 tonnes of these 6 centimetre shrimps every day.

Krill

Krill eat plant plankton and are then eaten themselves by sea birds, fish, squid, seals and whales.

A pile of baked beans weighing 4 tonnes (the weight of krill a whale eats in one day) would be 5.8 metres high.

The sea slugs and plankton on these pages are not drawn to scale.

6

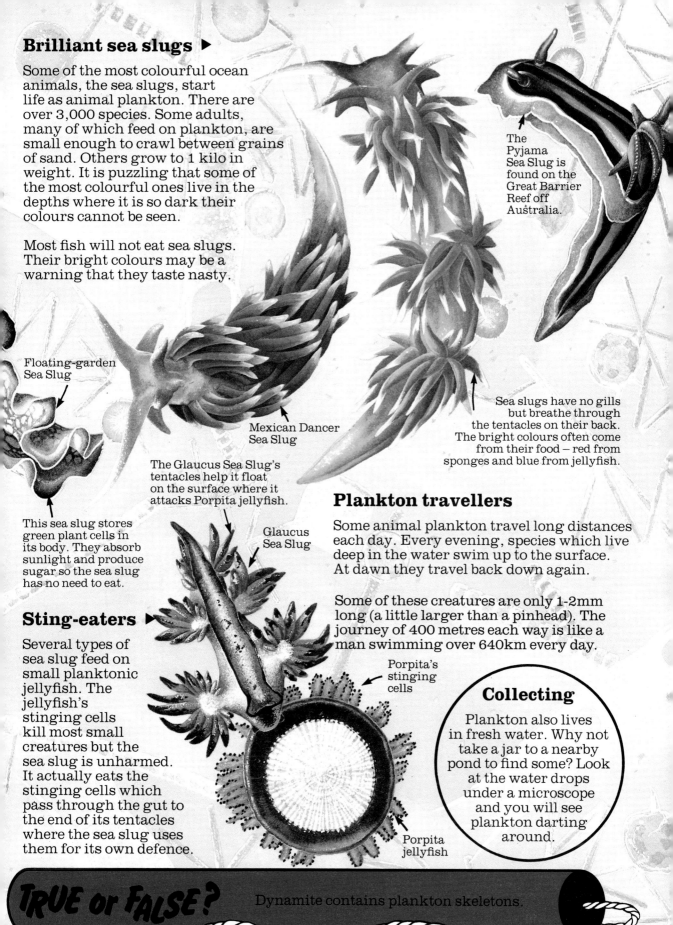

Brilliant sea slugs ▶

Some of the most colourful ocean animals, the sea slugs, start life as animal plankton. There are over 3,000 species. Some adults, many of which feed on plankton, are small enough to crawl between grains of sand. Others grow to 1 kilo in weight. It is puzzling that some of the most colourful ones live in the depths where it is so dark their colours cannot be seen.

Most fish will not eat sea slugs. Their bright colours may be a warning that they taste nasty.

The Pyjama Sea Slug is found on the Great Barrier Reef off Australia.

Floating-garden Sea Slug

Mexican Dancer Sea Slug

Sea slugs have no gills but breathe through the tentacles on their back. The bright colours often come from their food – red from sponges and blue from jellyfish.

This sea slug stores green plant cells in its body. They absorb sunlight and produce sugar so the sea slug has no need to eat.

The Glaucus Sea Slug's tentacles help it float on the surface where it attacks Porpita jellyfish.

Glaucus Sea Slug

Sting-eaters ▶

Several types of sea slug feed on small planktonic jellyfish. The jellyfish's stinging cells kill most small creatures but the sea slug is unharmed. It actually eats the stinging cells which pass through the gut to the end of its tentacles where the sea slug uses them for its own defence.

Porpita's stinging cells

Porpita jellyfish

Plankton travellers

Some animal plankton travel long distances each day. Every evening, species which live deep in the water swim up to the surface. At dawn they travel back down again.

Some of these creatures are only 1-2mm long (a little larger than a pinhead). The journey of 400 metres each way is like a man swimming over 640km every day.

Collecting

Plankton also lives in fresh water. Why not take a jar to a nearby pond to find some? Look at the water drops under a microscope and you will see plankton darting around.

TRUE or FALSE?

Dynamite contains plankton skeletons.

Twilight and deep sea fish

The background to these pages shows how sunlight quickly fades away below the sea surface. The sea 300 – 1,000 metres below the surface is known as the twilight zone. The deep sea below this is totally dark and very cold. No plants live there.

Creatures in the twilight zone and deep sea have developed ingenious ways to survive and to find food.

The Coelacanth produces very few eggs but these hatch internally. Giving birth to live young has probably ensured the species' long survival. It lives at depths of 200-400 metres.

Coelacanth

The unusual stout pectoral fins are very mobile and may be used to manoeuvre over the rocky sea floor.

The peculiar double tail is a feature of primitive fish. Most species alive today, which have evolved more recently, have only a single tail.

Although the Coelacanth was new to scientists, it had long been known to fishermen in the Comoro Islands off Madagascar. They catch one or two every year. The 1938 Coelacanth was a stray. Since then specimens have been caught around the Comoros, 2,900 kilometres (1,800 miles) to the north. The fish's oily flesh is not good to eat but the islanders use the rough scales as sandpaper.

The axe blade shape of its silver body led to the fish's common name of Hatchet Fish.

The re-discovered fish ▲

In 1938, a fish which was thought to have died out 70 million years ago was suddenly re-discovered. Just before Christmas, a trawler brought an odd-looking blue fish into a South African port. Although it was five times longer than a South African port. Although it was five times longer than fossil specimens known to scientists, the 1.6 metre fish was identified as a Coelacanth. Over 80 have since been caught.

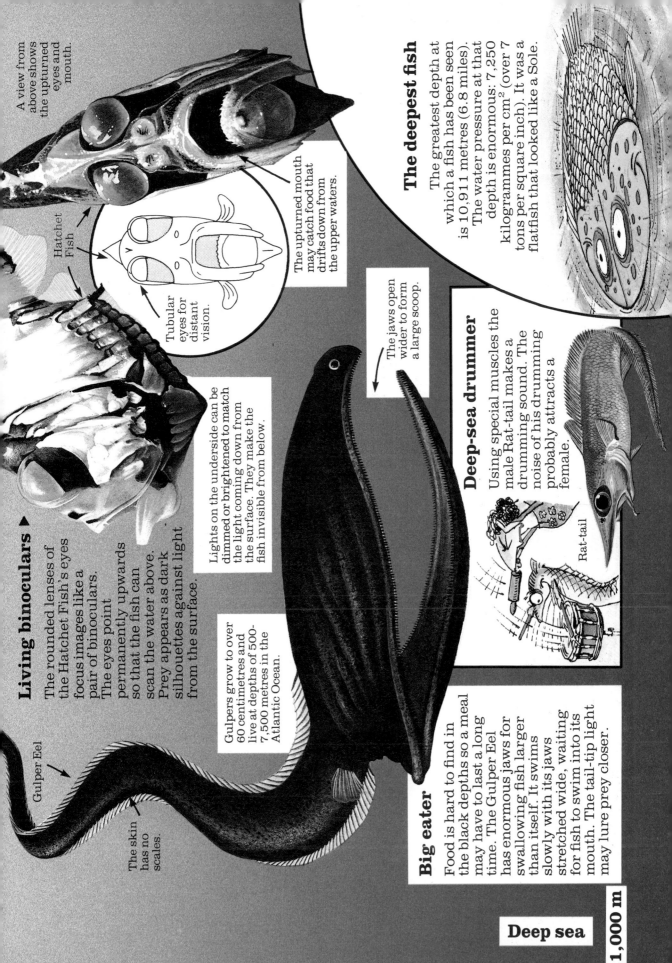

A view from above shows the upturned eyes and mouth.

Hatchet Fish

Tubular eyes for distant vision.

The upturned mouth may catch food that drifts down from the upper waters.

The deepest fish

The greatest depth at which a fish has been seen is 10,911 metres (6.8 miles). The water pressure at that depth is enormous: 7,250 kilogrammes per cm² (over 7 tons per square inch). It was a flatfish that looked like a Sole.

Living binoculars ▶

The rounded lenses of the Hatchet Fish's eyes focus images like a pair of binoculars. The eyes point permanently upwards so that the fish can scan the water above. Prey appears as dark silhouettes against light from the surface.

Lights on the underside can be dimmed or brightened to match the light coming down from the surface. They make the fish invisible from below.

The jaws open wider to form a large scoop.

Deep-sea drummer

Using special muscles the male Rat-tail makes a drumming sound. The noise of his drumming probably attracts a female.

Rat-tail

Gulper Eel

Gulpers grow to over 60 centimetres and live at depths of 500-7,500 metres in the Atlantic Ocean.

The skin has no scales.

Big eater

Food is hard to find in the black depths so a meal may have to last a long time. The Gulper Eel has enormous jaws for swallowing fish larger than itself. It swims slowly with its jaws stretched wide, waiting for fish to swim into its mouth. The tail-tip light may lure prey closer.

Deep sea

1,000 m

Lights and electricity

Many sea creatures can produce light. Some make their own luminous chemicals, others have colonies of light-producing bacteria living in them.

Flashing plankton

The dinoflagellates — a type of plant plankton — produce brief flashes of light. At night they make the sea surface sparkle when disturbed by waves or a boat's wake. Large numbers can throw out enough light to read a newspaper by.

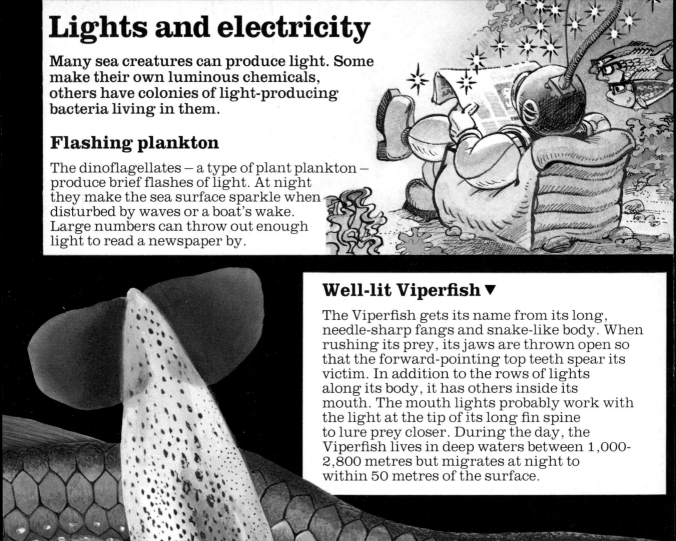

Well-lit Viperfish ▼

The Viperfish gets its name from its long, needle-sharp fangs and snake-like body. When rushing its prey, its jaws are thrown open so that the forward-pointing top teeth spear its victim. In addition to the rows of lights along its body, it has others inside its mouth. The mouth lights probably work with the light at the tip of its long fin spine to lure prey closer. During the day, the Viperfish lives in deep waters between 1,000-2,800 metres but migrates at night to within 50 metres of the surface.

◄ Sparkling squid

Many squid have light organs that shine through the body wall. The lights can be complex structures with reflectors and lenses. Other species use luminous bacteria which are passed on in the embryo. The pattern of lights may help squid to recognise their own species.

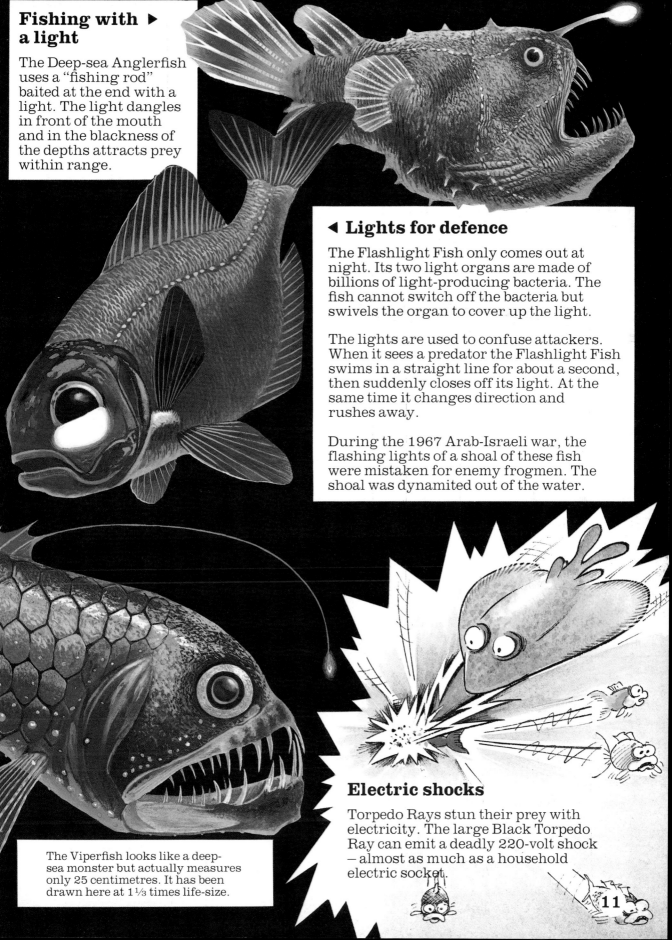

Fishing with ▶ a light

The Deep-sea Anglerfish uses a "fishing rod" baited at the end with a light. The light dangles in front of the mouth and in the blackness of the depths attracts prey within range.

◀ Lights for defence

The Flashlight Fish only comes out at night. Its two light organs are made of billions of light-producing bacteria. The fish cannot switch off the bacteria but swivels the organ to cover up the light.

The lights are used to confuse attackers. When it sees a predator the Flashlight Fish swims in a straight line for about a second, then suddenly closes off its light. At the same time it changes direction and rushes away.

During the 1967 Arab-Israeli war, the flashing lights of a shoal of these fish were mistaken for enemy frogmen. The shoal was dynamited out of the water.

Electric shocks

Torpedo Rays stun their prey with electricity. The large Black Torpedo Ray can emit a deadly 220-volt shock – almost as much as a household electric socket.

The Viperfish looks like a deep-sea monster but actually measures only 25 centimetres. It has been drawn here at 1⅓ times life-size.

11

Colourful characters

Sea creatures are amongst the most colourful animals in the world. The really brilliant species live in the sunlit surface waters of warm tropical seas.

Team colours ▼

In the busy waters around a coral reef each species of fish is decked out like a footballer in its own "team colours". This makes it instantly recognizable to other fish and to members of its own species.

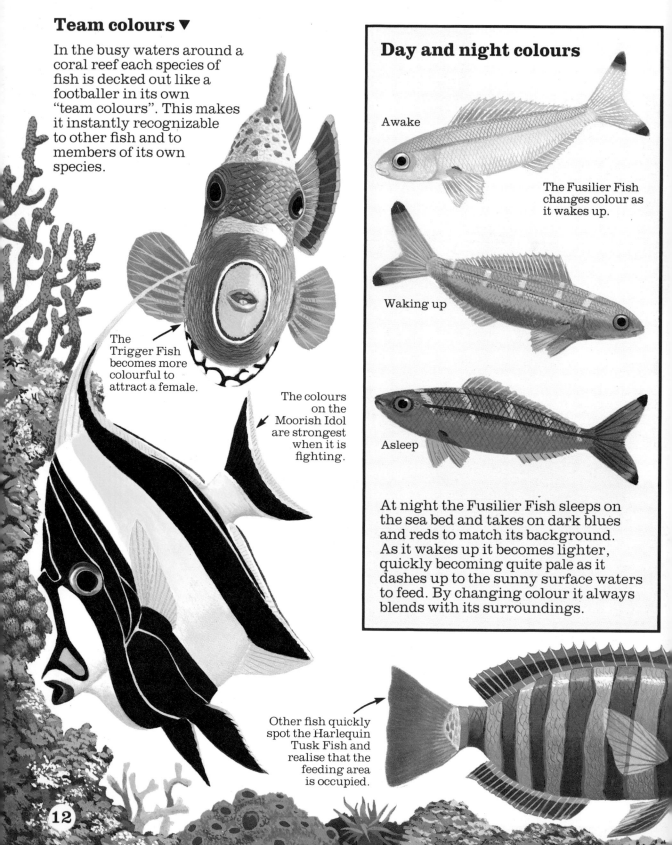

The Trigger Fish becomes more colourful to attract a female.

The colours on the Moorish Idol are strongest when it is fighting.

Day and night colours

Awake

The Fusilier Fish changes colour as it wakes up.

Waking up

Asleep

At night the Fusilier Fish sleeps on the sea bed and takes on dark blues and reds to match its background. As it wakes up it becomes lighter, quickly becoming quite pale as it dashes up to the sunny surface waters to feed. By changing colour it always blends with its surroundings.

Other fish quickly spot the Harlequin Tusk Fish and realise that the feeding area is occupied.

Warning colours ▼

Striking colours can be used to warn predators that an animal has a foul taste or is poisonous. The Sharp-nosed Puffer is extremely poisonous and other fish will not eat it.

In Japan people eat Puffer but it needs an expert chef to remove the poison and make the flesh safe. Known as *fugu* and regarded as a delicacy, the fish still kills people every year. In 1963, 82 people died of Puffer poisoning.

Puffers are protected by their warning colours.

Poison is found in the Puffer's liver, reproductive organs, intestine and muscles.

Camouflage colours ▼

Colours can be used for camouflage. Flatfish are the masters of this because they can change their colour and pattern to match almost any sea bed. They will alter their appearance in seconds when moving to a familiar sea bed. Unfamiliar backgrounds take them longer but tests have shown that they can even change to match a chessboard.

A Plaice takes on mottled colours to match a gravel sea bed. It will be overlooked by predators.

Multi-coloured mystery

Most starfish are slow-moving and live in the open. Dull colours would conceal them, so it is strange that they are brightly coloured.

Vermilion Biscuit Star

Rhinoceros Starfish

TRUE or FALSE?

An octopus turns white when scared.

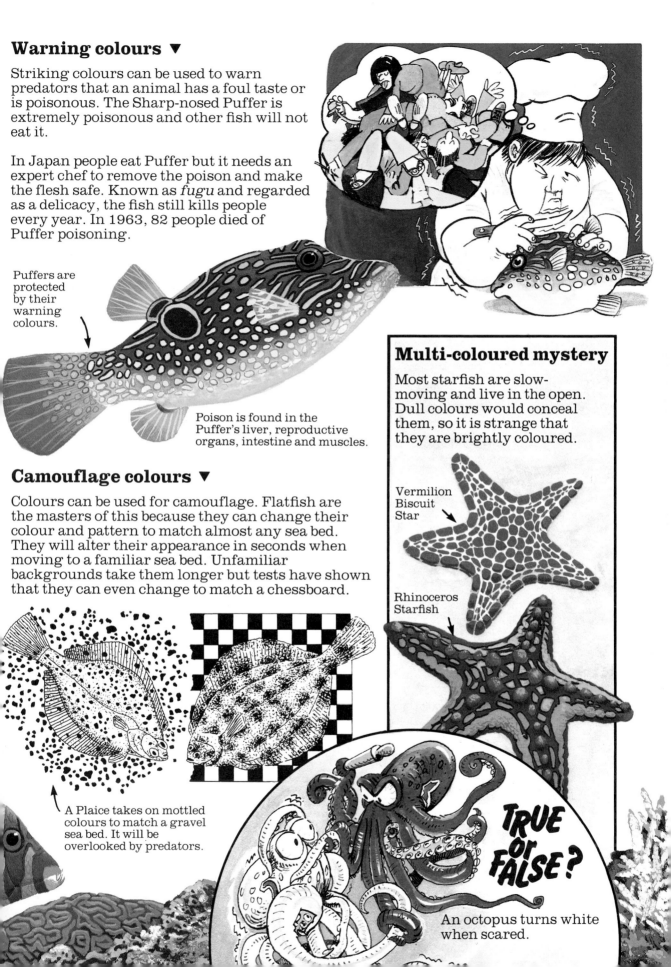

Living together

Doctor's surgery ▶

Grouper Fish

Cleaner Fish run regular "surgeries" for larger fish who visit them to have pests and dead skin nibbled away. The Cleaners work inside the gills and mouth as well as over the bodies of their patients. Cleaners get a free meal for their work by eating the parasites. As the Cleaner swims it flips sideways, flutters its fins or performs unusual dances. These movements identify it as a Cleaner and stop larger fish from eating it. Cleaners can even work safely down the throat of a shark.

Grouper Fish

Cleaner Fish

Groupers live around coral reefs and come in various colours. They regularly queue up for the Cleaners' surgery.

Cleaner Fish are important to the health of the ocean's fishes. If all the Cleaners are removed from an area, other fish quickly move away.

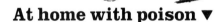

At home with poison ▼

Sea anemones have poisonous tentacles that kill the small fish they eat. Strangely, the Clownfish is unaffected by the poison and lives among the tentacles, where it is safe from predators. In return, the Clownfish attracts other fish which dart after it and are caught by the anemone.

Clownfish

A special liquid seems to protect the Clownfish from the anemone's poison.

The waving tentacles of a large sea anemone.

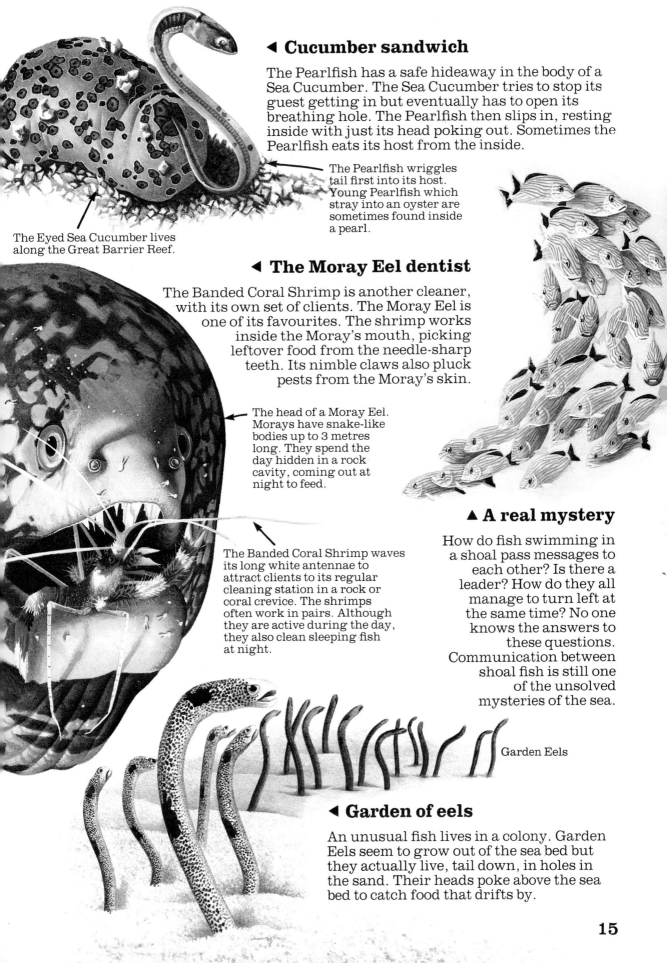

◄ Cucumber sandwich

The Pearlfish has a safe hideaway in the body of a Sea Cucumber. The Sea Cucumber tries to stop its guest getting in but eventually has to open its breathing hole. The Pearlfish then slips in, resting inside with just its head poking out. Sometimes the Pearlfish eats its host from the inside.

The Pearlfish wriggles tail first into its host. Young Pearlfish which stray into an oyster are sometimes found inside a pearl.

The Eyed Sea Cucumber lives along the Great Barrier Reef.

◄ The Moray Eel dentist

The Banded Coral Shrimp is another cleaner, with its own set of clients. The Moray Eel is one of its favourites. The shrimp works inside the Moray's mouth, picking leftover food from the needle-sharp teeth. Its nimble claws also pluck pests from the Moray's skin.

The head of a Moray Eel. Morays have snake-like bodies up to 3 metres long. They spend the day hidden in a rock cavity, coming out at night to feed.

The Banded Coral Shrimp waves its long white antennae to attract clients to its regular cleaning station in a rock or coral crevice. The shrimps often work in pairs. Although they are active during the day, they also clean sleeping fish at night.

▲ A real mystery

How do fish swimming in a shoal pass messages to each other? Is there a leader? How do they all manage to turn left at the same time? No one knows the answers to these questions. Communication between shoal fish is still one of the unsolved mysteries of the sea.

Garden Eels

◄ Garden of eels

An unusual fish lives in a colony. Garden Eels seem to grow out of the sea bed but they actually live, tail down, in holes in the sand. Their heads poke above the sea bed to catch food that drifts by.

Mimics

Like a Cleaner ▶

The Sabre-toothed Blenny looks just like the Cleaner Fish. It has similar colours and swims in the same way. Larger fish are fooled by this, allowing the Blenny to come close. It then snatches a small bite out of the unsuspecting large fish.

Cleaner Fish

Sabre-toothed Blenny

A Sabre-toothed Blenny makes a surprise attack on an angelfish.

The black stripe down its body helps to camouflage the Shrimpfish.

Black Spiny Sea Urchin

A safe hiding place ▲

The Shrimpfish mimics a sea urchin's spine. Hovering head downwards, it is safe from other fish when it hides among a sea urchin's spines. It also swims in the head-down position.

Prey ▶

Hidden in a shoal of Goatfish, Cheilinus closes in on its unsuspecting prey.

Cheilinus has changed colour to match the parrotfish.

Cheilinus stalks its prey, swimming in the shadow of the parrotfish.

Purple Parrotfish. It uses its beak-like teeth to scrape algae from coral reefs.

◀ Swimming under false colours

Cheilinus is a fish-eating hunter which disguises itself to look like a harmless plant-eating fish. It changes colour, mimicking one of several species of harmless fish. Then, swimming close to a single fish or within a shoal, it gets within range of its prey unseen. When near enough, Cheilinus darts out and attacks.

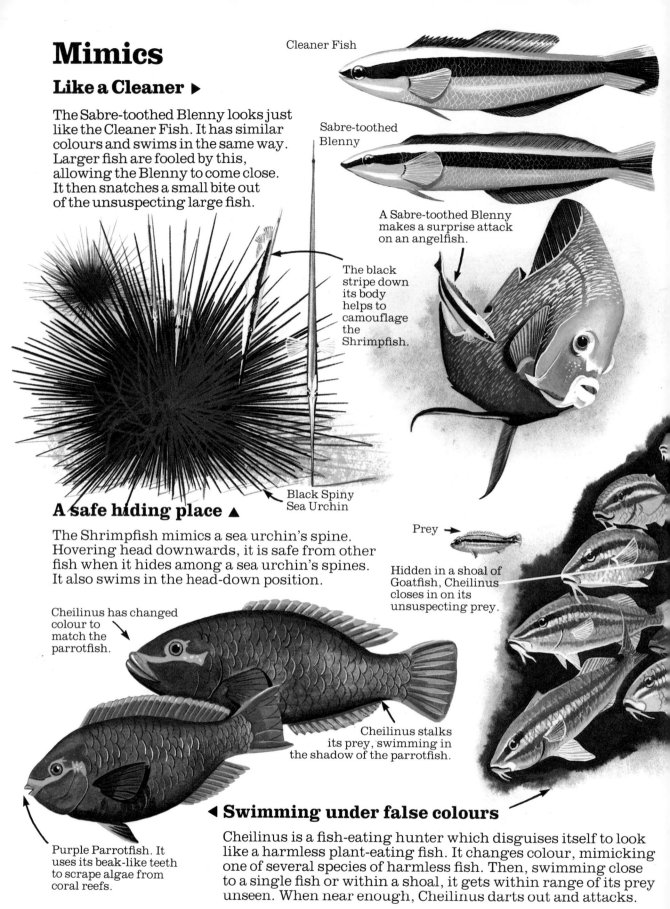

Small bags of yellow, orange, brown, red and black pigment are embedded in the skin. Muscles contract or expand the bags, combining them to produce a range of colours.

◀ Camouflage champion

The Cuttlefish mimics its background. Swimming over rocks covered with weeds and different coloured anemones it will change colour to match each background. Shoals of swimming Cuttlefish all change colour at the same time. Closely related to the squid and octopus, the Cuttlefish has eight arms and two longer tentacles.

Like squid and octopus, the Cuttlefish shoots out a cloud of "ink" to confuse predators. This ink is used to make the artist's brown paint known as sepia.

The cuttlebone, a Cuttlefish's internal shell, is often found washed up on beaches.

Matching the weed ▶

The Sargassum Fish mimics seaweed. Living in the Sargasso Sea, which is full of floating Sargassum Seaweed, the fish has clasping "fingers" on its front fins to pull itself through the thick weed. It is almost invisible to its prey, even having white body patches to match the casts of tubeworms on the weed.

Sea Dragon

The seaweed dragon ▲

The Sea Dragon imitates seaweed which grows off the Australian coast. A relative of the sea horse, it is covered with ragged flaps of skin that look like strands of seaweed. In common with other sea horses and pipefish, the male carries the female's eggs around until they hatch.

TRUE or FALSE?

The Pipefish mimics a pipe.

Marine hitchhikers

Hanging on ▶

The Remora is a hitchhiking scavenger, attaching itself by a sucker to larger fish. When its host finds food, the Remora lets go and feeds on the scraps. Remoras will also swim off in pursuit of shoals of passing fish. Hitchhiking is an easy way of travelling.

The vacuum sucker on top of the Remora's head is made from an adapted fin. It is designed so that the Remora cannot be detached from its host except by swimming forward. No matter how fast the host swims, the Remora cannot be shaken off.

Remoras grow to 90 centimetres, and up to a dozen may fix themselves to a large host, such as a Giant Manta Ray.

Green Turtle

The oval sucker is positioned where the first dorsal fin would normally be.

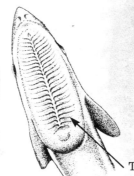

Remora

The ridges across the sucker are erected to create a powerful vacuum.

Whale passengers ▼

Whales – particularly the Gray Whale – carry around thousands of passengers. Barnacles, no bigger than a coin, need a solid base on which to glue their shells. The large, firm surface of a whale is just as good as a rock or a ship's hull. Barnacles feed by sifting food from the water around them. The patterns they make on a whale's skin identify individual whales to whalers.

Acorn Barnacles are also found on rocks along the seashore.

Barnacles

Gray Whale

Islanders in the Caribbean and off north Australia use Remoras to catch turtles. When a turtle is seen on the surface, a fisherman ties a line around the tail of a Remora and puts it over the boat's side. The Remora heads straight to the turtle and clamps on. The islander then reels them both back in.

Outrigger canoe

The vacuum in the sucker becomes stronger as the Remora is pulled backwards by the line.

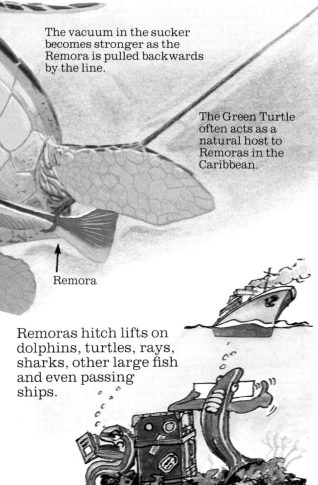

The Green Turtle often acts as a natural host to Remoras in the Caribbean.

Remora

Remoras hitch lifts on dolphins, turtles, rays, sharks, other large fish and even passing ships.

A crabby lift

The hermit crab's passengers are sea anemones. The sea anemones travel around on the crab's shell feeding on the crab's leftovers. In return the crab is protected from enemies by the anenome's stinging tentacles. Large shells can have up to ten anemones on them, sometimes bigger than the shell itself.

Sea anemone

Hermit crab

A male at the ready ▶

Finding a mate is difficult in the black depths of the sea. Some species of Deep-sea Angler get around the problem in an unusual way. When young males meet a female they attach themselves to her. Soon they become just another part of the growing female, living off her blood supply. When she lays her eggs the male is there, ready to fertilise them. The males spend the rest of their lives attached to the larger female.

Two male Anglers attached to a large female.

TRUE or FALSE?

Crabs hitch lifts on dolphins.

Sea changes

Male

Female

The striking colour
difference between
sexes is unusual
in fishes.

Courting male

The male takes on different
colours when courting.

The Cuckoo Wrasse puzzle

PUZZLE: Cuckoo Wrasse are all
born females, no young males are
ever found, most old fish are
males and there are many more
females than males. How can this
be true?

The answer to this strange
puzzle is that Cuckoo Wrasse
change sex. Females do not
begin to breed until they are 6
years old and some become males
between the ages of 7 and 13.
This happens because the shoals
are dominated by large, old
males. When one dies, its place
is taken by a large female changing
sex to become a leading male. It took
scientists years to solve this puzzle.

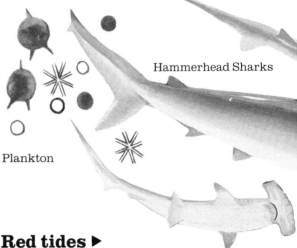

Hammerhead Sharks

Plankton

Changing tune

The haunting songs
of the Humpback
Whale have recently
been recorded and
studied by scientists.
They have found that
every whale's song is
different and that
each song changes
through the
breeding season.
Next season the
songs are
different again.
A single song
can continue
for thirty
minutes.

Red tides ▶

When some types of plant
plankton breed too rapidly they
produce poisons which turn the sea red.
These poisonous "red tides" kill everything.
The number of seabirds off South America
can drop from 30 million to 5 million
and a recent red tide off the Florida coast

Flattening out ▼

All flatfish start life as round fish. Young flatfish look like any other fish but after a few weeks their bodies begin to change shape. One eye slowly moves round the head and the fish swims to the sea bottom to lie on its blind side. Before long the round fish has become a flatfish. Its left and right side are now topside and underside.

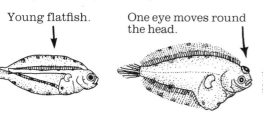

Young flatfish.

One eye moves round the head.

Adult with eyes on one side.

Flatfish are 2-4 years old before they start to breed.

About six weeks after hatching from an egg floating near the surface, flatfish begin living on the sea bed.

Front view of Turbot.

Plaice usually settle on their left side and Turbot settle on their right side. Reversed examples of each species are occasionally found. Flounders are less predictable, though two-thirds settle on their left side. Flatfish swim by undulating their bodies up and down.

This Flounder has settled on its right side. Its left side has become its topside.

The right eye has moved over the head to the left side.

The pelvic fin was on the underside of the young "round" fish.

Manta Ray

Flying fish

killed about 100,000 tons of fish. As the usual sea life dies, strange invasions of thousands upon thousands of Hammerhead Sharks move in. They are followed by jumping Giant Manta Rays and schools of flying fish. Slowly the sea returns to normal and the invaders retreat.

TRUE or FALSE?

Oysters frequently change sex.

The hunters' weapons

Teeth ▼

A shark's teeth are its weapons for catching and killing prey. The teeth also tear off lumps of flesh to be swallowed. This style of feeding quickly loosens teeth. Nurse Sharks cope by moulting their teeth and growing a new set every 8 days. Other sharks have one set of teeth in action and 3 or 4 rows in reserve, ready to move forward and replace teeth as they fall out.

A Tiger Shark's teeth. The top two rows are in use. Those below are reserves.

Tiger Shark

◀ Tusks

The Walrus roots in the mud of the sea bed, hunting for shellfish. It locates them with its sensitive whiskers and digs them out with its long tusks.

Cunning hunter ▶

...when near enough, the bear dives and then surfaces at speed under the ice floe...

The Polar Bear is a skilled hunter. When the ice is breaking up in Spring, it needs great cunning to catch a seal. Spotting one on an ice floe, it swims towards the seal with only its nose above water and...

Sonar clicks

Dolphins "talk" a lot, using whistles to communicate with each other. Much higher frequency clicks are used when hunting, probably to locate their quarry. Recent research suggests the high-pitched sounds may also stun fish, so the dolphin can make an easy catch.

Bottlenose Dolphin

TRUE or FALSE?

The Geographic Cone harpoons people.

Strong suckers ▶

The suckers on a starfish's arms are extremely powerful. They can exert a steady pressure for a very long time. Using this strength, a starfish can open shellfish that have very strong muscles. Starfish dine on oysters, mussels and scallops.

The shells are prised open just a couple of millimetres, enough for the starfish to squeeze its stomach through the gap to digest the shellfish's flesh. Starfish always eat by wrapping their stomach around their prey.

A starfish preparing to open a mussel.

... battering the floe so hard the seal is thrown into the water. It is swiftly killed with one blow of the bear's powerful paw.

Defence and escape

Fast tail-beats along the surface build up speed for take-off.

Four-winged Flying Fish

Taking off ▲

Flying Fish jump out of the water and glide, rather than fly, to escape enemies that are chasing them. They take off at about 64 kph (40 mph) and can travel over 1,000 metres. Most pursuers are confused but Dolphin Fish follow the flight and catch the Flying Fish as they land.

A movable cover polishes the Tiger Cowrie's shell, keeping it free from barnacles and algae.

Acid reply

The Tiger Cowrie has an unusual way of repelling enemies. It shoots out a cloud of sulphuric acid which stings the eyes of its attacker.

A Dab attacking a Common Brittle Star.

Unarmed ▲

The Brittle Star, a close cousin of the starfish, will lose an arm when tackled by an enemy. Part of an arm or a whole arm breaks off easily and will be deliberately abandoned as the Brittle Star escapes. It can lose all five arms and still survive to re-grow them. Brittle Stars move quickly, waving their arms to row themselves along.

Sticky tubes ▼

The harmless-looking Sea Cucumber repels nosey fish and crabs with a gut reaction. When upset, it lets out streams of sticky tubes from its gut, covering the predator. The Sea Cucumber then inches away to safety, leaving behind a baffled fish or crab. It can re-grow these sticky entrails in a few weeks.

The sticky tubes of some Sea Cucumbers are filled with poison.

Sea Cucumbers, relations of starfish, move on tube feet.

Blown out ▼

The Porcupine Fish looks quite small and ordinary until it is surprised by an attacker. Then it gulps in water, blowing itself up to football size. The spines on its body stick out all around like a porcupine. Most attackers are either scared off or unable to swallow the Porcupine Fish because it has grown so large.

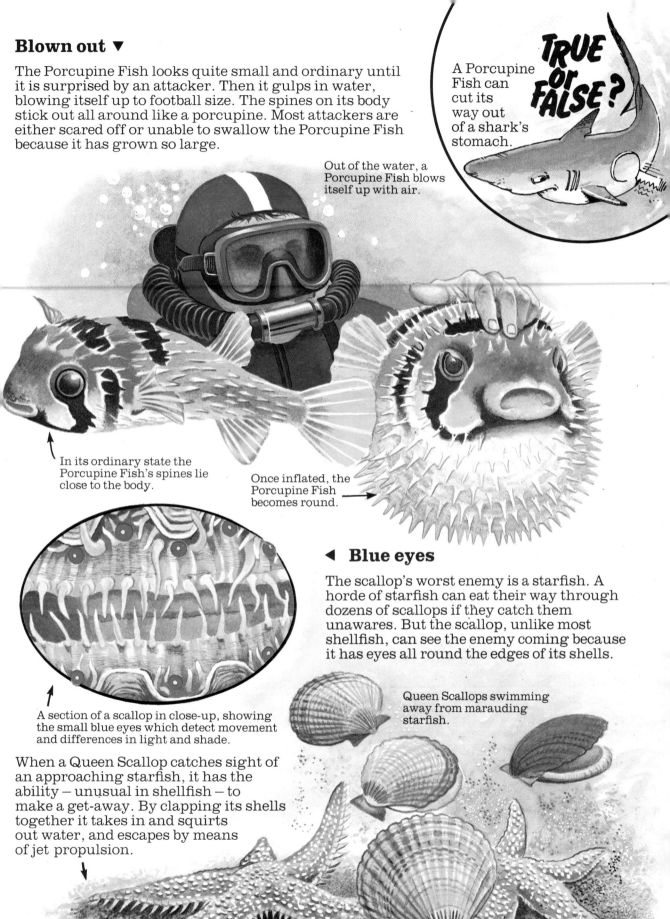

Out of the water, a Porcupine Fish blows itself up with air.

A Porcupine Fish can cut its way out of a shark's stomach.

TRUE or FALSE?

In its ordinary state the Porcupine Fish's spines lie close to the body.

Once inflated, the Porcupine Fish becomes round.

A section of a scallop in close-up, showing the small blue eyes which detect movement and differences in light and shade.

◄ Blue eyes

The scallop's worst enemy is a starfish. A horde of starfish can eat their way through dozens of scallops if they catch them unawares. But the scallop, unlike most shellfish, can see the enemy coming because it has eyes all round the edges of its shells.

Queen Scallops swimming away from marauding starfish.

When a Queen Scallop catches sight of an approaching starfish, it has the ability – unusual in shellfish – to make a get-away. By clapping its shells together it takes in and squirts out water, and escapes by means of jet propulsion.

25

Beware – poison!

The float is filled up by a gas gland.

Nomeid fish live among the tentacles.

Floating killer

Beneath its float, the Portuguese Man-of-war trails deadly stinging tentacles which paralyse and kill the fish on which it feeds. The tentacles – often over 15 metres long – are loaded with poison "harpoons" which, when touched, shoot into the victim.

The poison is extremely painful to human beings but, strangely, the Ocean Sunfish is unharmed by it, eating any Portùguese Man-of-war it comes across. Nomeid fish are also unaffected and can swim amongst the tentacles where they are safe from larger fish.

Ocean Sunfish feed on Portuguese Men-of-war.

Borrowed weapons ▶

The Mexican Dancer sea slug can feed on sea anemones without being harmed by the anemone's poison "harpoons". It actually swallows the minute spring-loaded harpoons without triggering them off. The harpoons travel through the sea slug to the tips of its orange "fingers". It is then armed with borrowed weapons which it shoots at anything that attacks it.

Anemone's stinging cell

trigger

barbs

discharged filament

lid

coiled filament

Blue-ringed Octopus

◀ Small but deadly

The Blue-ringed Octopus probably kills more people every year than any shark. The usual victims are bathers who pick up the octopus to look at it. Although the octopus's body is only 3 centimetres long it is one of the deadliest creatures in the world, producing poison more deadly than that of any land animal.

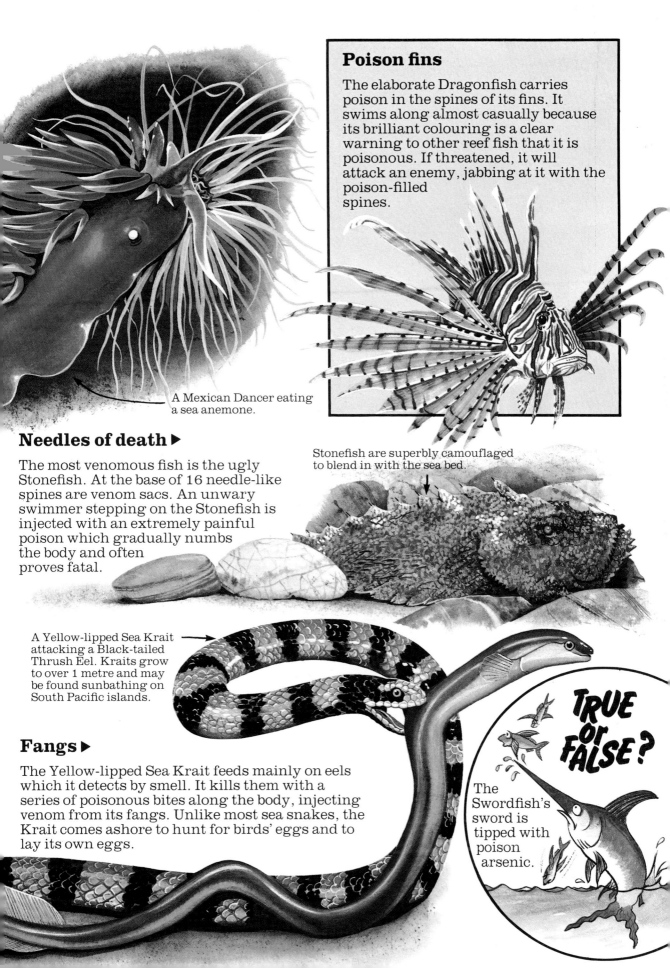

Poison fins

The elaborate Dragonfish carries poison in the spines of its fins. It swims along almost casually because its brilliant colouring is a clear warning to other reef fish that it is poisonous. If threatened, it will attack an enemy, jabbing at it with the poison-filled spines.

A Mexican Dancer eating a sea anemone.

Needles of death ▶

The most venomous fish is the ugly Stonefish. At the base of 16 needle-like spines are venom sacs. An unwary swimmer stepping on the Stonefish is injected with an extremely painful poison which gradually numbs the body and often proves fatal.

Stonefish are superbly camouflaged to blend in with the sea bed.

A Yellow-lipped Sea Krait attacking a Black-tailed Thrush Eel. Kraits grow to over 1 metre and may be found sunbathing on South Pacific islands.

Fangs ▶

The Yellow-lipped Sea Krait feeds mainly on eels which it detects by smell. It kills them with a series of poisonous bites along the body, injecting venom from its fangs. Unlike most sea snakes, the Krait comes ashore to hunt for birds' eggs and to lay its own eggs.

TRUE or FALSE?

The Swordfish's sword is tipped with poison arsenic.

Unusual events

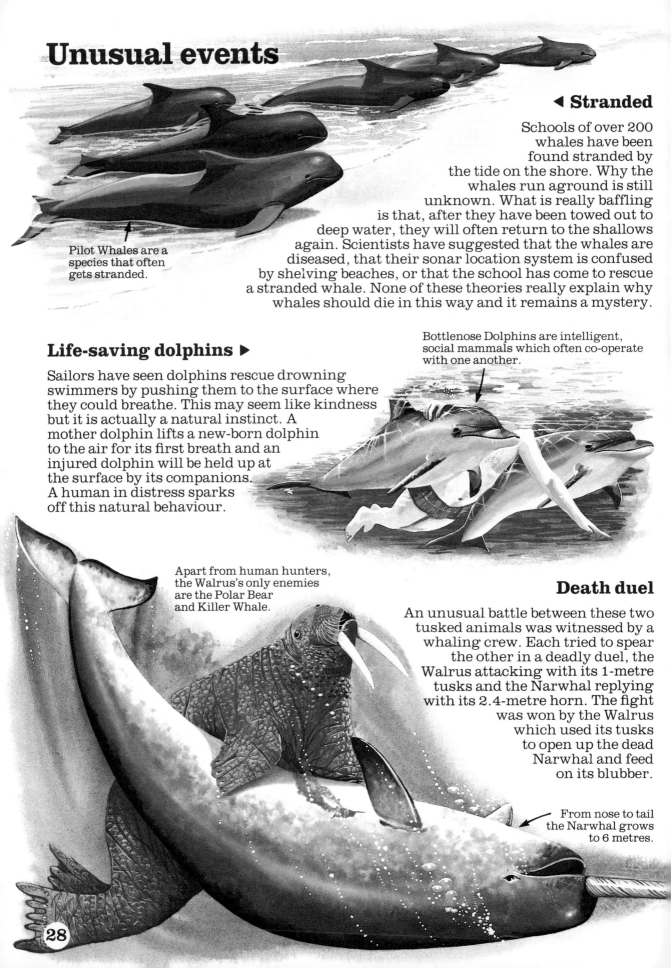

Pilot Whales are a species that often gets stranded.

◄ Stranded

Schools of over 200 whales have been found stranded by the tide on the shore. Why the whales run aground is still unknown. What is really baffling is that, after they have been towed out to deep water, they will often return to the shallows again. Scientists have suggested that the whales are diseased, that their sonar location system is confused by shelving beaches, or that the school has come to rescue a stranded whale. None of these theories really explain why whales should die in this way and it remains a mystery.

Life-saving dolphins ►

Sailors have seen dolphins rescue drowning swimmers by pushing them to the surface where they could breathe. This may seem like kindness but it is actually a natural instinct. A mother dolphin lifts a new-born dolphin to the air for its first breath and an injured dolphin will be held up at the surface by its companions. A human in distress sparks off this natural behaviour.

Bottlenose Dolphins are intelligent, social mammals which often co-operate with one another.

Apart from human hunters, the Walrus's only enemies are the Polar Bear and Killer Whale.

Death duel

An unusual battle between these two tusked animals was witnessed by a whaling crew. Each tried to spear the other in a deadly duel, the Walrus attacking with its 1-metre tusks and the Narwhal replying with its 2.4-metre horn. The fight was won by the Walrus which used its tusks to open up the dead Narwhal and feed on its blubber.

From nose to tail the Narwhal grows to 6 metres.

Sea anchors ▶

Families of Sea Otters swim and feed in the kelp beds (forests of seaweed) off the Californian coast. Rarely coming ashore, they sleep at sea. As night falls they twist and turn among the strands of kelp, wrapping it around their bodies. The kelp "anchors" keep the family together and stop them being swept away by fast-moving currents.

The otter's thick fur traps a warm layer of air.

◀ Bubble net

Fishing with a net of bubbles sounds an unlikely way to catch anything. Humpback Whales, though, have perfected a technique which works very well. Spotting a shoal of fish, a Humpback swims beneath it in a circle, releasing a stream of bubbles from its blowhole. The shoal is surrounded by a "net" of glistening bubbles and, although the fish could swim through them, they seem confused and remain inside. The Humpback then rises up to gulp down its captive prey.

▲ First one in . . .

The Adelie Penguin's chief enemy is the Leopard Seal which is large enough to swallow a penguin whole. Leopard Seals cruise around the ice-covered land where the Adelies breed. The penguins, wary of getting into the water, queue up on the ice, edging slowly closer to the water. Finally one dives in, or gets pushed, and if it survives the others quickly follow.

Adelies can leap considerable distances out of the sea on to land when fleeing from a pursuing Leopard Seal.

Leopard Seal

Only the male Narwhal has a horn. One of two upper teeth grows through his lip in an anti-clockwise spiral to form the horn.

Record breakers

Oldest fish

The Whale Shark is thought to live to 70 years or more. Halibut over 3 m long have been caught in the North Sea and are probably over 60 years old.

Largest shoal

The largest number of Herring in one shoal has been estimated at 3,000 million.

Longest migration

On their spawning migration from the Baltic to the Sargasso Sea, European Eels travel 7,500 km (4,660 miles).

Longest worm

One Bootlace Worm from the North Sea was recorded as 55 m in length (a lot longer than a Blue Whale).

Largest crab

The largest Giant Spider Crab, found off Japan, had a span, from claw tip to claw tip, of 3.69 m.

Most venomous

The Box Jellyfish's venom kills people in from 30 seconds to 15 minutes (exceptionally, 2 hours of excruciating pain). The poison of the Japanese Puffer Fish is 200,000 times more potent than curare, the deadly plant toxin used to tip poison arrows. Anyone unlucky enough to eat poisoned Puffer usually dies within 2 hours.

Most ferocious

Schools of Bluefin Tuna sometimes have "feeding frenzies", tearing into shoals of fish and cutting to pieces ten times as many fish as they can possibly eat.

Fastest fish

Incredibly, the Sailfish can cut through the water faster than a Cheetah can run. The Sailfish has been timed at 109 km/h (68.18 mph) whilst the Cheetah reaches 96-101 km/h (60-63 mph). Other sprinters are:

	km/h	mph
Wahoo	77.6	48.5
Marlin	92	57.6

Largest fish

The largest recorded Whale Shark was 18 m long, with an estimated weight of 43 tonnes.

Largest number of eggs

The Ocean Sunfish is the champion egg-layer, producing an astonishing 300 million eggs.

Largest jellyfish

The longest ever recorded was a Giant Jellyfish whose floating bell measured 2.29 m across with 36.5 m tentacles trailing beneath it.

Largest flesh-eating fish

The largest accurately measured Great White Shark was 7.92 m long. Larger sharks of 11.27 m and even 13.10 m have been reported.

Bulkiest bony fish

The Ocean Sunfish – a fish with bones rather than the cartilage that sharks have – is deeper than it is long. It grows to 3 m in length, 4.26 m high and weighs 2¼ tonnes.

Oldest crustacean

Large specimens of the American Lobster may be 50 years old.

Deepest diving whale

A Sperm Whale stayed underwater for 1 hour, 52 minutes. This whale surfaced with two bottom-living sharks in its stomach and, as the sea was over 3,193 metres deep, it seems likely that the whale dived to this depth.

Largest shellfish

The biggest Giant Clam collected from the Great Barrier Reef, Australia, was 1.09 m long by 0.73 m wide and weighed 262.9 kg (over quarter of a ton).

Largest mammal

The Blue Whale is the largest living animal. The largest measured was 33.58 m long and weighed over 160 tonnes.

Longest distance flier

The Four-winged Flying Fish has been recorded making flights of 1,109 m in length, 90 seconds in duration and 11 m in height.

Deepest ocean bed

The deepest part of the Pacific is 11,033 m (6.85 miles) deep. A 1 kg steel ball dropped at the surface would take nearly 63 minutes to reach the bottom.

Smallest fish

A fully-grown Marshall Islands Goby is just 16 mm from nose to tail. The slightly longer *Schindleria praematurus* is the lightest fish in the world, weighing only 2 mg. 14,175 fully-grown fish would weigh just 28.35 grms.

31

Were they true or false?

page 5 Big turtles cry.
TRUE. When ashore turtles do let tears fall. These are probably to clear sand from their eyes.

page 7 Dynamite contains plankton skeletons.
TRUE. Diatomaceous earth – produced from the dried skeletons of diatoms, a type of plankton – is inert and is used to make highly explosive nitro-glycerine safe to handle in the form of dynamite.

page 13 An octopus turns white when scared.
TRUE. An Octopus can make rapid and startling colour changes when frightened or angry. It also changes colour to match its background.

page 17 The Pipefish mimics a pipe.
FALSE. Although the Pipefish got its name because it looks something like an old clay pipe, it does not deliberately mimic a pipe.

page 19 Crabs hitch lifts on dolphins.
FALSE. Crabs get about on their own legs.

page 21 Oysters frequently change sex.

TRUE. Starting life as a male, an oyster gradually becomes a female. After laying her eggs the female reverts to being a male. In cold waters oysters change sex once a year but in warm waters they change sex frequently.

page 23 The Geographic Cone harpoons people.
TRUE. This attractive mollusc fires poisonous harpoon-like hollow teeth at its prey. Unwary shell collectors, attracted by its beauty, have been harpooned and at least four people have been killed.

page 25 A Porcupine Fish can cut its way out of a shark's stomach.
PROBABLY FALSE. One author suggests that the Porcupine Fish will "cut and crush the wall of the shark's stomach and body wall until it reaches the sea and freedom." There is no evidence to support this and it seems unlikely.

page 27 The Swordfish's sword is tipped with deadly arsenic.
FALSE. The Swordfish is pretty harmless and arsenic is a mineral found in the earth.

Further reading

First Nature: Fishes, A. Wheeler (Usborne)
The Nature Trail Book of Seashore Life, S. Swallow (Usborne)
Spotter's Guide to the Seashore, S. Swallow (Usborne)
Spotter's Guide to Fishes, A. Wheeler (Usborne)
The Sea, L. Engel (Time-Life)
Your Book of Fishes, H. Angel (Faber)
The Amazing World of the Sea, J. Cochrane (Angus & Robertson)
Killers in the Wild, J. Hatley (Macmillan Children's Books)
Discovering Life on Earth, D. Attenborough (Collins)
How Fishes Live, P. Whitehead (Elsevier-Phaidon)
A Closer Look at Whales and Dolphins, B. Stonehouse (Hamish Hamilton/Scimitar)
The Great Whale Book, J. Kelly et al, The Centre for Environmental Education (Acropolis Books, Washington DC)
Whales & Other Sea Mammals, T. Dozier (Time-Life)
The Whale, J. Cousteau & P. Diole (Cassell/Doubleday)

The Seashore and its wildlife, R. Burton (Orbis)
The Life of the Seashore, W. Amos (McGraw-Hill)
The Life of the Ocean, N. Berrill (McGraw-Hill)
All colour book of Ocean Life, M. & H. Angel (Octopus)
Underwater Life, P. Parks (Hamlyn)
The Guinness Guide to Underwater Life, C. Petron & J. Lozet (Guinness Superlatives)
The Fishes, F. D. Ommanney (Time-Life)
Fishes of Lakes, Rivers & Oceans, T. Dozier (Time-Life)
Fishes of the World, A. Wheeler (Ferndale Editions)
Encyclopedia of Fish, M. & R. Burton (Octopus)
Dangerous Sea Creatures, T. Dozier (Time-Life)
Migration, editor M. Ellis (J. M. Dent)
Hunters, editor M. Ellis (J. M. Dent)
The Hunters, P. Whitfield (Hamlyn)
Strangest Creatures of the World, G. Kensinger (Ridge Press/Bantam)
Animal Wonders of the World, D. Black (Orbis)
Weird & Wonderful Wildlife, M. Marten et al (Secker & Warburg)

PART 2

MYSTERIES & MARVELS
OF
PLANT LIFE

Barbara Cork

Consultant Simon Mayo

Designed by Anne Sharples

Illustrated by Ian Jackson
Kevin Dean, Sarah De Ath (Linden Artists)
Rob McCaig, Cynthia Pow, David Quinn
and Nigel Frey

Cartoons by John Shackell

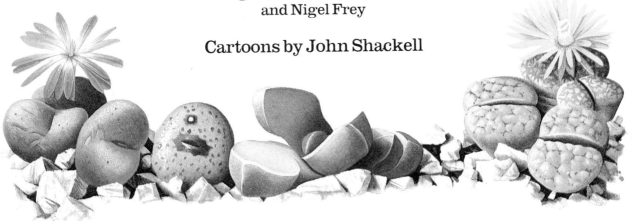

Contents

Tank plants,
ferns and mosses
on a jungle branch.

Orchids

Amethyst
Deceiver

Jack-in-the-Pulpit

Dragon Tree

Barrel
Cactus

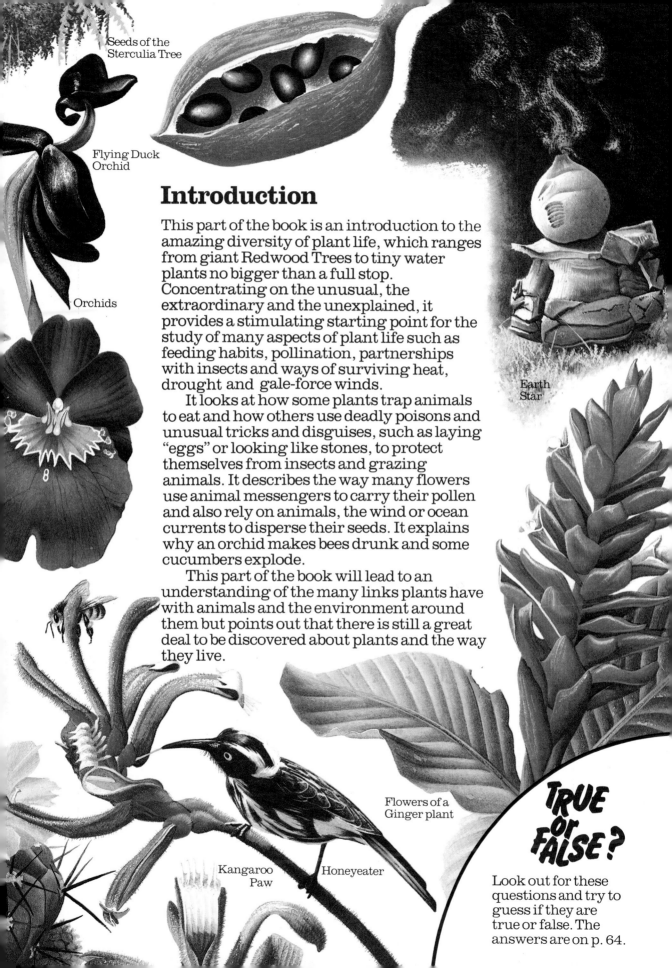

Seeds of the
Sterculia Tree

Flying Duck
Orchid

Orchids

Earth
Star

Introduction

This part of the book is an introduction to the
amazing diversity of plant life, which ranges
from giant Redwood Trees to tiny water
plants no bigger than a full stop.
Concentrating on the unusual, the
extraordinary and the unexplained, it
provides a stimulating starting point for the
study of many aspects of plant life such as
feeding habits, pollination, partnerships
with insects and ways of surviving heat,
drought and gale-force winds.

It looks at how some plants trap animals
to eat and how others use deadly poisons and
unusual tricks and disguises, such as laying
"eggs" or looking like stones, to protect
themselves from insects and grazing
animals. It describes the way many flowers
use animal messengers to carry their pollen
and also rely on animals, the wind or ocean
currents to disperse their seeds. It explains
why an orchid makes bees drunk and some
cucumbers explode.

This part of the book will lead to an
understanding of the many links plants have
with animals and the environment around
them but points out that there is still a great
deal to be discovered about plants and the way
they live.

Flowers of a
Ginger plant

Kangaroo
Paw

Honeyeater

**TRUE
or
FALSE?**

Look out for these
questions and try to
guess if they are
true or false. The
answers are on p. 64.

Climbers, stranglers...

Some jungle plants climb all over the jungle trees or perch on their branches. This helps them to escape from the dark, wet jungle floor and live nearer to the sunlight, which streams down on the roof of the jungle. They have special roots, stems and leaves to catch, carry and store water and nutrients.

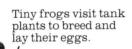
Tiny frogs visit tank plants to breed and lay their eggs.

The strangler strikes again

1. A Strangler Fig grows from a seed that a bird or bat drops high up on a tree branch. The seed soon sprouts roots and leaves.

2. The roots eventually reach the ground and start to take up water and nutrients from the soil. The fig then begins to grow more rapidly.

3. The fig competes with the tree for light, water and nutrients. The tree may lose the battle and die, rotting away inside a living coffin.

▲ Swimming pool plants

Tank plants have a watertight cup of leaves, which collects a pool of rainwater, leaf litter and animal droppings. Special scales on the leaves take up water and nutrients from their private pool. Tadpoles, tiny insects and even a plant that eats insects may live in these tree-top pools.

Vanda Orchid

Thick roots have lots of holes to soak up rainwater.

▲ Orchid water tricks

About half the orchids in the world grow on other plants. They usually have thick leaves with a waxy surface, which helps to stop water escaping. Some of them have swollen stems to store water.

Most plants use sunlight to make their own food from carbon dioxide (a gas in the air) and water. But some plants do not have the special green substance they need to capture the sun's energy. They steal their food from other plants instead and may eventually kill them.

Mistletoe suckers force their way into the pipes that carry food and water round their plant victims.

A plant robber

The strange Broomrape plant has no green leaves so it cannot make its own food. It has to break into the roots of other plants and steal their food. But it can live only on broom and gorse plants and its seeds will die if they cannot find one of these plants to grow on.

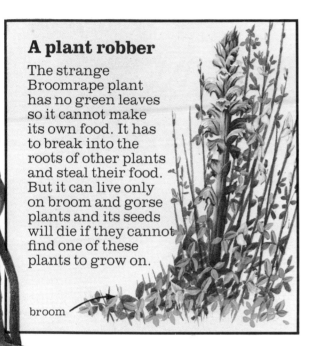

broom

◄ Ropes to the jungle roof

The living "ropes" that Tarzan used to swing on are the woody stems of climbing plants called lianas. Special cells in their stems carry water up from the roots to the leaves, which grow in the sun above the giant jungle trees. In some lianas, water flows as fast as 1-2½ metres a minute.

TRUE or FALSE?

Lianas grow as tall as the Eiffel Tower and are strong enough to take the weight of an elephant.

▲ Mistletoe – the vampire plant

Mistletoes have green leaves so they can make their own food but they also steal some food and water from the plant they grow on. Sometimes they kill the plants they feed from. There are even some mistletoes that grow on other mistletoes.

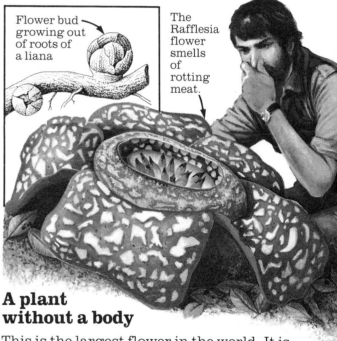

Flower bud growing out of roots of a liana

The Rafflesia flower smells of rotting meat.

A plant without a body

This is the largest flower in the world. It is the only part of the Rafflesia plant that appears above ground. The rest of the plant is a network of threads that lives inside the roots of a liana. The plant steals all its food from the liana so it does not need a body with green leaves to make its own food.

Plant battlegames

Plants are in constant danger of attack from the animals that try to eat them. They use disguises, tricks, poisons and deadly weapons to battle for their lives.

Heliconius butterfly

Do plants lay eggs?

Some passion flower vines do grow things that **look** like eggs on their leaves. Butterflies are less likely to lay real eggs if the plant looks as if it already has eggs on its leaves. So the vines that produce "eggs" trick butterflies into leaving them alone. They then have fewer caterpillars eating their leaves when the real eggs hatch out.

real egg

false egg

▼ Pebbles with flowers

Pebble plants are difficult to spot against a stony background. **How many different kinds of pebble plant can you find across these two pages?**
(The answer is on page 64.)

Their disguise may help them to hide from hungry animals.

Pebble plants

Plants of death

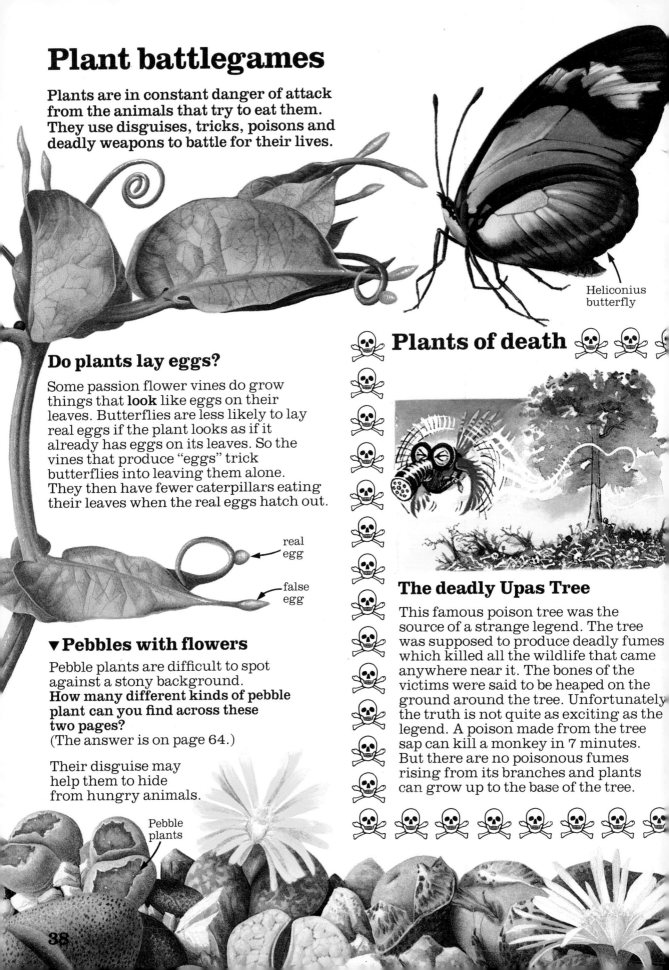

The deadly Upas Tree

This famous poison tree was the source of a strange legend. The tree was supposed to produce deadly fumes which killed all the wildlife that came anywhere near it. The bones of the victims were said to be heaped on the ground around the tree. Unfortunately the truth is not quite as exciting as the legend. A poison made from the tree sap can kill a monkey in 7 minutes. But there are no poisonous fumes rising from its branches and plants can grow up to the base of the tree.

Savage spines

Many plants, especially cacti, are covered in very sharp spines, which helps to protect them from grazing animals. Some cacti have spines up to 15 centimetres long. Cactus spines have such perfect points that people have managed to play records using a cactus spine as the needle.

TRUE or FALSE?

Green potatoes can poison children.

Barrel Cactus

The sharp spines are the leaves of the cactus.

Many plants contain deadly poisons, which may help to prevent animals from eating them. Fungi are the most poisonous. Some plant poisons can be used to treat human illnesses if they are given to the patient in very small amounts.

WORLD'S MOST POISONOUS FUNGUS

Death Cap

Deadly Nightshade
All parts poisonous to people but birds and rabbits can eat it. Used to widen pupils in eye surgery.

Koochla Tree
Source of strychnine. Causes convulsions and agonizing death. Can act as antidote to lead poisoning.

Foxglove
Eating 2½-4 leaves can cause death from heart attack. But used to treat heart disorders.

Laburnum
All parts poisonous. Children may mistake the seeds for peas. Causes convulsions, coma and death.

▼ The collapsing plant

The leaves of *Mimosa pudica* plants can suddenly collapse in just a few seconds. This may shake off insects that are trying to eat their leaves. The sudden movements may also help the plants to duck out of sight of grazing animals. As the plants also collapse at night and in cold weather, there is not a simple explanation for their strange behaviour.

A pair of swollen leaves on a pebble plant.

The strange ant plants

Some remarkable plants have their own special ants living inside their leaves, stems or even their thorns. The plants and their ants seem to help each other to survive by living together.

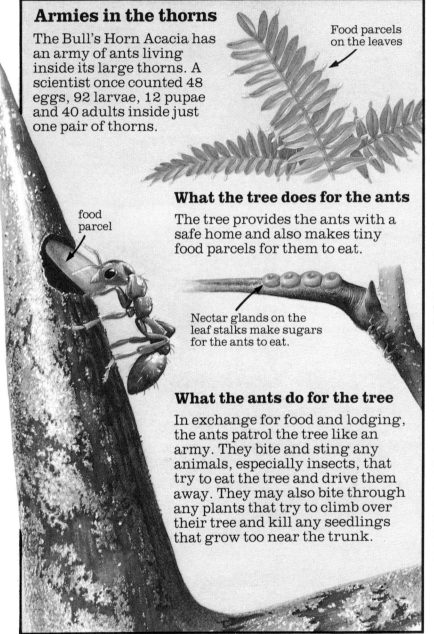

Armies in the thorns

The Bull's Horn Acacia has an army of ants living inside its large thorns. A scientist once counted 48 eggs, 92 larvae, 12 pupae and 40 adults inside just one pair of thorns.

Food parcels on the leaves

food parcel

What the tree does for the ants

The tree provides the ants with a safe home and also makes tiny food parcels for them to eat.

Nectar glands on the leaf stalks make sugars for the ants to eat.

What the ants do for the tree

In exchange for food and lodging, the ants patrol the tree like an army. They bite and sting any animals, especially insects, that try to eat the tree and drive them away. They may also bite through any plants that try to climb over their tree and kill any seedlings that grow too near the trunk.

▼Ants in the leaves

The Dischidia plant grows leaf pouches, which often have ants living in them.

Ants live in here

These pouches are too wet for the ants.

This is what a leaf pouch looks like inside. The roots of the plant grow inside its own leaves. The ants are sheltered and protected inside their unusual home. The rubbish that they leave in their nest is probably a source of food for the plant. The roots in the leaf can take up this food.

Ants in the stems ▶

The Hydnophytum plant has a weird swollen stem with an amazing network of tunnels inside. Some of the tunnels have rough walls and others have smooth walls. Ants often live in the tunnels with the smooth walls. They leave soil, insect remains and other rubbish in the tunnels with the rough walls. The plant probably takes up food from the ants' waste heap.

▲ Fungus farms

These ants are collecting leaves to feed to a special fungus that they grow inside their nest. They chew up the leaves to make a compost for the fungus to feed on. Something in the ants' saliva may help the fungus to grow. The ants harvest some of the fungus for food.

scale insect

Stem of Trumpet Tree

◄ Down on the ant farm

Many of the ants that live inside plants take their own crops and farm animals in with them.

Azteca ants live inside the hollow stems of the Trumpet Tree. They carry tiny scale insects into their home. The scale insects suck the sugary sap from the tree and the extra sugar that they do not need is eaten by their ant farmers. The ants also grow crops of fungus in the stems and collect part of the fungus as food.

Whole plant growing on tree trunk

Can trees whistle?

Whistling Thorn Trees can make eerie music when the wind blows. Some of the hollow balls on their branches have holes in them. These holes are made by ants that set up home inside. When the ants move out, the wind blowing across the holes makes the trees "whistle" in the wind.

Hole made by ants

Whistling Thorn Tree

roots

Tunnels with rough walls, which absorb nutrients.

Tunnels with smooth walls, where ants live.

Swollen stem of Hydnophytum plant

TRUE or FALSE?

Ants make apples grow on Oak Trees.

Plants that eat animals

Many plants are famous for their unusual habit of eating small animals, especially insects. But are there really killer plants that can eat elephants, dogs or even people?

Man-eating trees ▶

There are many legends of man-eating trees, which curl their long, spiny branches round people and crush them to death. It is unlikely that these trees do exist but no one can really be sure.

Tricky trappers

Meat-eating plants lure their victims into deadly traps with colours, scents or the promise of food. The plants absorb extra nutrients from these strange meals, which helps them to survive in poor soils. Did you know that a type of geranium, some petunias, tobacco and even the **seeds** of Shepherd's Purse can kill and eat insects? There are probably more plants that eat animals waiting to be discovered.

▼ Sticky sundews

Sundew plants catch insects on deadly tentacles that cover their leaves. Sticky drops at the end of the tentacles trap the insects. As they struggle to escape, the tentacles curl over and glue them firmly to the leaf so the plant can start its meal. The Portuguese Sundew takes about a day to eat a mosquito.

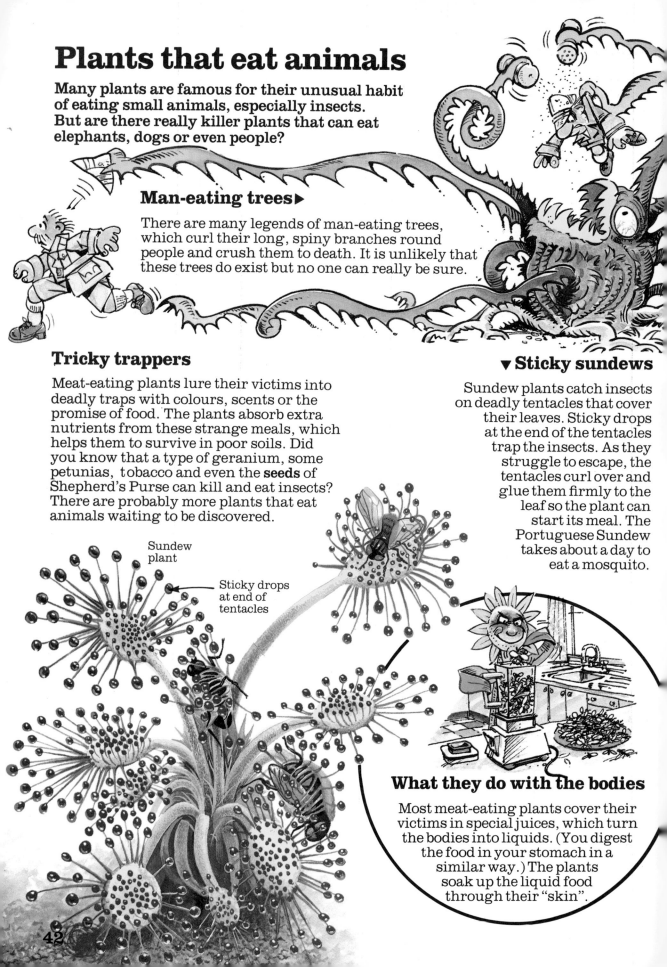

Sundew plant

Sticky drops at end of tentacles

What they do with the bodies

Most meat-eating plants cover their victims in special juices, which turn the bodies into liquids. (You digest the food in your stomach in a similar way.) The plants soak up the liquid food through their "skin".

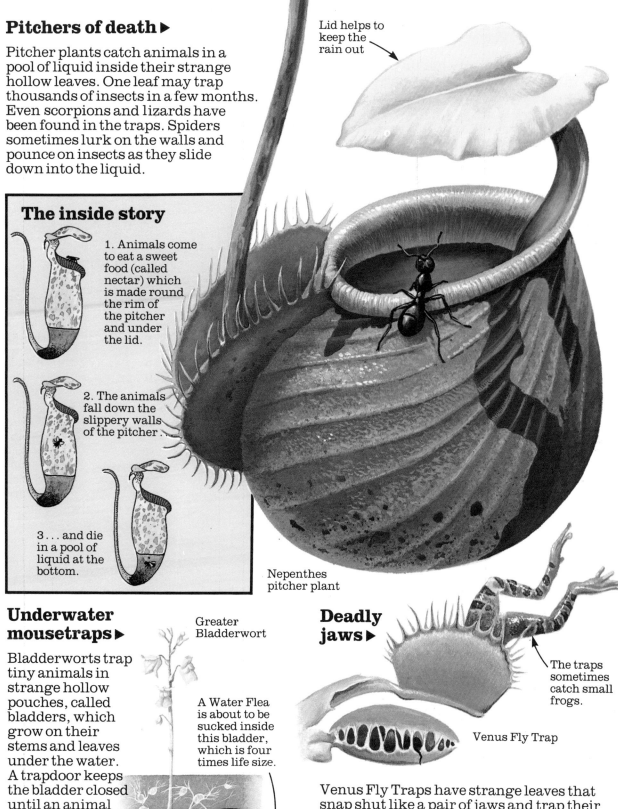

Pitchers of death ▶

Pitcher plants catch animals in a pool of liquid inside their strange hollow leaves. One leaf may trap thousands of insects in a few months. Even scorpions and lizards have been found in the traps. Spiders sometimes lurk on the walls and pounce on insects as they slide down into the liquid.

Lid helps to keep the rain out

The inside story

1. Animals come to eat a sweet food (called nectar) which is made round the rim of the pitcher and under the lid.

2. The animals fall down the slippery walls of the pitcher.

3 . . . and die in a pool of liquid at the bottom.

Nepenthes pitcher plant

Underwater mousetraps ▶

Greater Bladderwort

Bladderworts trap tiny animals in strange hollow pouches, called bladders, which grow on their stems and leaves under the water. A trapdoor keeps the bladder closed until an animal touches the hairs around the entrance. Some Bladderwort traps are only about the size of a full stop.

A Water Flea is about to be sucked inside this bladder, which is four times life size.

Deadly jaws ▶

The traps sometimes catch small frogs.

Venus Fly Trap

Venus Fly Traps have strange leaves that snap shut like a pair of jaws and trap their victims inside. The leafy jaws close only when something brushes against sensitive hairs on the surface of the leaf. Try growing a Venus Fly Trap yourself and see how many animals each leaf gobbles up.

Weird and wonderful flowers

Flowers are probably the most amazing structures in the plant world. Their wonderful shapes and colours are linked to their main purpose in life, which is to produce seeds. Some flowers need pollen from other flowers before their seeds can develop. They rely on the wind, water or animals to bring the pollen to them. Other flowers use their own pollen to produce seeds.

Marcgravia flower bud

Pouches full of sweet nectar

TRUE or FALSE?

Blue roses flower only in China.

Bird-of-paradise flower
Birds land here and pollen is brushed on to their feathers.

Pollen puzzle

These Birch Tree catkins are groups of male flowers, which produce the yellow dust called pollen.
How many pollen grains do you think each catkin produces?

One catkin can produce up to 5,500,000 pollen grains. Because there is so much pollen, at least some of it stands a chance of being blown by the wind to the female flowers so that seeds can develop.

The flower buds of the **Clove Tree** are dried and used as a spice in cooking.

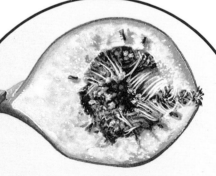

Fantastic fig flowers

The tiny flowers of figs are actually in the middle of the fig itself. Fig wasps carry pollen from the male to the female flowers.

◀ Curious clock flowers

Many flowers open and close at certain times of day. No one understands how these flower "clocks" work. They may help to protect the pollen from cold or rain, or they may make sure the flowers are open when animals are most likely to visit them. The famous botanist Carl Linnaeus planted a flower clock in his garden. He could tell the time by looking to see which flowers were open.

The rare **Lady's Slipper** is the largest European orchid with flowers up to 10 cm across.

male flowers

female flowers

The shoot lasts only a few days and smells of rotting meat.

Flowering shoot of *Amorphophallus prainii*

▼ Underground flowers

Two unusual Australian orchids live and flower below the surface of the soil. No one is sure how they manage to produce seeds. They may use their own pollen but if they do need pollen from the flowers on another plant, how does it reach them? This is still a mystery.

Trunks that sprout flowers

Many jungle trees have flowers that sprout straight out of their trunks and larger branches. This may make it easier for animals to find the flowers and feed from them. The trees rely on animals, such as bats, to pick up pollen while they are feeding and carry it to other trees.

Flower advertisements

Many flowers rely on animal messengers to carry their pollen to other flowers. They use colour and scent signals as well as tricks and disguises to persuade the messengers to visit their flowers at the right time.

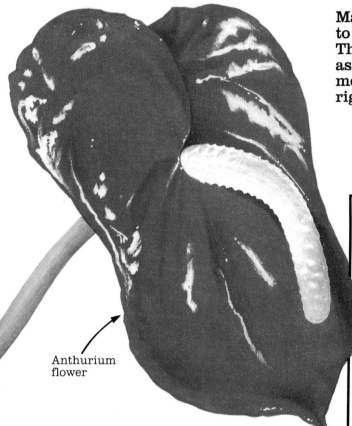

Anthurium flower

▲ Flowers in fancy dress

Brightly coloured structures around the flowers often attract animal messengers. The bright red hood on this Anthurium flower probably helps to attract insects to the yellow "tail" of tiny flowers.

Secret signals for bees

Did you know that flowers attract bees with colours and markings you cannot see? For example, a Wild Cherry flower looks white to you but bees see it as blue-green. Bees can also see ultra-violet light, which is invisible to you. So they can see markings on this Evening Primrose flower that you cannot see.

Bees can see these markings on the flower.

The flower looks like this to us.

Female impersonators ▶

Some extraordinary orchids attract male insects with flowers that look, smell and feel like females of their own species. This Mirror Orchid attracts a species of wasp. The male wasps appear earlier in the year than the females so the orchid flowers open when the males appear — before they have real female wasps to compete with.

furry "body"

folded "wings"

Smelly flowers ▶

Many flowers produce perfumes to attract animal pollen carriers. Sometimes these perfumes smell very unpleasant to us. This Stapelia flower reeks of decaying flesh. This smells like a tasty meal to flies that feed on rotting flesh so they are tricked into visiting the flower.

Stapelia flower

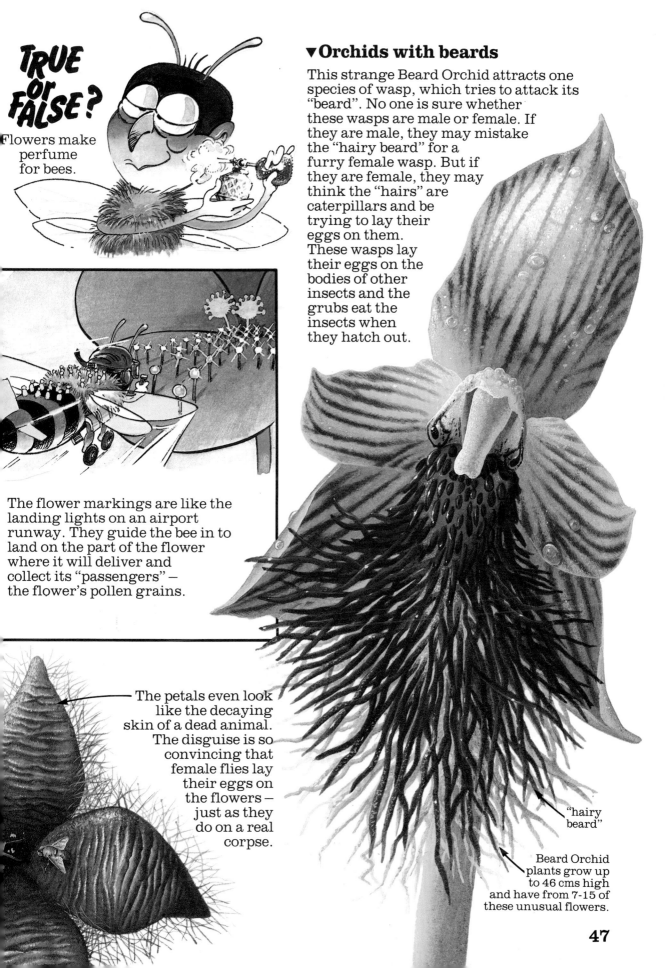

TRUE or FALSE?

Flowers make perfume for bees.

The flower markings are like the landing lights on an airport runway. They guide the bee in to land on the part of the flower where it will deliver and collect its "passengers" – the flower's pollen grains.

The petals even look like the decaying skin of a dead animal. The disguise is so convincing that female flies lay their eggs on the flowers – just as they do on a real corpse.

▼Orchids with beards

This strange Beard Orchid attracts one species of wasp, which tries to attack its "beard". No one is sure whether these wasps are male or female. If they are male, they may mistake the "hairy beard" for a furry female wasp. But if they are female, they may think the "hairs" are caterpillars and be trying to lay their eggs on them. These wasps lay their eggs on the bodies of other insects and the grubs eat the insects when they hatch out.

"hairy beard"

Beard Orchid plants grow up to 46 cms high and have from 7-15 of these unusual flowers.

47

Pollen take-aways

Once a plant has attracted an animal messenger to its flowers, it has to try and make sure the messenger delivers and collects some pollen. Many plants reward their messengers with a sweet food called nectar, or a place to lay their eggs. This means they are more likely to visit the flowers again.

Long-nosed Bat

Agave flower

Long, bristly tongue to lap up nectar.

◄ Bat postmen

Many tropical flowers use a bat messenger service to transport their pollen. This Agave flower hides the bats' wages of nectar deep inside the flower. As a bat licks up nectar with its long tongue, it collects pollen dust on its head. The bat may carry this pollen away to another flower.

Taking prisoners

The Aristolochia flower takes flies prisoner to make sure they deliver any pollen they have brought with them **before** they collect its own pollen. The flower only holds its prisoners in jail overnight and gives them a meal of sweet nectar. The next day, the flower sprinkles the prisoners with its own pollen before it allows them to escape through the entrance to the trap.

Flies deliver pollen here as they try to get out of a false window.

Aristolochia flower cut in half so you can see inside.

Flies slide down a chute of slippery hairs into the trap.

Flies are trapped in this prison overnight.

Yucca Moth

pollen

▲ A special messenger

Yucca flowers rely on a tiny moth to gather their pollen and carry it to exactly the right spot on another flower. The flowers cannot develop seeds without the help of their moth messenger. In return, the moth lays her eggs on the flower and the caterpillars eat some of the Yucca seeds.

Nectar – the super fuel ▶

Hummingbirds need the high-energy nectar they sip from flowers to power their amazingly rapid flight. They can beat their wings as fast as 80 times per second and hover motionless in front of flowers. If a person used up energy at the same rate as a Hummingbird, they would have to eat 150 kilograms of hamburgers every day.

Penstemon flower

Hummingbird

Yucca plant

▼Bees get drunk on orchids

The amazing Bucket Orchid produces a special nectar that makes bees drunk enough to fall into a pool of water inside one of its petals. As a bee staggers up an escape tunnel, the flower's pollen sacs stick to its body.

TRUE or FALSE?

Orchids are used to make ice cream.

A false female ▶

This male Ichneumon Wasp thinks the Tongue Orchid is a female wasp. He glues the orchid's pollen sacs to himself as he tries to mate with the flower.

pollen sacs

Tongue Orchid

◀ Bee transport

Milkweed flowers pack all their pollen into strange waxy bags. As bees sip nectar from the flowers, the bags may clip on to their legs and be carried off to another Milkweed flower.

49

Seed hitch-hikers

Seeds stand a better chance of growing into new plants if they do not have to compete with their parents for light, water and nutrients. They may travel away to a new area by hitching a ride on the wind, water currents, passing animals or sometimes even car tyres.

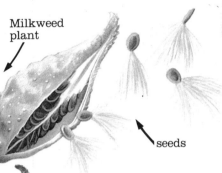

Milkweed plant

seeds

▲ Ocean travellers

Coconuts float away from their parent trees on the ocean currents. They may drift for several months and travel for up to 2,000 kilometres before reaching dry land. Special fibres around the seeds help the coconuts to float.

◀ Plant parachutes

Each Milkweed seed with its parachute of fluffy white fibres, can float on the wind for many kilometres. The fibres are so light that they have even been used to fill life jackets, which keep people afloat in water.

Exploding cucumbers

The Squirting Cucumber gets its name from its strange fruits. They burst open to shoot its seeds up to 8 metres away from the parent plant. The seeds zoom off like bullets from a gun and may travel as fast as a hundred kilometres per hour.

Wind witches ▶

Are there really giant witches that chase people over the plains in Russia? These legends are probably based on the unusual behaviour of a plant that uproots itself and rolls along in the wind to scatter its seeds. If large numbers of these plants become hooked together, they may look like "wind witches".

Seed stowaways

Many seeds stow away on the bodies of furry animals. Burdock seeds have rows of hooks to grip the coat of a passing animal. They may be carried several kilometres before they are brushed off by the undergrowth. If they land on a suitable patch of soil, they have a good chance of growing into new plants.

Burdock seed

The Durian is a favourite food of the Orang-utan.

The smelly Durian ▲

The Durian fruit attracts many mammals with its strange smell. It may grow as large as a football and has custard-like flesh around the seed. When animals eat the fruits, the seeds pass through their bodies unharmed and come out in their droppings. This may be some distance from the parent tree.

Some seeds get about in the mud on animals' feet. Charles Darwin once grew 80 plants from the mud he scraped off a bird's foot.

◄ Seed kites

The seeds of the Chinese Lantern are blown away from their parent plant inside shining red kites. The kite on the left is one that did not get away. You can see the seed inside.

Paeonia obovata

▲ A colourful peony

The bright pink seeds of this peony seem to develop just to attract birds. They cannot grow into new plants. Birds eat all the seeds, which eventually pass out in their droppings. If the blue seeds land on a suitable patch of ground, they may grow into new plants.

TRUE or FALSE?

Mexican beans jump away from their parent plant.

51

Fantastic fungi

Fungi are very curious plants. They have a "body" of tiny branching threads, which can absorb food from living or dead plants or animals. Sometimes the threads weave together to make fruiting bodies, which often look like mushrooms but may be more unusual shapes, such as "ears". The fruiting bodies produce the spores of the fungus, which can grow into new plants. They often seem to pop up from the ground with almost magical speed.

◀ Fur coat fungi

The ermine coat worn by this beetle is the white threads of a mould fungus, which is feeding on its body. Some fungi even feed on people. Athlete's foot and ringworm are caused by fungi feeding on human skin.

Ear fungus

▲ Even trees have ears

This strange "ear" is the fruiting body of a fungus that feeds on dead wood. If fungi did not eat up dead material, the world would be a huge rubbish dump piled high with litter.

TRUE or FALSE?

Fungi are strong enough to grow through roads and pavements.

Truffle

◀ Strange partners and pigs

Truffles are the fruiting bodies of a fungus that grows only in a strange partnership with tree roots. The fungus takes food from the tree but makes some nutrients in the soil available to the tree in return. Truffles rely on animals to dig them up, eat them and spread the spores in their droppings. They attract animals by producing some of the smells the animals make themselves.

Animal trappers ▼

A few microscopic fungi have special traps to catch tiny animals. These range from sticky threads and fishing lines to nooses, which squeeze shut when eelworms try to wriggle through. Some fungus **spores** can follow the scent trail worms leave in the soil.

Do fungi make nests?

Some strange fungi grow fruiting bodies that look like birds' nests. They even have eggs inside. The "eggs" are, in fact, cases full of spores, which often jump out of the nest when rain drops splash inside. Some spore cases even have sticky tails, which help them to cling on to another plant before they reach the ground.

spore case

A stinking cage ▼

This strange Cage Fungus takes only a few hours to grow. The black slime inside the cage contains spores and gives out a foul smell. This attracts flies, which eat the slime and spread the spores in their droppings.

Flies feeding on slime

Rich grass where fungi are releasing nutrients.

Grass may wither where fungi have used up nutrients.

▲ Fairy rings

People have blamed rings of toadstools on fairies, whirlwinds, haystacks, moles or underground smoke rings. But the strange rings are really formed by giant colonies of toadstools growing outwards year by year from a central point. Some rings may be 600 years old.

Puffball prizewinners

Puffballs release small clouds of minute spores, which are carried by the wind to new ground. An average-sized Giant Puffball 30 centimetres across can produce 7,000,000,000,000 spores. If all these spores grew into mature puffballs, they would stretch thousands of times round the earth.

Marvellous mini-plants

Some of the smallest plants in the world can trace their ancestors back over 2,000,000,000 years. A few of them can survive in blocks of ice or nearly boiling water. Some even live on hairs.

Diatom spaceships

These weird structures, which look like pill boxes, sieves or even spaceships are all kinds o tiny plants called diatoms. They live in water and in the soil and are so small about 2,500 would fit along this line _____. You need a microscope to see their strange shapes.

The sloths' hidden secret ▶

Some minute plants, called algae, live in grooves on the hairs of sloths, which makes the hair look greenish. This helps sloths to blend into the leafy background of their jungle home so that they are safer from enemies. Sloths never clean their fur so the algae do not get washed off the hairs.

What makes snow red?

Mysterious patches of red snow sometimes appear on mountains. They are caused by vast numbers of tiny algae. Each plant is about as big as this full stop.

▼ Strange spore holders

Some mini-plants produce their spores in strange structures, which look like horns, matchsticks, Chinese pagodas or even jam tarts.

Stag's-horn Clubmoss
Yellow "horns" a few cms high hold the spores. Clubmosses 30 metres high lived 300,000,000 years ago.

Sphagnum Moss
The capsule fires its spores into the air like airgun pellets. The spores may land up to 2 metres away.

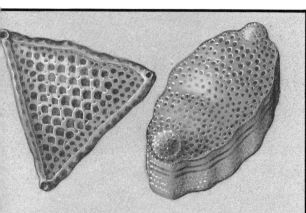

Diatoms are very simple plants consisting of one cell with a coat of silica round it. Each species of diatom has a different pattern of ridges, furrows and holes in its silica coat.

Plants that eat rocks ▶

The amazing coloured patterns on these rocks are actually tiny plants called lichens. The brilliant colours are lichen acids, which help to protect the plants from strong sunlight. The lichens also produce different acids, which eat into the rocks and make them crumble. Then they send out tiny "roots" to absorb minerals from the rocks. By breaking up the rocks in this way, the lichens slowly turn them into soil, where other plants can grow.

TRUE or FALSE?

Clubmosses are used to make fireworks.

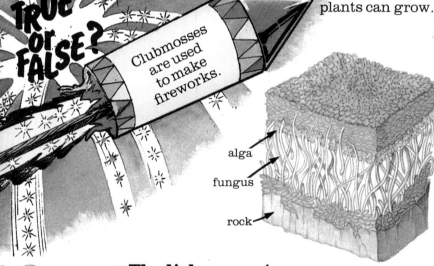

alga
fungus
rock

◀ Living together

Lichens are two plants, an alga and a fungus, which live together in a strange partnership. The alga provides the fungus with food. In return, the fungus holds water for the alga and protects it from fierce winds and too much strong sunlight.

▼ The lichen mystery

These lichen fruiting bodies are made by the fungus partner in the lichen. The spores inside them cannot grow into a new lichen unless they find the right sort of alga to grow with. No one is sure how this happens.

Cup Lichen
Spores are produced round the rim of the cups.

Devil's Matches
Red tips of lichen produce spores.

Lecanora Lichen
Brown discs hold the spores.

Lunularia Liverwort
Special cups have small "buds" inside, which can form new plants. The "buds" splash out in raindrops.

55

Life at the top

High up on mountains, the strong sunlight, fierce winds, thin soils and freezing night-time temperatures make life very difficult for plants. Yet some amazing plants manage to survive there.

The flowering spike of the Silversword is about 2 metres high.

Silversword

Silverswords from Hawaii

The spectacular Silversword lives only on the tops of old volcanoes on two Hawaiian islands. Only about 7 centimetres of rain fall each year so the Silversword may take 20 years to store enough water for flowering. A few weeks later, the plant dies.

Furry flowers ▶

The white colour helps to reflect strong sun, which may harm the flower.

The European Edelweiss has a thick coat of hairs, which help to trap the warmth of the sun and stop water escaping from the plant.

Vegetable sheep

Some mountain plants grow close to the ground with their short stems packed tightly together to form strange cushions. This helps them to escape from the wind and they can also trap heat in the cushion. In some places, these cushions grow so big they have been mistaken for sheep.

Elfin woods ▶

Did you know that the trees on some mountains are so small you can walk over the top of them? Dwarf Willows grow in dense carpets only a few centimetres high. Their branches bend easily so they can twist and turn close to the ground. There they are out of reach of the fierce winds, which may be strong enough to blow a person over.

Plants with central heating

The tiny shoot of the Alpine Snowbell produces enough heat to melt a hole in the snow. It can then reach the surface to flower in early spring.

TRUE or FALSE?

Flowers grow at the top of Mount Everest.

The plants are often surrounded by a swirling mist.

Dwarf Willow

Spike of flowers on a giant Lobelia.

The flowers are buried under these bracts.

Mystery of the Mountain Giants

Extraordinary giant plants grow in the mountains of Central Africa. Bizarre Lobelias and Tree Groundsels grow in a landscape that looks like a scene from a science fiction film. Why they grow several metres high here is a mystery. Elsewhere in the world, they usually grow no more than a $\frac{1}{3}$ of a metre high.

Dead leaves lag the trunk of a Tree Groundsel and keep it warm.

Not a drop to drink

It takes a very special sort of plant to cope with the boiling hot days (up to 83°C), freezing nights and the dry soils of a desert. Desert plants have special features such as spines, vast root systems and deadly poisons to help them survive.

The **Gila Woodpecker** may nest in a Saguaro Cactus. It can be up to 30°C cooler inside.

▲ Blooming magic

Many plants survive the dry season as seeds buried in the desert sands. As soon as there is enough rain, they suddenly sprout and produce flowers and seeds. The seed of one African plant (*Boerhavia repens*) takes only 8 to 10 days to grow into a mature plant, and produce seeds of its own.

▲ The leaf trick

In the dry season, the Ocotillo plant sheds all its leaves so that it does not lose moisture through them. It grows a new set of leaves as soon as it rains.

Barrel Cactus spines have been used as fish hooks.

◄ Saguaro skyscrapers

Giant Saguaro Cacti may grow up to 15.2 metres high and live for over 200 years. They do not usually grow "arms" until they are 75 years old. Large Saguaros may weigh as much as two elephants. Three quarters of this weight is the water they store in their huge stems. The pleats in the stem expand like a concertina as the cactus takes up water. A waxy outer skin helps to stop water escaping.

TRUE or FALSE?

Plants scream when they are thirsty.

Joshua Trees are such a strange shape because their branches bend in a new direction whenever a fresh blossom forms.

Teddy Bear Chollas have a lot of spines, which lose less water than leaves.

Woolly cacti

Some strange cacti are covered in a fine "wool". This probably helps to protect them from the extremely hot days and cold nights in the desert. The "wool" may also work like a net to trap moisture near to the stem of the cactus.

Keeping the neighbours away

Creosote Bushes are often spaced out at surprisingly regular intervals. The secret ingredient that keeps the neighbours away is a poison given off by their roots. This stops other plants from growing too close so each bush has a good space and all the available water to itself.

Creosote Bush

Prickly Pear Cacti have a vast network of shallow roots to soak up moisture.

Plant mysteries

▼ Strange seed showers

Many people claim to have been pelted with thousands of seeds that suddenly fell down from somewhere high in the sky. Rice, wheat, barley and even hazelnuts have been reported in these strange showers. The cause is a mystery although people have blamed the showers on whirlwinds or strong winds high up in the atmosphere.

The secret life of plants

Plants seem to respond to people, noises and other things around them in ways that no one really understands. But many people claim to have made startling new discoveries that could change the way we think about plants. Try testing some of these ideas on your own plants.

This fungus glows green but other species produce blue, white or yellow light.

◄ Night lights

Many plants, especially fungi, produce an eerie light at night. Some fungi even produce enough light to read by. No one knows why they do this. Some scientists have suggested that the fungi use the light to attract the flies they need to scatter their spores. But why should some geraniums, marigolds and mosses glow in the dark?

People with "green fingers"

Why are some people especially good at growing plants? No one is really sure but plants seem to be able to respond to people praising them and wanting them to grow well. Some people produce chemicals in their sweat that may help plants to grow better.

Can plants read your mind?

Some people claim that a plant will react if you just **think** about burning one of its leaves. Other experiments seem to show that plants will grow badly or even die if people keep thinking nasty thoughts about them.

Do plants grow better to music?

Many people think they do. Some people even claim that Bach and classical Indian Sitar music is better for plants than rock music. Research has shown that crop plants grow better to the vibrations of an electric motor and loud noises can make seeds sprout more quickly.

Can plants remember?

Some people claim that a plant "remembered" the killer of a plant that was growing next to it and even picked out the guilty person from a group of people. Other experiments have shown that plants can "remember" injuries to their leaves.

▲The twisted tree mystery

The reason for the weird twisted trunk of this tree is a mystery. Some people think that a radioactive meteor may have caused the trunk to start growing in this strange way hundreds of years ago.

◀The mystery of the veiled lady

No one is sure why this tropical Stinkhorn Fungus has such a fantastic lacy veil. It may help to make the fungus more attractive to the flies that it needs to carry its spores away. The fungus grows as fast as 5mm a minute and some people believe it is magical.

How do bamboos count?

Some bamboos flower at very strange times. A few species wait 20 or 30 years before flowering and then die. Other species flower at odd intervals for many years. One species flowered at 14, 39 and then 7 year intervals. All bamboos of the same species flower at the same time even if they are taken to the other side of the world. How do bamboos count the years? People have suggested that sunspots may be involved but no one really knows.

Record breakers

The amazing Welwitschia

The *Welwitschia mirabilis* plant only ever grows two leaves although it may live for 100 years or more. The leaves grow about 5-8 centimetres a year and the largest recorded leaves were 8.2 metres by 2 metres.

Largest leaves

The Raffia Palm has the largest leaves in the world. Its leaves measure up to twenty metres in length and are taller than most trees.

Smallest flowering plant

A floating duckweed called *Wolffia arrhiza* is the smallest flowering plant in the world. Its fronds are only 0.5 – 1.2 millimetres across and 25 of these plants would fit across your fingernail.

Deepest roots

The deepest roots ever reported were those of a wild fig tree in South Africa, which grew to a depth of 120 metres.

Largest living thing

The largest living thing on earth is a Giant Sequoia Tree from California, U.S.A., which is called "General Sherman". It is 83 metres tall and measures 24.11 metres round the trunk. It contains enough timber for forty bungalows or 5,000,000,000 matches.

First space plant

The first plant to flower and produce seeds in the zero gravity of space is called Arabidopsis. It has a short life cycle of about forty days and was grown on board the Soviet Union's Salyut-7 space station in 1982.

Largest water plant

The Giant Water Lily from the Amazon is the world's largest water plant. Its leaves can grow up to two metres across and they are strong enough to take the weight of a child. Thick ribs under the leaf help it to float.

Largest rose tree

A "Lady Banks" rose tree at Tombstone, Arizona, U.S.A. has a trunk 101 centimetres thick, stands 2.74 metres high and covers an area of 499 square metres. It is supported by 68 posts and 150 people can sit underneath it.

World's oldest living thing

A lichen from Antarctica is thought to be at least 10,000 years old and could be much older. Other lichens in Alaska are at least 9,000 years old and grow only 3.4mm in a hundred years.

World's oldest seed plant

The ancestors of the Gingko or Maidenhair Tree first appeared in China about 180,000,000 years ago. This was the Jurassic Period, when dinosaurs roamed the earth. The Gingko trees alive today look very much like their ancestors from these ancient times.

Most and least nutritious fruit

The **most** nutritious fruit in the world is the Avocado. It contains 741 calories per edible pound. The **least** nutritious fruit in the world is the cucumber. It contains only 73 calories per edible pound.

Slowest flowering plant

The rare *Puya raimondii* from the Andes does not flower until it is about 150 years old. After this the plant dies.

Hardiest seeds

Arctic Lupin seeds found frozen in the soil in the Canadian Yukon were believed to be between 10,000 and 15,000 years old. Some of them sprouted and grew into plants; one even developed flowers.

Monster fruit and vegetables

Here are just some of the largest fruit and vegetables ever recorded.
Cabbage...51.8 kg
Cauliflower...23.9 kg
Tomato...1.9 kg
Pumpkin...171.4 kg
Mushroom...190 cm (round the edge of the cap)
Lemon...2.65 kg
Pineapple...7.5 kg
Melon...40.8 kg

Were they true or false?

page 37. Lianas grow as tall as the Eiffel Tower and are strong enough to take the weight of an elephant.
Possibly true. The Eiffel Tower is 320 metres high and there are a few lianas on record with stems over 300 metres long. A tangle of liana stems can hold up a giant jungle tree so several lianas together **might** be able to take the weight of an elephant (about 5.7 tonnes).

page 39. Green potatoes can poison children.
True. Green potatoes contain large amounts of strong poisons called solanines, which are especially dangerous to children. The poisons are not destroyed by boiling or cooking.

page 41. Ants make apples grow on Oak Trees.
False. A structure called an oak apple gall does grow on some Oak Trees but a female **wasp** causes the tree to grow the "apple" by laying her eggs in an Oak bud.

page 44. Blue roses flower only in China.
False. There is, as yet, no such thing as a true blue rose – or a black rose.

page 47. Flowers make perfume for bees.
Partly true. A species of Euglossa bee from Latin America collects scent from orchids. The scent attracts other male bees and the sight of a glittering group of male bees in turn attracts female bees.

page 49. Orchids are used to make ice cream.
Partly true. The flavouring in some kinds of vanilla ice cream comes from the cured seed pod of an orchid called *Vanilla planifolia*.

page 51. Mexican beans jump away from their parent plant.
False. A caterpillar living inside the beans of the Mexican Arrow Plant makes them leap into the air.

page 52. Fungi are strong enough to grow through roads and pavements.
True. Fungi such as the Ink Cap can break up asphalt and even lift paving stones.

page 55. Clubmosses are used to make fireworks.
True. The spore cases of the Stag's Horn Clubmoss produce a bright yellow powder, which was used at one time to make fireworks.

page 57. Flowers grow at the top of Mount Everest.
False. Everest is 8,848 metres high and the highest altitude at which any flowering plant has been found is 6,135 metres. This was for a plant called *Stellaria decumbens* in the Himalayas.

page 59. Plants scream when they are thirsty.
Partly true. An Australian scientist found that plants make clicking noises when they are thirsty. The noises are caused by the vibrations of the tiny water pipes inside plants.

---

page 38. How many pebble plants?

There are **10** different kinds of pebble plant in the picture.

Further reading

Flowers, R. Kidman Cox & B. Cork and *Trees*, R. Thomson (Usborne First Nature series)
The Nature Trail Book of Wild Flowers, S. Tarsky (Usborne)
The Nature Trail Book of Trees & Leaves, I. Selberg (Usborne)
Spotter's Guide to Wild Plants, (Usborne)
The Macmillan Colour Library: Plants, M. Chinery (Macmillan Children's Books)
The Life of Plants, R. Wilson (Ward Lock)
Discover the World of Plants, (Arrow Books)
A Closer Look At Plant Life, B. Stonehouse (Hamish Hamilton or Scimitar)
Discovering Life on Earth, D. Attenborough (Collins)
Strange Plants and their Ways, R. E. Hutchins (Burke)
The Hidden Life of Flowers, J. M. Guilcher & R. H. Noailles (Sterling)
Plant and Planet, A. Huxley (Penguin)
The Secret Life of Plants, P. Tompkins & C. Bird (Penguin)
Nature, Mother of Invention, F. Paturi (Penguin)

Botanic Man, D. Bellamy (Hamlyn)
The Plants, F. R. Went (Time-Life International)
Nature's Use of Colour in Plants and their Flowers, J. & S. Proctor (Peter Lowe)
Poisonous Plants and Fungi in Colour, P. M. North (Blandford)
Carnivorous Plants, A. Slack (Ebury Press)
The Sex Life of Plants, A. Bristow (Barrie & Jenkins)
The Love of Mushrooms and Toadstools, G. Kibby (Octopus)
The Wonderful World of Mushrooms and other Fungi, H. L. Pursey (Hamlyn)
Lichens, Fungi, H. Angel (Angus & Robertson)
Popular Exotic Cacti in Colour, E. & B. Lamb (Blandford)
Jungles, E. S. Ayensu (Jonathan Cape)
The Life of the Jungle, P. W. Richards (McGraw-Hill)
The Life of the Desert, A. & M. Sutton (McGraw-Hill)
The Desert: Young Readers Library, A. Starker (Time Life International)

PART 3

MYSTERIES & MARVELS
OF THE
ANIMAL
WORLD

Karen Goaman and Heather Amery

Consultant: Joyce Pope

Designed by Anne Sharples
and Nigel Frey

Illustrated by David Quinn
Sarah DeAth (Linden Artists), Ian Jackson,
Rob McCaig, Chris Shields (Wilcock Riley),
and David Wright (Jillian Burgess)

Cartoons by John Shackell

The Fennec Fox lives in hot deserts.

A Lioness carries her cub to a new resting place.

Contents

The Spiny Anteater, lays eggs.

A Gorilla uses a large leaf as an umbrella.

A Grizzly Bear lives on a wide variety of food.

The Aardvaark is almost naked.

The Duck-billed Platypus feeds underwater but breathes air.

Introduction

Part Three is a fascinating introduction to the world of land mammals. By concentrating on the unusual, the extraordinary and the unexplained, it provides a stimulating starting point to a study of many aspects of mammal life, such as the way they live in different habitats, find food, move about and communicate.

Mammals are different from other land animals, such as birds, insects, snakes or frogs, although they do have some things in common. All mammals breathe air and are warm-blooded and most have fur or hair. Mammals give birth to live young (except two which lay eggs) and all females produce milk for their babies and care for them. Many mammals are intelligent and curious, using tools, trying new foods and exploring new environments.

This part of the book will lead to an understanding of the huge variety and interdependence of mammal life but points out that there is still much to be discovered about mammals and the way they live in the wild.

A Giant Panda mainly eats bamboo.

A Kongoni calf feeding on its mother's milk.

TRUE or FALSE?

Look out for these questions and try to guess if they are true or false. The answers are on p. 96.

Strange start to life

Most mammals give birth to babies which are fully formed. But two strange mammals lay eggs and the young of marsupials, such as the Kangaroos, develop in their mothers' pouches.

Spiny Anteater

The eccentric egg-layers

The Platypus lays her eggs in a nest at the end of a long burrow in a river bank. After the babies hatch, they lick the milk which oozes from their mother's skin on to the fur of her tummy.

Platypus at entrance to burrow

Platypus nest

The eggs are sticky and have soft shells.

The Spiny Anteater, or Echidna, keeps her egg in her pouch but no one knows how she gets it in there. One suggestion is that she curls up very tightly as she lays an egg so that it pops straight into the pouch.

Long crawl into the pouch

A newborn Kangaroo is like a small lump of pink jelly with arms. Blind and helpless, it has to crawl up its mother's fur from the birth opening into the pouch where it will develop.

Kangaroo's tummy

Entrance to pouch.

New born Kangaroo

Birth opening.

Grey Kangaroo and Joey

Inside the pouch, the baby Kangaroo fastens on to a teat to suck milk.

A Joey feeds on its mother's milk until it is about a year old.

◄ Jumping joeys

A young Kangaroo is called a joey. When it is about six months old, it starts to spend time outside its pouch. To get back in, it dives in head first, then turns a somersault to come up the right way again.

Growing up

Back packers ▶

A Koala baby spends its first six months in its mother's pouch and another six months riding around on her back.

The young koala feeds on eucalyptus leaves over its mother's shoulder.

Opossum with young

The Opossum feeds at night, climbing trees with hands and feet and clinging on with its claws.

Koala with baby

Clinging on all over ▶

The female Opossum has a big pouch for her eighteen or so babies. But after about ten weeks they grow too big to fit in it. Then she carries them about and they cling on anywhere they can — on her back, tummy and even on her tail.

When a Hippo mother goes off to feed, she finds a baby sitter.

TRUE or FALSE?

Trailing along behind ▼

When a Shrew mother goes out for food, she takes her young with her in a long line, each holding on firmly to the one in front.

White-toothed shrews

Fantastic feeders

Some mammals have some fantastic
ways of getting at food and of storing it.

Mole's worm larder ▶

The Mole hunts for earthworms and
insects in its tunnels. If it finds more
than it can eat, it bites them in the
back. This prevents the worms from
wriggling away but keeps them
alive and fresh for future meals. The
Mole then stores the worms in an
underground larder, which may
contain hundreds of worms. Moles
can eat their own weight in worms
each day, finding them with a keen
sense of smell and a sensitive nose.

Mole with store
of worms.

Leopards are good climbers
and can drag heavy weights
up trees.

Toothless wonder

The Giant Anteater has no
teeth. It tears open ant hills and
termites' nests with its long
curved claws. Then it pokes in
its tongue – 60 cm long – to
pick up the insects. These are
crushed by the strong
walls of its stomach. A
Giant Anteater will
swallow several
thousand ants or
termites for a single
meal.

Gazelle lodged in
the fork of a tree.

Spends much of the
day resting in trees
and hunts at night.

Leopard's tree larder

A Leopard often stores its
prey in a tree larder. It will
drag an animal it has killed
up a tree and lodge it in a
forked branch. Here it is
safe from scavengers and
the leopard has a ready
meal when hungry.

Leopard

Aye-Aye

Fantastic finger ▲

The Aye-Aye has an amazingly long and very useful middle finger. It knocks on the dead wood of a tree, listens for insects inside and pulls them out with its finger.

Giant Anteater

The Anteater can collect 500 ants with one lick!

Giraffe tongue ▶

The Giraffe uses its immensely long tongue and strong upper hairy lip to pull leaves off branches.

A giraffe has an extra-large heart to pump blood up its neck to its head. →

45 cm long black tongue.

TRUE or FALSE?

Goats in Tunisia jump on donkeys' backs to reach leaves on high branches of trees.

Salt miners ▶

Elephants living on Mount Elgon in Kenya walk into deep caves at night to mine salt. In total darkness, they strike the salty rock with their tusks, pick off lumps with their trunks and grind the rock up in their mouths. They need the salt as part of their diet. The caves have probably been carved out by elephants mining the rock over thousands of years.

Sniffs at rock to see how salty it is.

Strikes rock with tusks.

Supermovers

Swinging through the trees ▶

The Gibbon can hurl itself at top speed through the forest, swinging from tree to tree. It quickly grasps branches with alternate hands, hurling itself on again with each grasp. Moving like this, it can swing across spaces of 15 metres. Its long arms are its main way of getting about in the treetops.

A tail-less ape, a Gibbon can move through the trees faster than a man can run on the ground underneath.

Has a top speed of 16 kph through the trees.

Extremely long arms and very mobile wrists and shoulders.

Sugar Glider feeding on buds and flowers.

Outstretched skin in flight.

Fold of skin.

Gliding parachutist

The Sugar Glider can glide downwards for about 45 metres between trees. It takes a leap and stretches out the flaps of skin between its front and back legs like a parachute. Landing with great accuracy, it quickly climbs up the tree for another leap.

TRUE or FALSE?

The Gibbon is a tightrope artist.

Red Kangaroo

Leaps and bounds ▶

The Red Kangaroo can jump over obstacles as high as 3 metres. Using its very powerful hind legs, it can travel as far as 9 metres in one huge bound. It holds up its thick tail to help it balance when travelling fast. Over short distances, it can reach a speed of about 55 kilometres an hour.

A Cheetah is the fastest land animal.

Flexible spine moves up and down.

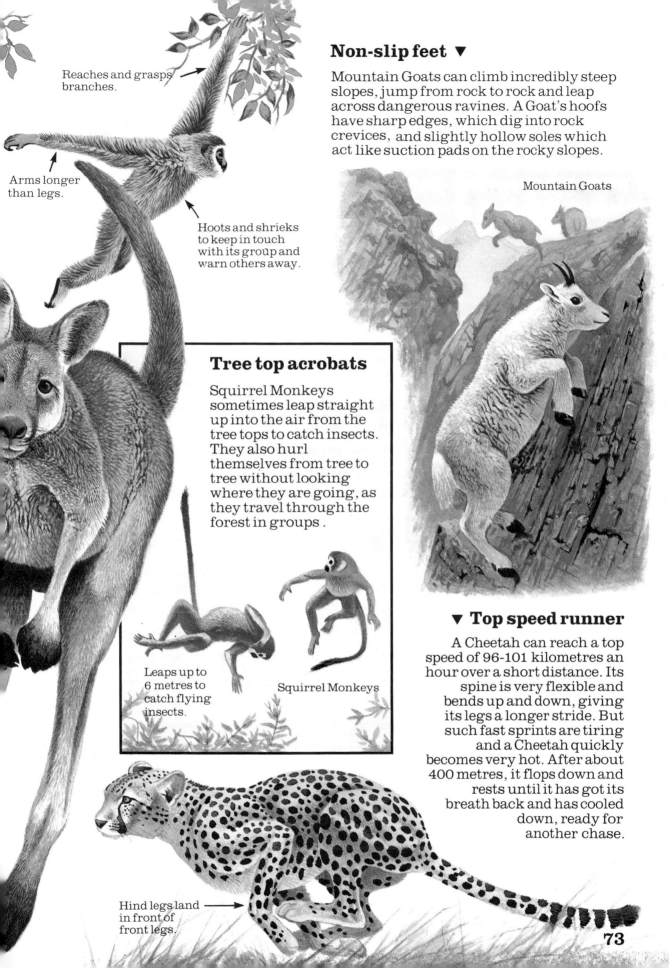

Reaches and grasps branches.

Arms longer than legs.

Hoots and shrieks to keep in touch with its group and warn others away.

Non-slip feet ▼

Mountain Goats can climb incredibly steep slopes, jump from rock to rock and leap across dangerous ravines. A Goat's hoofs have sharp edges, which dig into rock crevices, and slightly hollow soles which act like suction pads on the rocky slopes.

Mountain Goats

Tree top acrobats

Squirrel Monkeys sometimes leap straight up into the air from the tree tops to catch insects. They also hurl themselves from tree to tree without looking where they are going, as they travel through the forest in groups.

Leaps up to 6 metres to catch flying insects.

Squirrel Monkeys

▼ Top speed runner

A Cheetah can reach a top speed of 96-101 kilometres an hour over a short distance. Its spine is very flexible and bends up and down, giving its legs a longer stride. But such fast sprints are tiring and a Cheetah quickly becomes very hot. After about 400 metres, it flops down and rests until it has got its breath back and has cooled down, ready for another chase.

Hind legs land in front of front legs.

Midnight feasts

Some mammals sleep during the day, waking up at dusk for a busy night.

Blood-sucking vampires ▶

Vampire bats drink the blood of sleeping victims. During the night, they settle on a large animal, such as a cow. They make a very shallow bite which does not wake up the animal. Then they lap up the blood which runs from the wound. Their saliva contains a substance which prevents the blood from clotting and closing up the wound.

The black "devil"

How did the Tasmanian Devil get its name? Because it has a devilish snarl and a gaping mouth with strong teeth. It hunts at night, ambushing its prey which it pushes into its mouth with its front feet. But it looks more like a small, stubby bear than a devil.

Its heavy jaws can open to nearly a right angle.

Eats any flesh, alive or dead.

Tasmanian Devil

The laughing hyaenas ▶

Hyaenas set out at night to hunt in packs of up to 30. They run down a large animal, such as a wildebeest, biting it with their powerful jaws until it falls. After about 15 minutes, they have eaten every scrap, even cracking up bones with their strong teeth, and leaving no trace of the night's meal.

Uses ears and nose more than eyes to find its prey.

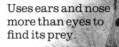
Spotted Haenas

TRUE or FALSE?

Frog-eating Bats choose the juiciest frog by listening to its mating call.

Daytime earplugs ▼

The Bushbaby has amazingly sharp hearing to help it find food in the dark. Its hearing is so good that when it sleeps during the day, it has to fold its ears inwards to plug up its earholes. Otherwise all the noises of the forest would keep it awake all day. It takes great care of its ears, curling them up before it leaps so that they do not catch on branches.

It can turn its head right round to look directly behind it.

Tarsier

Bushbaby

It can make huge leaps — up to 6 metres — from tree to tree.

The Bushbaby gets its name from the cries it makes at night which sound like a new-born baby.

The hyaena's call is a sad howl but when excited it gives a mad cackle.

Huge eyes ▲

The Tarsier's enormous eyes help it to see in the dark. It leaps like a frog, with jumps up to 2 metres, through the forest at night, searching for insects, young birds, eggs and lizards to eat. It has sticky round toe pads to help it cling to branches.

Curious and confusing colours

The changing colours

The Arctic Fox is smoky grey or brown in summer but in winter it turns white, making it hard to see against a background of snow and ice.

As the days get longer, it loses its white fur and grows grey fur. As the days shorten, white fur grows back again.

Summer coat

Under the coarse outer fur is a thick woolly layer which protects it from the Arctic cold.

Winter coat

Golden Lion Marmoset

Confusing stripes ▼

A Zebra's stripes may seem to make it very easily seen but, in the heat haze of the African plains, the stripes blur its outline. They act as a camouflage, especially when it is moving, and confuse its predators.

TRUE or FALSE?

Black Panthers really do exist in the forests of South America.

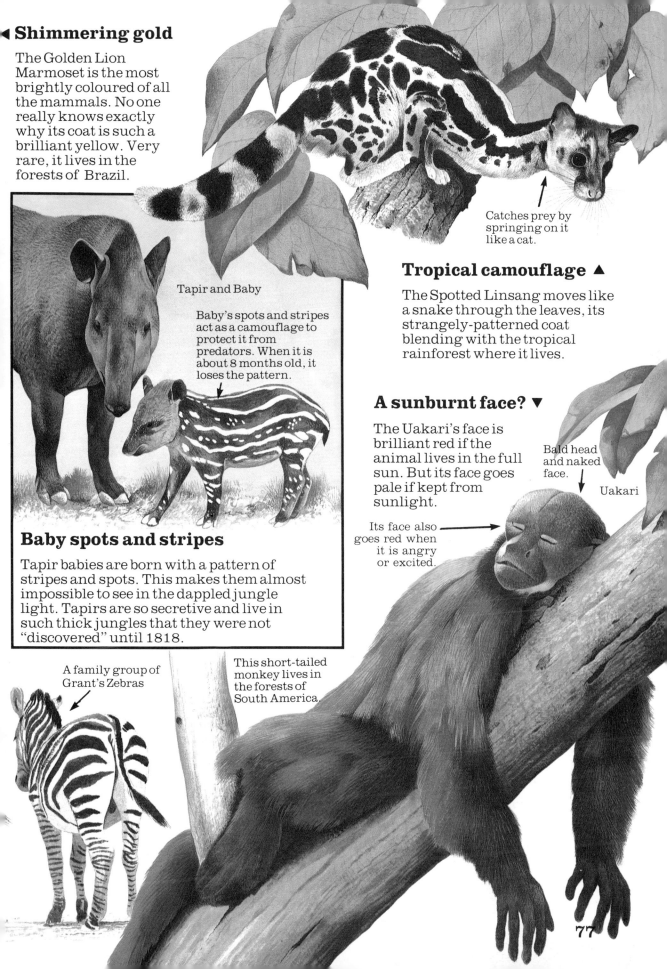

◀ Shimmering gold

The Golden Lion Marmoset is the most brightly coloured of all the mammals. No one really knows exactly why its coat is such a brilliant yellow. Very rare, it lives in the forests of Brazil.

Catches prey by springing on it like a cat.

Tapir and Baby

Baby's spots and stripes act as a camouflage to protect it from predators. When it is about 8 months old, it loses the pattern.

Baby spots and stripes

Tapir babies are born with a pattern of stripes and spots. This makes them almost impossible to see in the dappled jungle light. Tapirs are so secretive and live in such thick jungles that they were not "discovered" until 1818.

Tropical camouflage ▲

The Spotted Linsang moves like a snake through the leaves, its strangely-patterned coat blending with the tropical rainforest where it lives.

A sunburnt face? ▼

The Uakari's face is brilliant red if the animal lives in the full sun. But its face goes pale if kept from sunlight.

Bald head and naked face.

Uakari

Its face also goes red when it is angry or excited.

A family group of Grant's Zebras

This short-tailed monkey lives in the forests of South America.

Escape artists

A Springbok jumping or "pronking".

Springs and bounces ▶

When surprised or alarmed, the Springbok jumps straight up in the air, as high as 3 metres, with its body arched and legs stiff. This sets the whole herd springing and bouncing. No one knows why they do this. It may be a way of warning the herd of danger or it may confuse a predator, such as a cheetah, when it attacks the Springboks.

Springs up, arching back and lowering head.

TRUE or FALSE?

A porcupine shoots its quills at an enemy.

The Spotted Skunk does a handstand to squirt smelly liquid at an enemy.

In spite of their smell, Skunks are sometimes killed by golden eagles, foxes and coyotes.

◀ The smelly squirters

The Skunk, when disturbed, raises it tail, stamps its feet, growls and hisses. If this does not make an enemy retreat, it squirts a horrible-smelling liquid from glands under its tail. Its aim is very accurate with a range of up to 3 metres. The foul scent can be smelt half a kilometre away.

The Striped Skunk turns its back on its enemy to squirt at it.

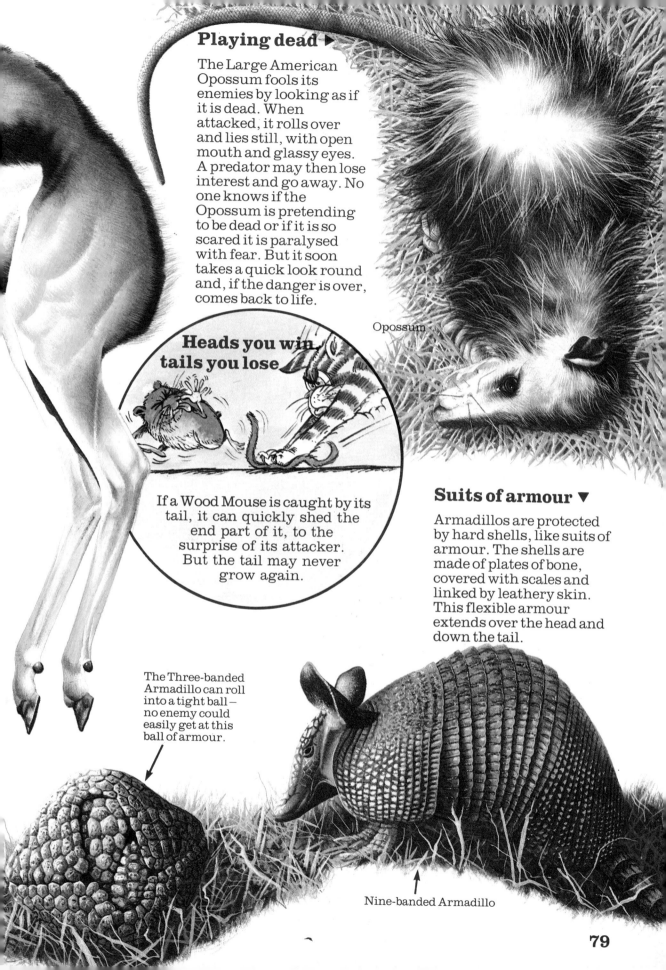

Playing dead ▶

The Large American Opossum fools its enemies by looking as if it is dead. When attacked, it rolls over and lies still, with open mouth and glassy eyes. A predator may then lose interest and go away. No one knows if the Opossum is pretending to be dead or if it is so scared it is paralysed with fear. But it soon takes a quick look round and, if the danger is over, comes back to life.

Opossum

Heads you win, tails you lose

If a Wood Mouse is caught by its tail, it can quickly shed the end part of it, to the surprise of its attacker. But the tail may never grow again.

Suits of armour ▼

Armadillos are protected by hard shells, like suits of armour. The shells are made of plates of bone, covered with scales and linked by leathery skin. This flexible armour extends over the head and down the tail.

The Three-banded Armadillo can roll into a tight ball – no enemy could easily get at this ball of armour.

Nine-banded Armadillo

Attack, fight or bluff?

Bighorn rams

The horns grow longer each year, adding a new ridge and curling round at the tips.

Fighting rams ▲

These Bighorn rams clash heads in a fight for the females of the herd at the start of the mating season. Often one ram will give in to another with larger horns but two rams of equal size may end with bruised heads. For the rest of the year, rams live peacefully in a herd separate from the females.

Massive horns

An African Buffalo bull can fight off an attack by a lioness with slashing sweeps of its horns. It also charges other buffalo bulls during the mating season but the smaller, younger ones usually give in without injury.

The antlers, which are made of bone, begin to grow again each spring.

A bull Moose has the biggest horns of all deer.

Rubbing off the itching velvet to polish the antlers.

◄ Annual display

The bull Moose grows a new, larger set of antlers each year, adding two more points until they are up to 2 metres wide. At the end of the summer, the covering of soft, furry skin, called velvet, begins to drop off. The bull then cleans and polishes his antlers before challenging other bulls to duels to win females of the herd. When mating is over, the antlers fall off.

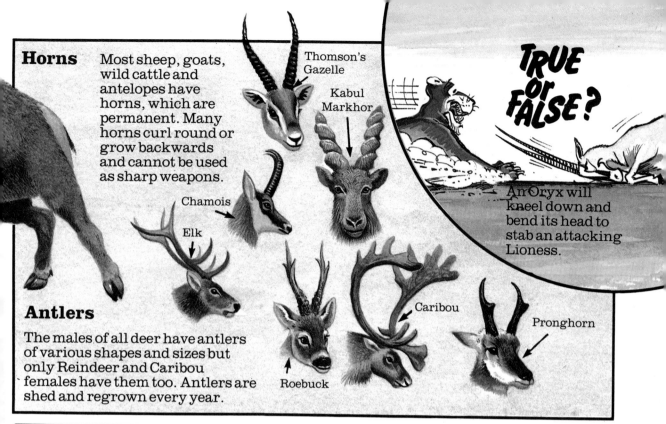

Horns

Most sheep, goats, wild cattle and antelopes have horns, which are permanent. Many horns curl round or grow backwards and cannot be used as sharp weapons.

Thomson's Gazelle

Kabul Markhor

Chamois

Antlers

The males of all deer have antlers of various shapes and sizes but only Reindeer and Caribou females have them too. Antlers are shed and regrown every year.

Elk

Roebuck

Caribou

Pronghorn

TRUE or FALSE?

An Oryx will kneel down and bend its head to stab an attacking Lioness.

Threatening tusks ▼

The Hippopotamus has huge teeth but it only feeds on plants, tearing them off with its rubbery lips. A female Hippo may use her teeth to defend her calf against a hungry crocodile. And a bull, fighting to establish his territory against other bulls, may cause terrible wounds with his teeth.

Sharp fangs ▼

A Lioness uses her long, sharp fangs to kill her prey with one deep bite. Her other teeth act like shears for cutting meat and grinding it up. Several Lionesses hunt together, stalking and ambushing food for the pride.

Hippopotamus

A Hippo's yawn is a threat to other bulls and may start a fight.

Strong jaws for holding on to prey.

Lioness

Deep freeze mammals

Snowshoes ▶

The Snowshoe Hare gets its name from its huge hind feet which act like snowshoes when it runs and leaps across soft snow. Long hair grows between the toes and the side of the feet, keeping them warm and giving a grip on frozen snow. The Hare is white during the North American winter but turns brown in spring.

In winter the Hare feeds on twigs and bark, or scrapes away the snow to find roots.

The huge footprints leave little scent for predators to follow. →

The Beaver's "lodge" has a room above the water and underwater entrances. ↘

Lodge built of branches and mud.

Macaques groom each other when sitting in hot pools.

Japanese Macaques

Beaver dragging felled branch to underwater foodstore.

Food in the freezer

Beavers collect branches in the autumn and store them in a pile next to their "lodge". During the winter they feed on the bark, reaching the store through an underwater tunnel when the lake is frozen over. Each family has its own lodge. It can be so warm inside that steam sometimes rises from its ventilation hole in very cold weather.

Making hay while the sun shines ▼

A Pika makes a short piercing whistle as it works at "haymaking".

The Pika makes hay during the summer to eat in the winter when the ground is covered with snow. It collects grass and herbs, spreads them out in the sun to dry and then carries them to a "haystack" in a rocky crevice. Each Pika builds its own haystacks, guarding them fiercely against the rest of the colony.

The supply of food has to last for over four months during the winter.

Food under the snow ▶

When snow covers the ground, Reindeer scrape holes in it to eat the "moss" underneath. No one knows how they find the plant, which is really a lichen, but they may be able to smell it.

The Reindeer has broad, splayed hoofs for walking on snow and soft ground.

It needs 12 kilos of spongy green lichen a day in winter.

TRUE or FALSE?

When hunting seals, Polar Bears cover up their black noses with a paw.

◀ Long hot baths

Macaques in northern Japan keep warm in winter by taking baths in hot volcanic springs. They come out, wet and dripping, to search for meals of seeds and bark.

Living with heat and drought

A Kangaroo Rat hops about the desert collecting seeds, pushing them into its cheek pouches with its front paws.

Leaps over 2 metres up into the air to escape predators.

◀ Desert drought

Kangaroo Rats can survive without water by living on dried seeds. They make their own fluids from these seeds and keep cool during the heat of the day by sealing themselves up in underground burrows. This preserves the moisture they breathe out. They also eat their own droppings for the moisture and vitamins they contain.

Mud bather

After feeding in the early morning, Rhinos wallow in mud holes, swamps or lakes in the heat of the afternoon. A cooling bath lowers the body temperature and protects a Rhinoceros from biting insects which get into the folds and wrinkles of its thick skin.

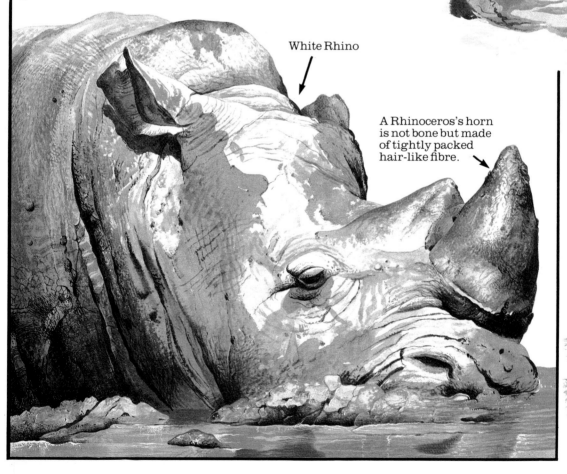

White Rhino

A Rhinoceros's horn is not bone but made of tightly packed hair-like fibre.

A cooling dip ▼

Tigers do not like very hot weather and spend the day lying in long grass or taking a cooling dip in shallow water. They are strong swimmers and will catch fish and turtles when food is scarce.

A solitary hunter, a tiger silently stalks its prey. When close enough it pounces, holding on and biting until the animal is dead.

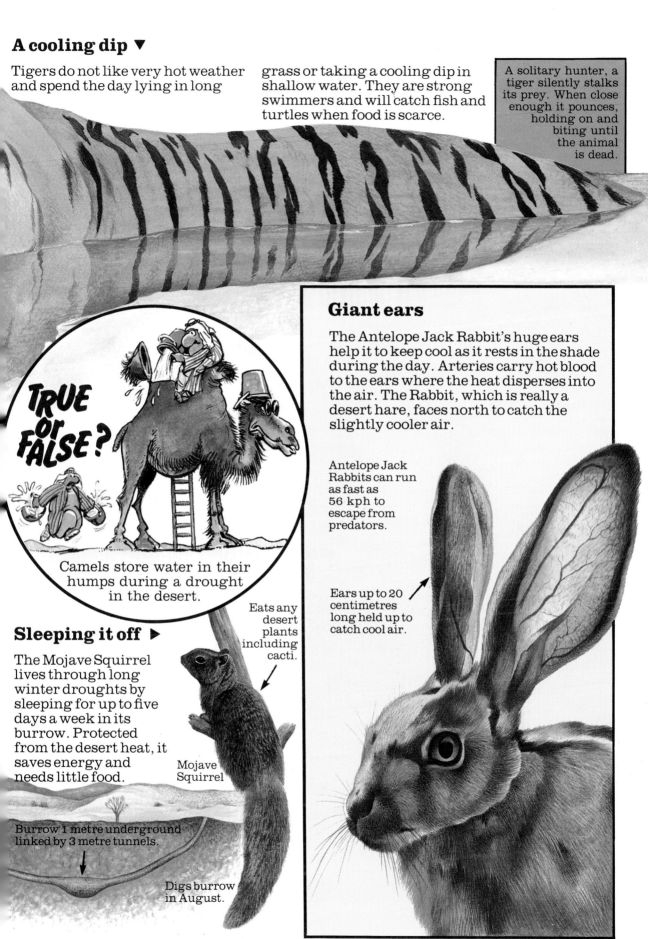

TRUE or FALSE?

Camels store water in their humps during a drought in the desert.

Giant ears

The Antelope Jack Rabbit's huge ears help it to keep cool as it rests in the shade during the day. Arteries carry hot blood to the ears where the heat disperses into the air. The Rabbit, which is really a desert hare, faces north to catch the slightly cooler air.

Antelope Jack Rabbits can run as fast as 56 kph to escape from predators.

Ears up to 20 centimetres long held up to catch cool air.

Sleeping it off ▶

The Mojave Squirrel lives through long winter droughts by sleeping for up to five days a week in its burrow. Protected from the desert heat, it saves energy and needs little food.

Eats any desert plants including cacti.

Mojave Squirrel

Burrow 1 metre underground linked by 3 metre tunnels.

Digs burrow in August.

Clever co-ordinators

Defending the young ▼

Musk oxen live in small herds in the Arctic tundra. When attacked by wolves, the adults form a defensive wall to protect the calves. A male ox steps forward to do battle. If he falls, others follow, one by one, until the attack is repelled.

African Oxpeckers on a Warthog's back may warn it of danger by retreating to the far side of the animal and making noisy calls.

Musk oxen's shaggy coats have two layers, a long coarse outer with a fine wool one underneath.

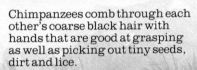

Chimpanzees comb through each other's coarse black hair with hands that are good at grasping as well as picking out tiny seeds, dirt and lice.

They travel and rest on the ground but feed and sleep in the trees.

Friendly groomers

Chimpanzees spend many hours a day grooming each other. This keeps their fur clean and also helps to keep them together in a friendly group. Grooming is such a pleasure that chimpanzees sometimes sit in chains, stroking and picking at each other's fur. But during these times of rest, they must always be alert for prowling leopards and other predators.

Oxpecker

Warthog

Ants under the scales

The Pangolin eats ants but it also uses them as cleaners. It raises its scales to let the ants crawl underneath. They eat the parasites that the Pangolin cannot scratch off itself.

There are stories that the Pangolin will then go off to the nearest pool. When it is underwater, it opens its scales so that the ants float out and it licks them up with its tongue.

The Pangolin has sharp overlapping scales. When curled in a ball it is safe from any attack.

TRUE or FALSE?

Do rats help each other to move eggs which are too large for one rat to carry?

Insect-pecking birds ▲

Oxpecker birds spend most of their day perched on large animals, such as Giraffes, Antelopes or Warthogs, busily pecking at ticks and biting flies. The animal ignores them unless they peck too painfully in ears, round eyes or at wounds.

Honey Guide Bird

Honey Badger

Wild bees' nest

A Honey Badger's thick, loose coat is good protection against bee and wasp stings.

◀ The nest robbers

The Honey Guide Bird works with the Honey Badger to find their favourite foods. The Bird flits from tree to tree, calling noisily, to lead the Badger to a bees' nest. The Badger claws it open and they feast together — the Badger on honey and grubs, the Bird on beeswax.

87

Communicating

The Indri lives in the forests of Madagascar.

Colourful heads and tails

A male Mandrill bares his teeth to show that he submits to an older male.

The male Mandrill's brilliantly coloured face, and bottom of the same colours, warn other males to keep away from his family group.

Wailing Indri ▲

The Indri has a very loud, wailing call. A family group often wails in concert for several minutes. This seems to alert straying members of the group and warns other groups to keep their distance.

Kissing friends ▼

Prairie dogs "kiss" when they meet to find out if they are from the same group. If they are, they groom each other. If not, they fight and the intruder is driven away. Prairie dogs live in huge underground burrows or "towns" containing hundreds, even thousands, of animals. Each family group has its own section which it defends against strangers.

TRUE or FALSE?

Lonely Wolves howl at the moon.

Prairie Dogs

Sentries keep watch at the entrance to Prairie Dog burrows, barking a warning at the first sign of danger.

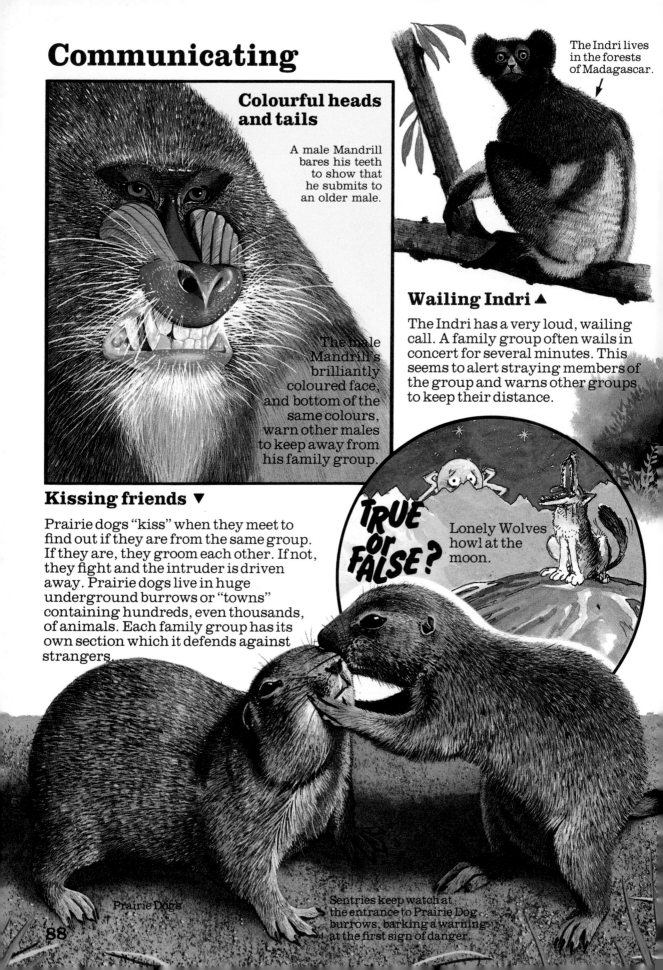

Booming pouches ▼

A male Orang Utan calls and "burps" to tell other males to keep out of his territory. He fills his throat pouch with air, swelling his face, and lets out a long call, ending with bubbling burps and sighs.

The heaviest of all the tree-dwellers, male Orang Utans may be over 1½ metres tall and weigh 200 kilos.

Old male Orang Utans have huge cheeks which are stores of fat for times when fruit is scarce.

A Ring-tailed Lemur spends most of the time on the forest floor. It keeps its tail up to show the rest of the troop where it is.

Living in family groups of about 20, they sleep in the trees, moving on each morning in search of fruit to eat.

Scent signals

The Ring-tailed Lemur rubs its bottom on trees as it goes through the forest, leaving its scent to mark its trail for the rest of the troop.

Before the annual mating season, males have "stink fights" for females. A male rubs his wrists against scent glands near his armpits, brings his tail between his legs and rubs scent all over it. Then he faces his rival, fanning the scent forwards with his bristling tail. These battles also take place when two troops meet at the edges of their territories.

Mysterious behaviour

◄ Give and take rats

The Trade Rat, or Pack Rat, gets its name from its curious habit of stealing a bright, shiny object during the night and leaving a small stone or twig in its place. It stores these in its large untidy nest. There are stories of stolen jewellery, spectacles and even of a Trade Rat carrying away a burning candle.

Brown Hare

The swimming monkey ▼

Proboscis Monkey

This male monkey's huge nose probably boosts the sound of its honks as it calls through the mangrove swamps of Borneo. The female's nose is much smaller. Good swimmers, they jump into the water to search for mangrove shoots on which they feed.

In 1950, a Proboscis Monkey was seen swimming in the China sea, far out from the Borneo coast. A lifeboat was lowered from a cruise ship and the exhausted monkey climbed aboard. After resting for a while, it dived back into the sea and swam away. No one knows where it was going or if it reached dry land.

Alert ears catch the slightest sound of danger.

Strong hind legs for leaps of up to 5 metres.

Mad March boxers

In Spring, Hares have boxing matches and wild acrobatic games, which gave them their name of Mad March Hares. For years, no one really knew why they behaved like this. The latest theory is that it is part of their courtship ritual. Before mating, males and females – it is very difficult to tell them apart at a distance – chase each other. A female may also punch a male on the nose and tear fur from his back with her teeth if he tries to mate with her before she is ready.

Chimpanzees

Dancing chimps

At the beginning of a heavy storm male chimpanzees have been seen performing amazing rain dances. They stamp their feet, sway from side to side, tear the branches off trees and may race wildly up and down slopes in the forest. Watched by females and young chimpanzees sitting in the trees, these wild dances can last for 15 minutes or more.

Apple thieves

A Hedgehog carrying apples is an unusual sight. Reports say that a hedgehog collects a pile of apples and rolls on them so that some stick to its spines. It then takes them back to its nest in a hollow wall or empty rabbit burrow.

Mass migrations ▶

Every three or four years lemmings suddenly set off on mass migrations. Thousands swarm down the mountains of Norway and try to swim across rivers and even the sea. So many drown that it was thought they were on a suicide trek. It is now known that when food is plentiful, lemmings breed at a fantastic rate. As the population grows, food and places to live become scarce. Then the lemmings migrate in search of food and new homes.

Fact or fiction?

Mysterious monster ▼

Many people claim to have seen a monster in Loch Ness, Scotland. Underwater cameras and sonar have produced no proof but it has been suggested the monster is really a line of otters or a herd of swimming elephants.

Trunk of elephant swimming in Loch Ness?

Gazelle boy ▼

In a desert in the Middle East, a boy was spotted running with a herd of gazelles. He was later captured and adopted by a foster-mother. She said he behaved and ate like a gazelle, he refused the food she gave him and wanted to eat grass. She believed he had been brought up from a baby with the gazelles.

A boy was found living with a herd of gazelles.

Apeman's hands

In China an apeman was said to have been killed after it attacked a small girl in 1957. Its hands were preserved and hair, a nest and footprints were also found in the area.

The ape-man's palms were 14 cm long.

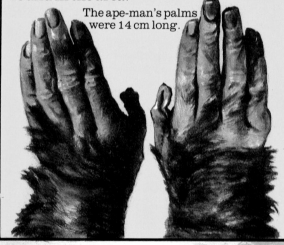

The long-armed creature, it is said, stands upright except when climbing up steep ground.

Huge footprints ▶

There have been many reports of wild men – half human, half ape – from the remote parts of the world. They come from the Soviet Union, the United States, India and China. Usually only huge footprints are seen in snow or mud and these are quite different from the prints of any large animal, such as a bear. People living in the Himalayas say they have seen the Yeti, a tall shambling figure which stands upright and makes high-pitched calls.

Footprints of a Yeti in hard snow were 80 cms long and 40 cms wide.

Animal showers ▶

Do animals fall from the sky? On the Indonesian island of Lambok, the people said that in 1968 rats fell on to their rice fields. The rats came down in bunches of seven, led by a huge white rat. There have also been stories of showers of frogs, fish, snails, lizards and rattlesnakes.

A shower of rats falling on rice fields on an Indonesian island.

Wolf children ▼

Many stories have been told of children brought up by wolves. The most famous is of two Indian girls, aged about seven and two years old, who were found in 1920 romping with a pack of wolves. They crawled about, eating only meat and howling. Taken to an orphanage, the eldest learned to stand up and say a few words but died when she was about 17.

Indian girls grew up with a pack of wolves.

Apeman

This strange creature, which had been shot through the head, was kept in a block of ice by a showman in the United States. He would not say where it came from or how he got hold of it in 1968. A Belgian zoologist, who examined it through the cloudy ice, was sure it was not a fake. This ape-man was 2 metres tall with long arms and huge hands. In many ways it was like the short, stocky Neanderthal Man, an ancestor of human beings, who was thought to have lived about 50,000 years ago.

Record breakers

Highest jumper

Both Pumas and African Leopards have been seen to jump 5½ metres up into a tree. A hunted kangaroo leapt over a pile of timber 3 metres high.

Fastest mammal

The Cheetah has been timed at 110 kph over short distances. Over longer distances, a Pronghorn Antelope clocked 67 kph for 1.6 km, and one was reportedly timed at 98 kph for 183 metres. A race horse runs at about 70 kph.

Largest land animal

The largest land animal is the male African Elephant. The largest recorded was 3.8 metres high at the shoulder, 10 metres from the tip of its tail to the end of its trunk, and weighed about 10.8 tonnes.

Slowest mammal

The Three-toed Sloth moves along the ground at a speed of about 2 metres a minute. Through the trees, it is a little faster—about 3 metres per minute. Answering a distress call from her baby, a mother sloth was seen to "sprint" 4 metres in a minute.

Smallest land mammal

From head to tail adult Etruscan Shrews measure between 6 and 8 cms—the tails are about 2.5 cms long—and weigh 1.5-2.5 grams.

Tallest animal

Bull Giraffes are usually 5 metres tall although there are reports of 7 metre ones being shot. The tallest recorded bull lived at Chester Zoo, England, and grew to 6 metres.

Man-eating cats

A Tigress in Nepal and Kumaon killed 437 people in eight years, before being shot in 1911. A Leopard in Panar, India, accounted for over 400 victims.

Largest litter

The Common Tenrec, which is found mainly in Madagascar, gives birth to litters of 32 or 33 babies.

Oldest animal

The Asiatic Elephant can live to be 70 years old and may survive to be 80.

Longest horn

The longest front horn on a White Rhinoceros measured 158 cm. Explorers' reports of a beast with a horn may had led to the myth of the unicorn.

Most dangerous bat

The Vampire Bat of tropical America can transmit a number of diseases when it sucks blood. In Latin America 1 million cattle die every year from rabies passed on by this bat and there are a number of human deaths too.

Largest wingspan

The Kalong, a fruit bat of Malaysia, has a wingspan of 170 cms.

Largest herd

In the 19th century, vast herds of Springbok, numbering perhaps 100 million, migrated in search of food. One herd was said to be 24 kilometres wide and more than 150 kilometres long.

Longest tusks

The right tusk of the longest pair of elephant tusks measured 3.48 metres along its outside curve. Together the tusks weighed 117 kilograms.

Smallest flying mammal

Thailand's Bumblebee Bat has a wingspan of 160 mm, a length of 29-33 mm and weighs about 2 grams.

Longest pregnancy

The Asiatic Elephant usually carries its young for about 20 months but pregnancies can last for over 2 years before the single calf is born.

Rarest animal

— The rarest animal, which may already be extinct, is the Thylacine, or Tasmanian Wolf. It has not been positively seen for over 50 years and has probably never been photographed in the wild.

Highest living

The Yak sometimes climbs up to an altitude of 6,100 metres in the Himalayas.

Were they true or false?

Page 69 When a Hippo mother goes off to feed, she finds a babysitter.
True. Each group of Hippos has a central nursery where the females and young gather. If a mother goes out of it, she leaves her calf with another female.

Page 71 Goats in Tunisia jump on donkeys' backs to reach leaves on high branches of trees.
Maybe. There are reports that the goats have been seen butting the donkeys into position under the trees but they have never been photographed.

Page 72 The Gibbon is a tightrope artist.
True. The Gibbon will walk upright on its hind legs along tree-top vines. Other monkeys use legs and arms to walk along vines.

Page 75 Frog-eating Bats choose the juiciest frog by listening to its mating call.
True and false. These Bats can tell edible frogs from the poisonous ones by the mating calls, but cannot tell which ones will make the biggest meal.

Page 76 The Black Panther really does exist.
True, but it is just a black form of the Leopard.

Page 78 A Porcupine can shoot its quills at an enemy.
False, but if an enemy touches the quills, they come loose and stick in its skin.

Page 81 An Oryx will kneel down and bend its head to stab an attacking Lioness.
True. Instead of running away, an Oryx will sometimes bravely face a Lioness. When kneeling down with bent head, its backward-sloping horns point forwards and can cause serious injuries.

Page 83 When hunting seals, Polar Bears cover up their black noses.
Probably false, although one scientist claimed that a Polar Bear sometimes covers its nose so that it does not show up against its white fur and the snow.

Page 85 Camels store water in their humps during a drought in the desert.
False. Their humps are lumps of fat which they live on when food is scarce.

Page 87 Rats help each other to move eggs which are too large for one rat to carry.
Maybe. There have been reports that Rats move eggs by forming chains and passing the egg along, or one Rat drags another holding an egg. But there is no real scientific proof.

Page 88 Lonely Wolves howl at the moon.
False. Wolves do howl at night but this is to keep in touch with the rest of the pack and to warn other packs away from their territory.

Further reading

The NatureTrail Book of Wild Animals, R. Hartill (Usborne)
How Animals Live, A. Civardi & C. Kilpatrick (Usborne)
Animal Specialists: Nocturnals, M. Ellis, (Dent)
The World of Young Animals, A. Guilfoyle, (Allen & Unwin)
Mammals in Colour, L. Lyneborg (Blandford)
Mountain Animals, M. Chinery (Ward Lock)
Chimpanzees, R. Whitlock (Wayland)
The Mammals, R. Carrington (Time-Life Young Readers Library)
The Predators, I. E. Cohen (Quarto)
The Secret Life of Animals, L. & M. Milne & F. Russell (Weidenfeld & Nicolson)
The Big Cats, G. Badino (Orbis)

How Mammals Live, M. Burton (Elsevier Phaidon)
Mammals, C. König (Collins)
Foxes, Squirrels, Bats, Hedgehogs and other titles (Young Naturalist Books, Priority Press)
Elephants and Other Land Giants (Wild, Wild World of Animals series, Time-Life Films)
Animals of the African Plains, M. Cuisin (Nature's Hidden World series, Ward Lock)
The Red Deer, B. Staines, (Animals of the World series, Wayland)
The Red Squirrel, A. Tittensor (Mammal Society series, Blandford)
Illustrated Encyclopedia of Mammals, V. Hanak & V. Mazak (Octopus)

PART 4

MYSTERIES & MARVELS
OF
INSECT LIFE

Dr. Jennifer Owen

Edited by Rick Morris

Designed by Anne Sharples
and Teresa Foster

Illustrated by Ian Jackson
and Alan Harris

Cartoons by John Shackell

Some shieldbugs, unlike most insect parents, stand guard over their eggs and young.

The 13 cm Goliath Beetle is the heaviest flying insect.

Not thorns, but tree-hoppers.

Contents

A Seven Spot Ladybird to the same scale.

Largest and smallest butterflies drawn life-size: a female Queen Alexandra's Birdwing and a Dwarf Blue.

Assassin bugs inject saliva into their prey, then suck its juices.

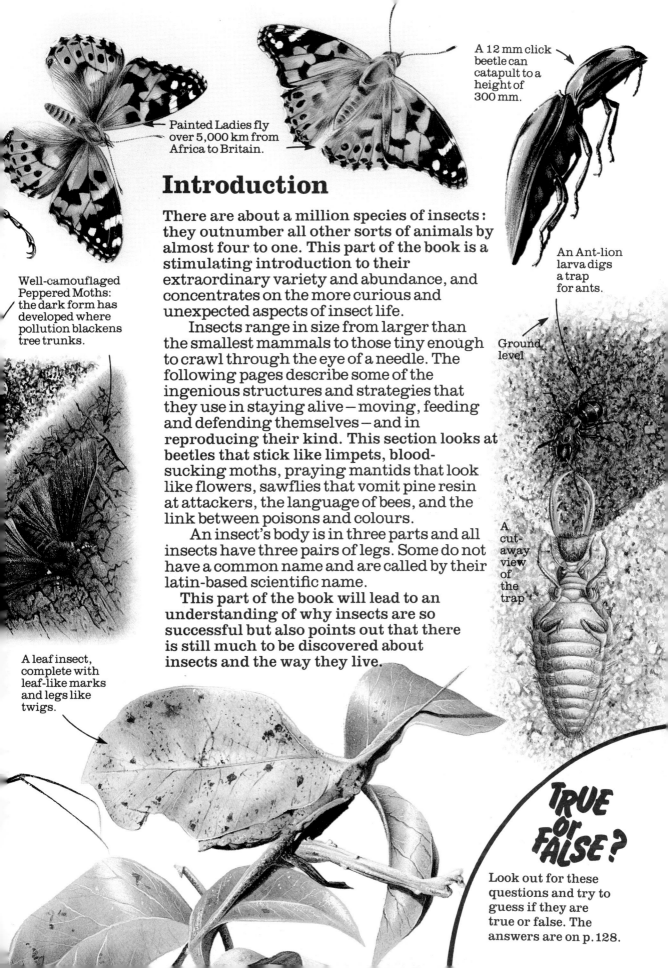

Painted Ladies fly over 5,000 km from Africa to Britain.

A 12 mm click beetle can catapult to a height of 300 mm.

Introduction

There are about a million species of insects: they outnumber all other sorts of animals by almost four to one. This part of the book is a stimulating introduction to their extraordinary variety and abundance, and concentrates on the more curious and unexpected aspects of insect life.

Insects range in size from larger than the smallest mammals to those tiny enough to crawl through the eye of a needle. The following pages describe some of the ingenious structures and strategies that they use in staying alive – moving, feeding and defending themselves – and in reproducing their kind. This section looks at beetles that stick like limpets, blood-sucking moths, praying mantids that look like flowers, sawflies that vomit pine resin at attackers, the language of bees, and the link between poisons and colours.

An insect's body is in three parts and all insects have three pairs of legs. Some do not have a common name and are called by their latin-based scientific name.

This part of the book will lead to an understanding of why insects are so successful but also points out that there is still much to be discovered about insects and the way they live.

Well-camouflaged Peppered Moths: the dark form has developed where pollution blackens tree trunks.

A leaf insect, complete with leaf-like marks and legs like twigs.

An Ant-lion larva digs a trap for ants.

Ground level

A cut-away view of the trap

TRUE or FALSE?

Look out for these questions and try to guess if they are true or false. The answers are on p.128.

Ingenious design

The bodies of insects are amazingly varied in shape and
form. All these designs are answers to the problems of
moving, breathing, keeping warm, eating and avoiding
being eaten.

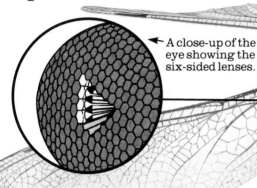

← A close-up of the
eye showing the
six-sided lenses.

Between the compound
eyes are three small
simple eyes which
respond to light.

Aerial hunters ▶

The large second and third segments of a dragonfly's body
are tilted, bringing all the legs forward below the jaws,
where they form a basket for catching other insects in flight.
Dragonflies strike with deadly accuracy, guided by the enormous
compound eyes, each made up of as many as 30,000 separate lenses.
Each lens reflects a slightly different view of the world.

Dragonfly hunting
a butterfly.

Each foot has
5,000 bristles
which end in
pairs of flat
pads.

▼ A gripping story

When threatened, a tiny
leaf-eating beetle,
Hemisphaerota cyanea,
can clamp down like a
limpet. Just as water
between two sheets of
glass sticks them
together, so the beetle
uses a film of oil between
the 60,000 pads on its
feet and the leaf.

Ants heave
unsuccessfully
at the rounded
"shell".

Water-skiing

In an emergency, the rove beetle, *Stenus*,
only 5 mm long, can zoom across the
surface of water. Glands at the tip of
the abdomen release a liquid that
lowers the surface tension of water.
The beetle is pulled forward by the
greater surface tension of the
water in front of it.

*Hemisphaerota
cyanea*

There are over 40,000 species of weevil. They lay eggs in nuts, such as chestnuts, hickory and hazel, which the grub eats from the inside.

← Antennae

← Jaws

Elephant Weevil →

All the colours of the rainbow

Butterfly wings are covered with tiny over-lapping scales. Iridescent colours result from the way some scales reflect light, and depend on structure not pigment. Other scales have colour pigments.

In this close-up of scales, the orange and deep purple ones have pigment colours. The iridescent blue and green scales have little pigment but reflect blue or green light.

Morpho butterfly

Two views of an iridescent wing. Colour depends on the light angle.

Scales increase "lift" when flying.

A boring story ▷

The jaws of weevils are at the end of a long snout which, in nut weevils, may be as long as the rest of the body. The tiny weevils bore holes in hard nutshells by using the snout as a lever to increase pressure.

Scuba diving and air lines

Some diving beetles use an air bubble trapped between their bodies and their wing cases for breathing under water. Oxygen from the water replaces some of the air used but slowly the bubble shrinks and the beetle must re-surface. Other insects have breathing tubes: the Rat-tailed Maggot's tube is telescopic.

The Water Scorpion has an air tube.

Some diving beetles tow an air bubble.

The Rat-tailed Maggot's tube is 27 cm.

TRUE or FALSE?

Bumblebees have central heating.

101

Colourful confusion

Many insects fool predators by looking like something else or by camouflage colours which match their backgrounds.

Which way? ▶

Hairstreak butterflies have a dummy head on their hind wings. On landing, they move their wings up and down. This waggles the false antennae and makes them look real. A bird will probably peck at the false head rather than the real one. The butterfly then escapes with only slightly damaged wings.

Bay-headed Tanager

Head

This South American hairstreak will fly "the wrong way" to escape, confusing the bird.

False antennae

The Mocker Swallowtail ▼

Birds quickly learn the colour patterns of poisonous butterflies and leave them alone. Edible butterflies which have the same patterns are protected. Female Mocker Swallowtails have the added advantage of looking like several poisonous species. Males, strangely, never mimic and so are unprotected.

One model: a poisonous Friar butterfly.

Another model: a poisonous African Monarch.

Two mimics: both are female Mocker Swallowtails.

Curious caterpillars ▶

Caterpillars make juicy meals but protect themselves from birds by various disguises. Some look like bird droppings, others like twigs, and some match the colours of leaves. The Lobster Moth caterpillar even squirts acid.

This threatening "snake" is actually a hawk moth caterpillar. It waves its body to look like a snake.

Not a twig but a caterpillar holding itself rigid.

The false eyes are on the underside.

Careful disguise ▼

Birds remember being stung and avoid insects that resemble wasps. Yellow and black are warning colours in nature.

The harmless Hornet Moth of Europe and North America mimics the stinging Hornet.

A flash of colour

Camouflage gives no protection once a hungry predator has spotted its meal. But a sudden display of bright colours and patterns startles the predator and gives the prey a few seconds in which to escape.

A flightless Australian Mountain Grasshopper shows its bright body.

This Hairy Buprestid beetle looks like a wasp even when flying, because it keeps its wing-cases over its back.

Dangerous flower ▶

Flower mantids feed on insects and seem to lie in wait on flowers that match their own colours. Some are green to match green petals while others are pink, matching pink petals. Markings and projections on their bodies and legs perfect the camouflage.

Flower mantis with butterfly prey.

A Puss Moth caterpillar, when attacked, spits out its stomach contents and acid from a special gland. Large false eyes form a fierce "face".

Tail "whips" wave menacingly.

TRUE or FALSE?

Zebras have black and white fleas.

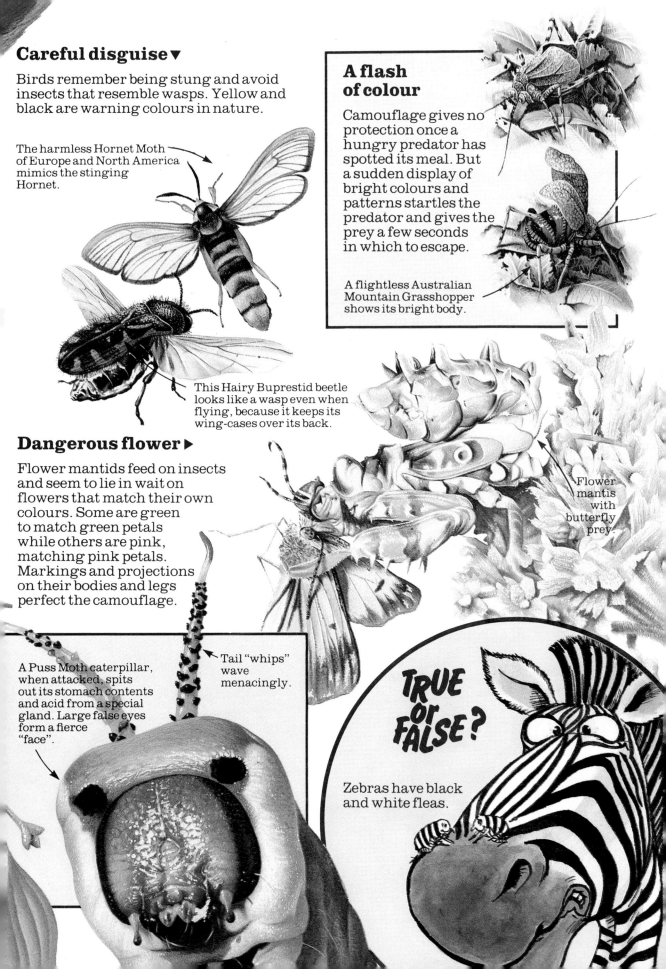

Food and feeding

Insects eat plants or animals, alive or dead, as well as substances produced by them. Some have amazing methods of using unlikely sources of food.

Toad-in-the-hole ▶

The larvae of a horsefly lie buried in mud at the edge of ponds in the U.S.A., ready to grab tiny Spade-foot Toads as they emerge from the water. A larva grasps a toadlet with its mouth hooks and injects a slow-acting poison. Then it drags its meal into the mud and sucks out the juices. It leaves the rest of the body to rot. Adult horseflies, however, are likely to be eaten by adult toads.

Young Spade-foot Toad.

The toadlet and the horsefly larva are each about two centimetres long.

The larva is a grub-like stage between the egg and adult horsefly.

Disappearing dung

Dung beetles bury the dung of grazing mammals and lay their eggs on it. They react to smell, moving towards buffalo dung before it hits the ground. A single mass of fresh elephant dung may hold 7,000 beetles. Within a day or two, they will have buried it all.

Some beetles roll away dung with their back legs.

▼ Turning the tables

A sundew plant feeds on insects which are trapped by sticky droplets on the stalks on its leaves. But caterpillars of a small plume moth feed on sundews in Florida, U.S.A. Detachable scales on the moth probably save it from being caught. The caterpillars drink the sticky droplets, then eat the stalks and any trapped insects.

Plume moth caterpillar.

A fly trapped by a sundew.

▼ Feeding on stones

Males of some butterflies — Purple Emperor, Red Admiral and White Admiral — are sometimes seen licking dry stones on woodland tracks. They are probably taking in sodium salts. Why only males? The packet of sperms passed to the female during mating contains a rich soup of nutrients. Scientists in North America have found that some butterfly species need to make up this loss of sodium after mating.

Purple Emperor

The butterfly makes a damp patch on the stone, then sucks it dry.

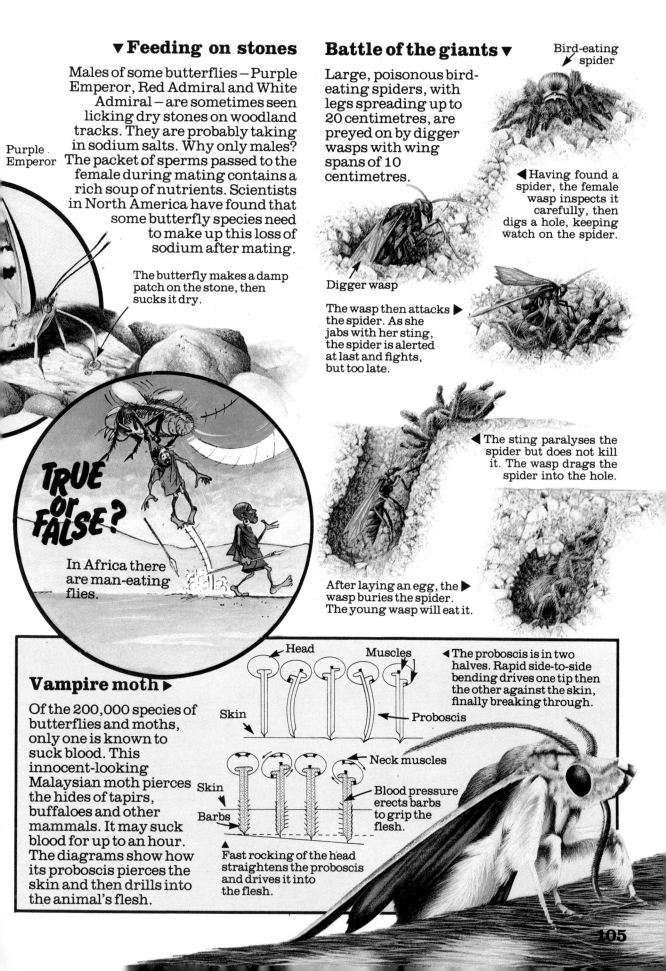

Battle of the giants ▼

Large, poisonous bird-eating spiders, with legs spreading up to 20 centimetres, are preyed on by digger wasps with wing spans of 10 centimetres.

Bird-eating spider

Digger wasp

◄ Having found a spider, the female wasp inspects it carefully, then digs a hole, keeping watch on the spider.

The wasp then attacks ► the spider. As she jabs with her sting, the spider is alerted at last and fights, but too late.

◄ The sting paralyses the spider but does not kill it. The wasp drags the spider into the hole.

After laying an egg, the ► wasp buries the spider. The young wasp will eat it.

TRUE or FALSE?

In Africa there are man-eating flies.

Vampire moth ►

Of the 200,000 species of butterflies and moths, only one is known to suck blood. This innocent-looking Malaysian moth pierces the hides of tapirs, buffaloes and other mammals. It may suck blood for up to an hour. The diagrams show how its proboscis pierces the skin and then drills into the animal's flesh.

Head

Muscles

Skin

Proboscis

◄ The proboscis is in two halves. Rapid side-to-side bending drives one tip then the other against the skin, finally breaking through.

Neck muscles

Skin

Barbs

Blood pressure erects barbs to grip the flesh.

Fast rocking of the head straightens the proboscis and drives it into the flesh.

Chemical warfare

Harmful chemicals are used by insects as repellents, in defence and attack. Most advertise this by their colour pattern, often some combination of black with yellow, orange or red. These colours are a universal code meaning "don't touch!"

Frothing at the mouth ▶

Flightless Lubber Grasshoppers are large and slow. When disturbed, however, they ooze foul-smelling froth from the mouth and thorax with a hissing noise. Air is bubbled into a mixture of chemicals which include phenol and quinones. Both these chemicals are widely used as repellents by insects.

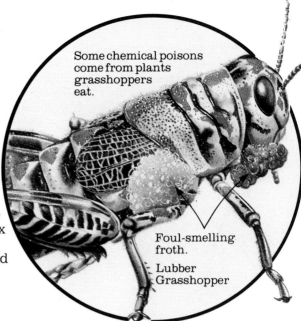

Some chemical poisons come from plants grasshoppers eat.

Foul-smelling froth.

Lubber Grasshopper

◀ Painful jabs

The stings of ants, bees and wasps are modified ovipositors (egg-laying tools), used to inject poison in defence or to paralyse prey. More than 50 different chemicals have been identified from various species. Some cause itching, pain, swelling and redness; others destroy cells and spread the poison. Honeybees cannot pull their barbed stings from human skins, and tear themselves away, dying soon afterwards.

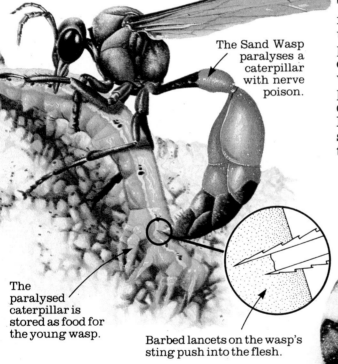

The Sand Wasp paralyses a caterpillar with nerve poison.

The paralysed caterpillar is stored as food for the young wasp.

Barbed lancets on the wasp's sting push into the flesh.

Bombardment ▶

When provoked, a bombardier beetle swivels the tip of its abdomen and shoots a jet of boiling chemicals at its attacker. The chemicals are produced in a "reaction chamber" with an explosion you can hear. The spray of foul-tasting, burning vapour is a result of rapid firing. It shoots out at 500 to 1,000 pulses per second at a temperature of 100°C.

Bottoms up ▶

Darkling beetles respond to trouble by doing a hand-stand. They tilt up at an angle of 45° and point their abdomen at the attacker. They then spray a foul-smelling liquid from glands that open at the tip of the abdomen. Darkling beetles are slower than bombardier beetles and are often swallowed by toads before discharging their spray.

The foul spray contains quinone.

Darkling beetle

A Grasshopper Mouse disarms a beetle by ramming its hind end into the soil. It eats all but the poison.

Multi-purpose hairs

The hairs of Yellow-tail Moth caterpillars can cause a nasty rash. Adult females keep a tuft of these irritant hairs and shed them over their eggs for protection.

Food as a weapon ▶

Sawfly larvae that feed on pine needles, store the scented resins in pouches which open into the gut just behind the head. Under attack, a larva vomits a sticky blob of resin, twists itself round, and daubs the attacker, gumming its legs together.

A sawfly larva gumming up an ant.

The bombardier beetle's spray can be fired accurately in any direction.

Ladybirds bite when annoyed.

TRUE or FALSE?

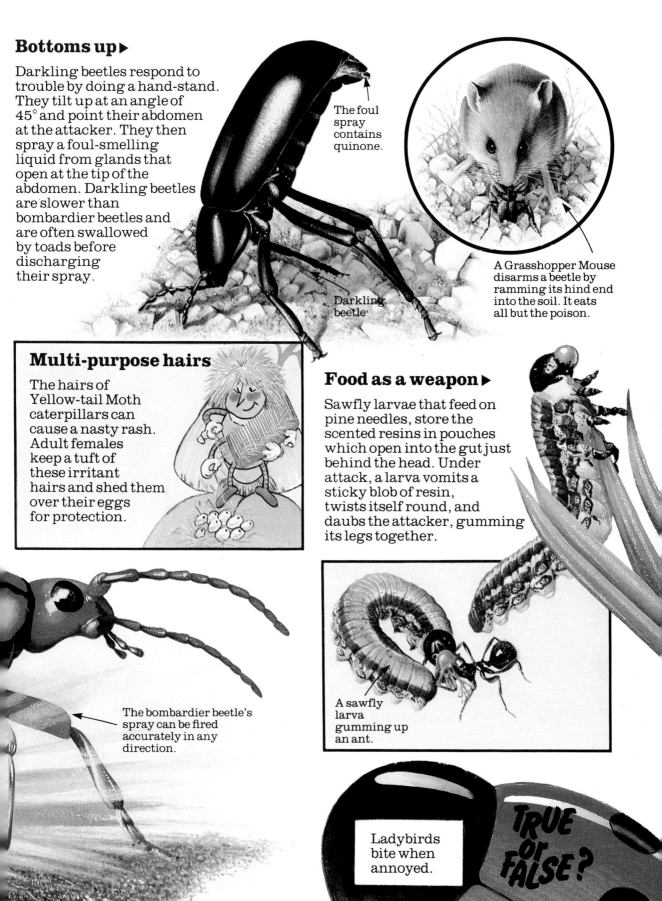

Curious courtship

Insects have many ways of attracting and recognising a mate, of arousing their interest, calming their fears, and overcoming their aggression.

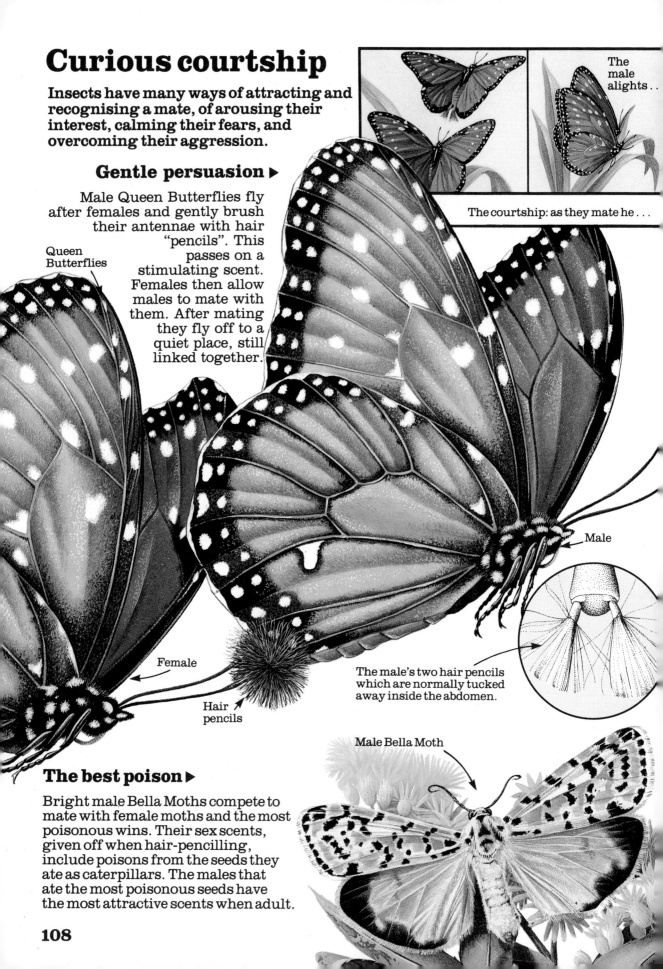

The courtship: as they mate he . . .

The male alights . .

Gentle persuasion ▶

Male Queen Butterflies fly after females and gently brush their antennae with hair "pencils". This passes on a stimulating scent. Females then allow males to mate with them. After mating they fly off to a quiet place, still linked together.

Queen Butterflies

Female

Hair pencils

Male

The male's two hair pencils which are normally tucked away inside the abdomen.

Male Bella Moth

The best poison ▶

Bright male Bella Moths compete to mate with female moths and the most poisonous wins. Their sex scents, given off when hair-pencilling, include poisons from the seeds they ate as caterpillars. The males that ate the most poisonous seeds have the most attractive scents when adult.

... they mate ...

... and fly off together.

... strokes her antennae as if to calm her.

TRUE or FALSE?

Singing crickets attract more females.

Off with his head!

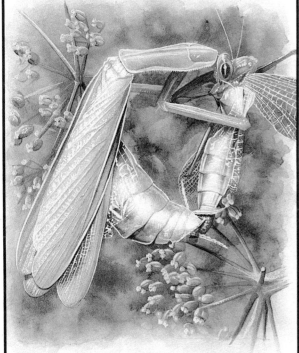

In some species of praying mantis, the female begins to eat the male while they are mating. She starts at his head and by the time she reaches his abdomen, mating is completed. By becoming a nourishing meal, the father provides a supply of food for the eggs that are his children.

Bribing the lady ▼

Courtship and mating are dangerous for males if females are insect-eaters. Many male Empid flies distract their females with the gift of a captured insect. This stops the female eating the male. Some wrap the "gift" in silk.

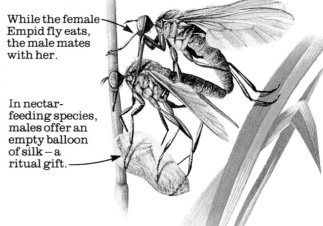

While the female Empid fly eats, the male mates with her.

In nectar-feeding species, males offer an empty balloon of silk — a ritual gift.

Fatal attraction ▼

Male and female fireflies recognise and find each other by light signals. Each species has its own pattern of flashes. Predatory female *Photuris* mimic the signals of female *Photinus* to lure male *Photinus* to their deaths. As their male prey approaches, they take off and "home in" like light-seeking missiles.

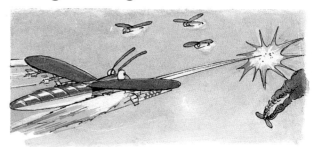

Female firefly

A female flashing in answer to a male.

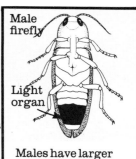

Male firefly

Light organ

Males have larger lights than females.

Magical changes

Grasshoppers and several other sorts of insects hatch out of eggs as miniature adults, except for their wings and reproductive organs which develop later.▶

In many other groups of insects, such as beetles and flies, the young insect (the larva) is quite unlike the adult. The larva concentrates on feeding and growing before turning into a pupa. Great changes of the body take place in the pupa to produce the winged adult.▼

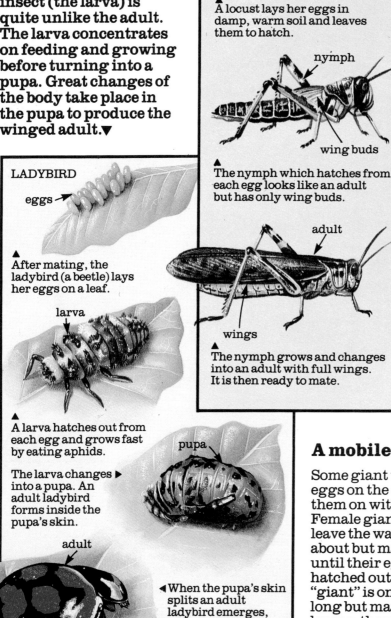

LOCUST

▲ A locust lays her eggs in damp, warm soil and leaves them to hatch.

— eggs

nymph

wing buds

▲ The nymph which hatches from each egg looks like an adult but has only wing buds.

adult

wings

▲ The nymph grows and changes into an adult with full wings. It is then ready to mate.

LADYBIRD

eggs —

▲ After mating, the ladybird (a beetle) lays her eggs on a leaf.

larva

▲ A larva hatches out from each egg and grows fast by eating aphids.

The larva changes ▶ into a pupa. An adult ladybird forms inside the pupa's skin.

pupa

adult

◀ When the pupa's skin splits an adult ladybird emerges, ready to find a mate.

▼ Egg machines

Moth caterpillars, known as bag-worms, build a protective case of silk and fragments of twigs and leaves. They pupate in the case, and the wingless females never leave. Many females are worm-like, with no legs, eyes or mouthparts. Their only function is to mate and lay eggs. Males are normal. Three of the many different bag-worms are shown here.

A North American bag-worm caterpillar eating leaves

A case becomes a cocoon.

A male Malayan bag-worm mating. The female is still inside her case.

A mobile nest ▶

Some giant water bugs lay their eggs on the male's back, sticking them on with waterproof "glue". Female giant water bugs often leave the water and fly about but males stay until their eggs have hatched out. This "giant" is only 2-5 cm long but many are larger: they lay eggs on water plants.

The male "nursemaid"

Beauty and the beast ▶

The nymphs of dragonflies are fearsome underwater predators, even eating small fish. By pumping water in and out of its rectum, where its gills are, a nymph can move by jet propulsion.

A fully-grown nymph climbs out of the water and a dragonfly emerges.

Adult dragonfly

A nymph eating a tadpole, caught by hooks on its lower lip.

TRUE or FALSE?

Butterflies live for only one day.

Coming out together

The periodical cicadas of the eastern United States spend 17 years (13 in the south) below ground as nymphs feeding on tree roots. All in one place emerge together. They change into adults, lay eggs, and after a few weeks die. None is seen again for 17 (or 13) years.

A red aphid giving birth. Other daughters cluster behind her.

Nymphs hatch from the eggs.

Inside a Russian doll is a smaller doll and within that is a still smaller doll, and so on . . .

Giant water bug

Russian dolls ▲

For most of the year, female aphids produce young without mating. Eggs develop into small daughters inside the mother. Inside each daughter eggs also start to develop. So when a mother gives birth to her daughters, they already contain her grand-daughters, like a set of dolls.

Royal households

The social life of two different groups of insects: ants, bees and wasps, and termites, has evolved separately. Most nests have only one egg-laying female, known as the queen. The teeming members of a nest are her offspring. Most are workers who never breed. The queen keeps her ruling position and controls the nests' activities by chemical communication.

The queen honeybee is at the centre of the swarm.

Deciding where to go ▶

A new honeybee nest starts when thousands of workers, all female, leave the old nest with the old queen, or with some virgin queens, when a few males (drones) go too. Before they fly off, scout bees find suitable nesting sites and report back, telling of their finds by "dancing". After several hours, by unknown means, the site for the new nest is chosen.

Bees swarm on the ground, on branches and even on post-boxes in towns.

To fill her crop with nectar, a bee worker visits up to 1,000 flowers. She flies 10 such trips a day if it is sunny.

To make 1 kg of honey, bees make up to 65,000 trips, visiting 45-64 million flowers.

Large colonies have 80,000 workers and eat 225 kg of honey a year. Surplus honey is stored for bad weather.

Honeycomb cells are six-sided.

TRUE or FALSE?

Bees make jellies.

Nest bullies ▲

Dominant *Polistes* worker biting a subordinate.

Bullying ends in food exchange.

Dominant *Polistes* wasp workers bully their sister workers. A dominant one will bite a subordinate, as she crouches motionless, until she regurgitates her food. This seems to bind the colony together.

Incredible industry ▶

Vespula wasps build their football-sized nests with paper made of chewed-up wood mixed with saliva. A large nest has 12 combs containing 15,000 cells, surrounded by walls of layered paper. Unlike the honeybees, wasps abandon their nests in autumn and build a new one in spring, sometimes underground in an old animal burrow.

Wasps do not make honey but feed their larvae on pellets made of chewed-up insects.

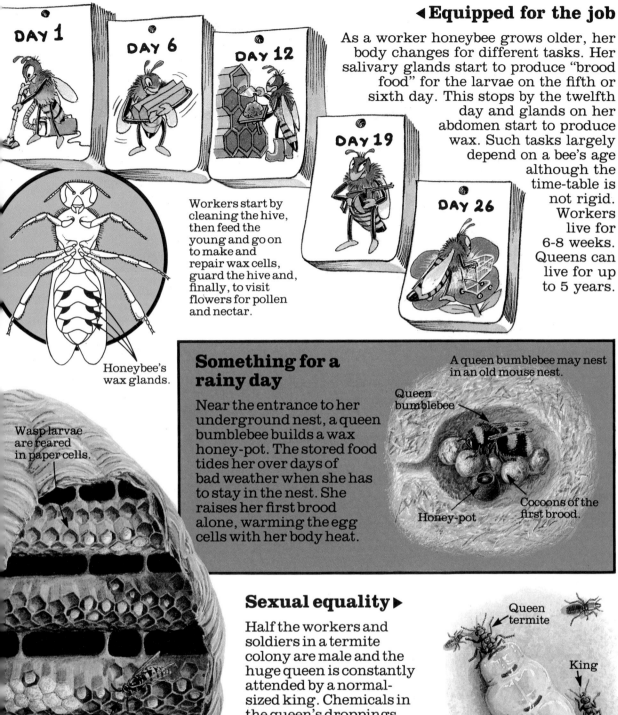

◄ Equipped for the job

DAY 1

DAY 6

DAY 12

DAY 19

DAY 26

As a worker honeybee grows older, her body changes for different tasks. Her salivary glands start to produce "brood food" for the larvae on the fifth or sixth day. This stops by the twelfth day and glands on her abdomen start to produce wax. Such tasks largely depend on a bee's age although the time-table is not rigid. Workers live for 6-8 weeks. Queens can live for up to 5 years.

Workers start by cleaning the hive, then feed the young and go on to make and repair wax cells, guard the hive and, finally, to visit flowers for pollen and nectar.

Honeybee's wax glands.

Wasp larvae are reared in paper cells.

Wasps drink a sweet secretion produced by their larvae.

Something for a rainy day

Near the entrance to her underground nest, a queen bumblebee builds a wax honey-pot. The stored food tides her over days of bad weather when she has to stay in the nest. She raises her first brood alone, warming the egg cells with her body heat.

A queen bumblebee may nest in an old mouse nest.

Queen bumblebee

Honey-pot

Cocoons of the first brood.

Sexual equality ▶

Half the workers and soldiers in a termite colony are male and the huge queen is constantly attended by a normal-sized king. Chemicals in the queen's droppings, which are eaten and regurgitated by the termites, prevent the production of more kings and queens. The queen of an African termite species grows up to 140 mm long and can lay 30,000 eggs a day. Queens may live for 15 years and more.

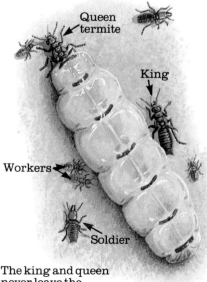

Queen termite

King

Workers

Soldier

The king and queen never leave the royal chamber.

113

Farmers, tailors, soldiers and builders

Large insect colonies, particularly those of termites and ants, have different members which are specialized for different types of jobs. By working together efficiently, they have developed unusual ways of using and feeding on plants and other animals.

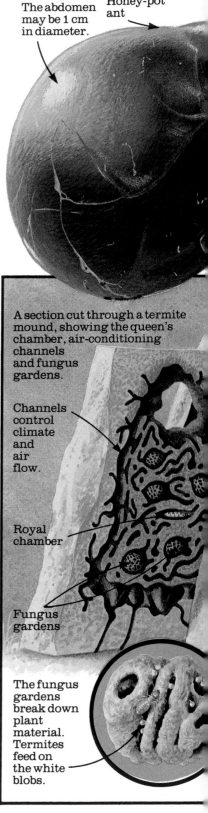

The abdomen may be 1 cm in diameter.

Honey-pot ant

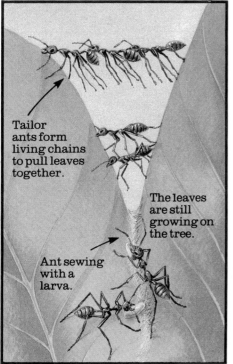

Tailor ants form living chains to pull leaves together.

The leaves are still growing on the tree.

Ant sewing with a larva.

◄ Tailor ants

Oecophylla ants sew leaves together to form a nest, using silk produced by the saliva glands of their larvae. A line of workers stand on the edge of one leaf, and pull another towards it with their jaws. Other workers wave larvae to and fro across the leaves until they are joined by the silk. Tailor ants live in the forests of Africa, S.E. Asia and Australia.

A section cut through a termite mound, showing the queen's chamber, air-conditioning channels and fungus gardens.

Channels control climate and air flow.

Royal chamber

Fungus gardens

Minders ►

When cutting or carrying bits of leaf, leaf-cutter ants cannot defend themselves against parasitic flies. Tiny workers, too small to cut and carry leaves, go with the larger workers to fight off the flies. The ants carry the leaf pieces back to their nest.

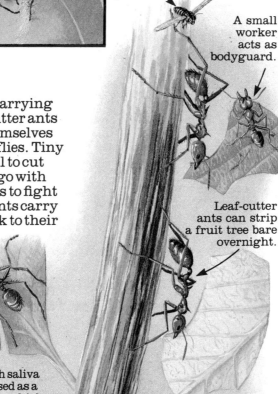

Parasitic fly

A small worker acts as bodyguard.

Leaf-cutter ants can strip a fruit tree bare overnight.

Once in the nest the leaves are chewed up, mixed with saliva and droppings, and used as a compost for the fungus which the ants feed on.

The fungus gardens break down plant material. Termites feed on the white blobs.

A worker feeding.

Honey-pot ants are a sweet delicacy to Mexican villagers and Australian aborigines. An ant colony may have up to 300 living "honey-pots".

Living storage tanks ▲

Some honey-pot ant workers are fed so much nectar and honeydew that their abdomens swell to the size of a grape. Unable to move, they hang motionless from the roof of the nest and are looked after by other workers. The "honey-pots" store food for the colony to eat when the nectar season is over in the deserts where they live. When empty they shrivel up.

Soldiers and weapons

Soldier termites have enlarged heads and defend the nest against intruders. Most have formidable pointed jaws as weapons, but not *Nasutitermes* soldiers. Their heads extend forwards as a pointed nozzle from which they spray a sticky, irritating fluid.

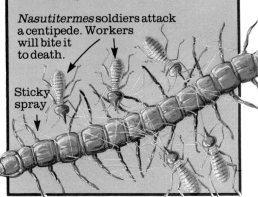

Nasutitermes soldiers attack a centipede. Workers will bite it to death.

Sticky spray

Master builders

Fungus garden termites build enormous, rock-hard mounds with sand, clay and saliva. One vast mound contained 11,750 tonnes of sand, piled up grain by grain. The nest may be in or below the mound and the shape varies with species, soil type and rainfall. Some mounds are 9 m tall.

Some mounds are like pagodas, with roofs to shed rain.

Mounds of the Australian Compass Termite all face the same way. The broad sides, facing east-west, catch maximum heat from the weak sun at dawn and dusk.

5 m

▼ Laying in a store

Harvester termites cut grass into short pieces and store it in their warm, damp underground nests where temperatures are constant. Harvester ants bring seeds from the desert floor into their underground granaries. Husked and chewed into "ant bread", it provides food during shortages.

Fresh grass is stored in chambers near the surface. When dry it is then moved close to the nest.

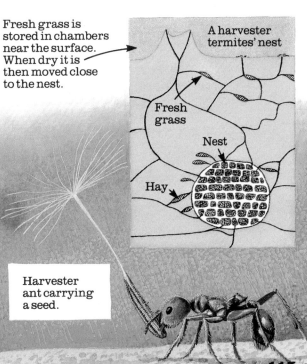

A harvester termites' nest

Fresh grass

Nest

Hay

Harvester ant carrying a seed.

Recognition and deception

Scent, sight and sound are used by insects to identify each other and to pass on information to members of the same species. They may also be used for defence and disguise.

A colony of aphids.

Lacewing larva covered with aphid wax.

Tiger moth

Flexing this cuticle makes a clicking noise.

The ear picks up a bat's clicks.

Bright colours deter daytime predators.

Noises in the night

Many nasty-tasting tiger moths make high-pitched clicks at night. Bats, which hunt by echo-location, veer away from clicking moths. The Banded Woolly Bear Moth is quite edible but it clicks like other tiger moths and so is left alone by the bats.

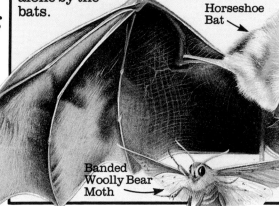

Horseshoe Bat

Banded Woolly Bear Moth

Wolf in sheep's clothing

Woolly Alder Aphids are eaten by Green Lacewing larvae in disguise, despite being protected by ants that feed on their honeydew. The larvae pluck wax from the aphids, and attach it to hooks on their backs.

If stripped of its wax, a lacewing larva is removed by an ant.

Turning up the volume

Mole crickets broadcast their songs from specially built burrows. The Y-shaped burrow acts as an amplifier so that the call can be heard from further away.

Noses on stalks ▶

An insect's antennae carry dozens of tiny structures which are sensitive to scent. They are also sensitive to touch. Antennae are used both to smell and to touch and stroke. They provide an insect with much information.

Cockchafers spread their antennae to find food.

Antennae

Emperor Moth

Grasshopper band ▶

Male grasshoppers stridulate, or sing, by rubbing a "file" across a "scraper". They mainly sing to attract female grasshoppers.

"Ear"

A line of pegs on the inside of the "thigh" acts as the file. They rub across a hard vein on the wing.

Close-up of pegs.

Short-horned grasshoppers rub the hind legs against the wings. Their "ears" are on the side of the body.

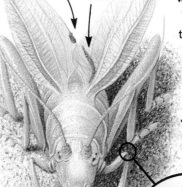

Scraper

File

A scraper on one wing rubs against a file on the other.

"Ears" are in their front "knees".

Long-horned grasshoppers rub their wings together.

TRUE or FALSE?

Crickets have thermometers.

The large feathery antennae of the male Emperor Moth can detect a female's scent from several miles.

No one is sure why these antennae are so long.

Timberman Beetle

Dancing bees ▼

Honeybees tell others where to find food by "dancing" on the comb. Sound, scent and food-sharing also pass on information about the type of food and where it is.

Round dance
A round dance means food within 80 m. The richness of the source is shown by the energy and length of dance. Other bees pick up the scent of the flowers.

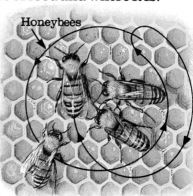

Honeybees

Waggle dance

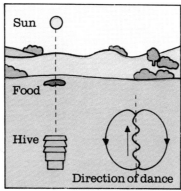

Sun

Food

Hive

Direction of dance

Sun

Food

Hive

45°

45°

Direction of dance

A waggle dance describes food over 80 m from the hive. Speed and number of waggles on the straight run indicate distance. The angle between

straight run and vertical shows the direction of the food relative to the sun. As the sun moves across the sky, the angle of dance changes.

117

Living – and dying – together

Many insects live with and make use of a wide variety of other animals and plants. Some even share ants' nests and many are "milked" of sweet liquids by ants. These relationships have led to special ways of feeding, finding shelter and breeding. Sometimes the association is good for both sides. More often, one makes use of the other, usually by eating it.

Over 100 moths, of seven species, have been found in the coat of one sloth.

Special delivery ▼

Human Botflies use biting flies, such as mosquitoes, to deliver their eggs to human, bird or mammal hosts. Grubs hatch from the eggs and burrow into the host's skin.

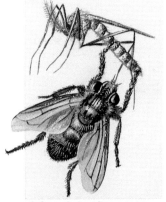 

A female botfly catches a mosquito and glues a cluster of 15-20 eggs on the mosquito's body.

When the mosquito settles on a person, the eggs hatch immediately in response to warmth.

Three-toed Sloth

Moths and sloths ▲

Sloths are so sluggish that moths infest their long coats which are green with algae. About once a week, a sloth slowly descends its tree to excrete. Its moths lay eggs in the dung, which the caterpillars eat. Since their "home" never moves far or fast, moths have no trouble finding it again.

Velvet ant →

Solitary wasp pupa.

◄ Pretty but painful

Velvet ants are not ants. They are really densely hairy, wingless, female wasps. Most break into the nests of solitary bees or wasps to lay their eggs on a pupa, which the velvet ant grub will eat. The brilliant colours of the wasps perhaps warn that they have a sting so powerful they are called "cow-killers".

A houseful of lodgers ▶

Robin's pincushions on wild rose are galls caused by a tiny wasp which lays eggs in young leaf buds. After the gall has formed, another gall wasp enters and lays its eggs. The larvae of both owner and lodger are parasitized by chalcid and ichneumon wasps, and these in turn may also be parasitized.

The original Robin's pincushion gall wasp.

Gall wasp larvae inside the pincushion.

TRUE or FALSE?

Springtail "jockeys" ride soldier termites.

Treacherous guest ▼

Although they eat ant larvae, caterpillars of the Large Blue Butterfly are allowed to live in the nests of *Myrmica* ants. They produce a sweet fluid which the ants love.

Tiny caterpillars eat Thyme flowers. Older ones will produce a sweet fluid for an ant, which responds by carrying it into its nest.

Caterpillar in ant nest.

Ants' nest.

Adult Large Blue

Parasites on parasites

The Mexican Bean Beetle eats leaves and is a pest in North America. It is parasitized by a tachinid fly, which is itself parasitized by an ichneumon wasp.

Mexican Bean Beetle

Tachinid fly

Ichneumon wasp

Beetle's larva

Wasp laying eggs in the fly's pupa

Fly larva inside beetle larva

Travellers and hitchhikers

Insects not only make long journeys under their own power but are also carried, often accidentally, by people or other animals.

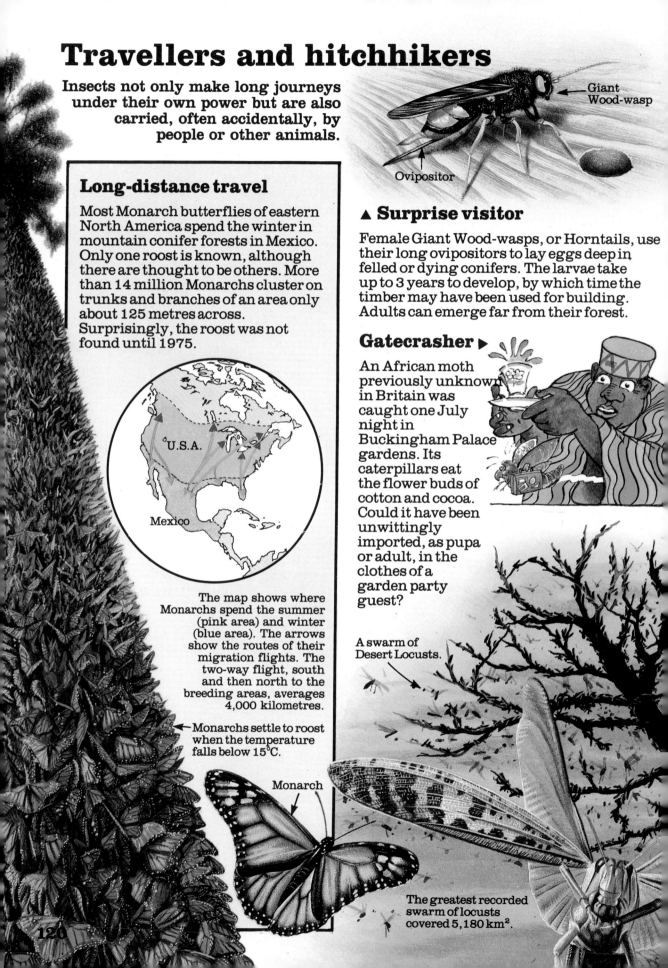

Giant Wood-wasp

Ovipositor

Long-distance travel

Most Monarch butterflies of eastern North America spend the winter in mountain conifer forests in Mexico. Only one roost is known, although there are thought to be others. More than 14 million Monarchs cluster on trunks and branches of an area only about 125 metres across. Surprisingly, the roost was not found until 1975.

U.S.A.

Mexico

The map shows where Monarchs spend the summer (pink area) and winter (blue area). The arrows show the routes of their migration flights. The two-way flight, south and then north to the breeding areas, averages 4,000 kilometres.

← Monarchs settle to roost when the temperature falls below 15°C.

Monarch

▲ Surprise visitor

Female Giant Wood-wasps, or Horntails, use their long ovipositors to lay eggs deep in felled or dying conifers. The larvae take up to 3 years to develop, by which time the timber may have been used for building. Adults can emerge far from their forest.

Gatecrasher ▶

An African moth previously unknown in Britain was caught one July night in Buckingham Palace gardens. Its caterpillars eat the flower buds of cotton and cocoa. Could it have been unwittingly imported, as pupa or adult, in the clothes of a garden party guest?

A swarm of Desert Locusts.

The greatest recorded swarm of locusts covered 5,180 km².

120

Drifts of butterflies ▶

White butterflies in the drier parts of Africa fly off in huge clouds at the start of the dry season when there is no food for the caterpillars. One observer in East Africa reported 500 million butterflies passing each day on a 24 kilometre wide front. Migrating butterflies are sometimes blown out to sea and then washed up on beaches.

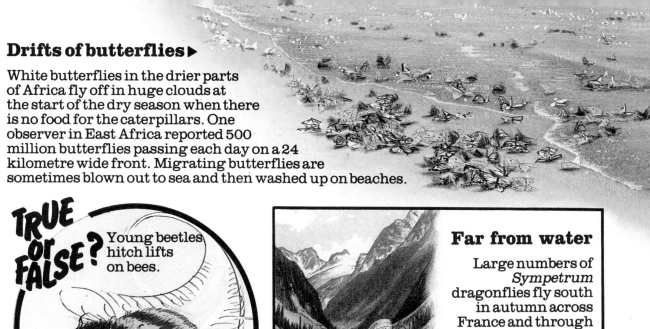

TRUE or FALSE?

Young beetles hitch lifts on bees.

Far from water

Large numbers of *Sympetrum* dragonflies fly south in autumn across France and through mountain passes in the Pyrenees. The exact route of their migration is not known but some turn up in Portugal. On northward migrations the dragonflies often reach south-eastern England from Europe.

Migrating dragonflies

▼ Locust plagues

From time to time Desert Locusts breed rapidly and millions fly long distances in search of food. An area of 26 million km², from West Africa to Assam, and Turkey to Tanzania is at risk of invasion. A large swarm eats 80,000 tonnes of grain and vegetation a day.

Mulberry Silkworm Moth

The caterpillar is called a silkworm.

Caterpillars are fed on mulberry leaves, and pupate in a cocoon spun from a single thread of silk over 900 m long.

Cocoon

Home-grown moths ▲

Silkworm Moths have been reared in China for their silk for over 4,000 years. The moth's wings are so small it cannot fly and it no longer exists in the wild.

The Chinese kept silk-making a secret. One story says that it did not leave China until 350 AD when a princess hid eggs in her head-dress when she went to India to marry a prince.

121

Citizens of the world

Wherever you go on land you find insects. They can live in the harshest climates, eat whatever there is, and adapt quickly to change.

TRUE or FALSE?

Insects make long-distance 'phone calls.

Drinking fog ▶

Darkling beetles manage to live in the hottest, most barren parts of the Namib desert. When night-time fogs roll in from the sea, *Onymacris* beetles climb to the top of sand dunes and, head down, stand facing into the wind. Moisture condenses on ridges on their backs and runs down into their mouths.

Mount Kilimanjaro

A flightless crane fly

Staying on top of the world ▶

Above 5,000 metres on Kilimanjaro, just below the snow cap, is a bleak, windy, alpine desert, with little vegetation. Moths, beetles, earwigs, crane flies and grasshoppers live there but many are wingless. Flying insects might be in danger of blowing away.

Hot as your bath ▶

In the USA's Yellowstone National Park, famous for its geysers, nymphs of the Green-jacket Skimmer dragonfly live in hot spring water at 40°C.

Hissing Cockroaches push air through holes, hissing as they fight.

Cockroaches nibble at book-bindings, photographic film, starched linen, leather goods and any food, fouling them with strong-smelling droppings.

Easy to please

Tropical cockroaches have spread worldwide as scavengers in people's heated houses. They can and do eat anything of animal or plant origin, and this accounts for their success.

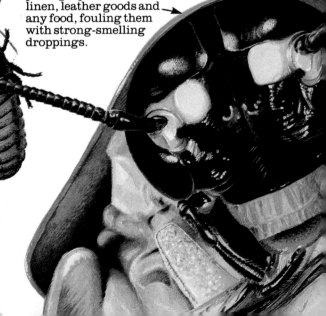

This cave cockroach from Trinidad feeds on bat droppings.

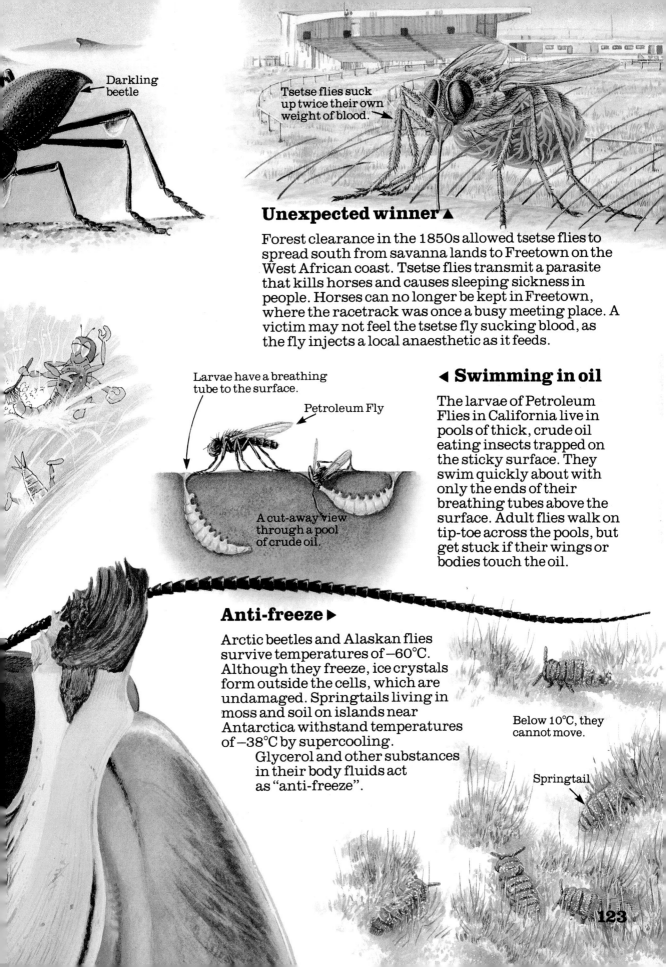

Darkling beetle

Tsetse flies suck up twice their own weight of blood.

Unexpected winner ▲

Forest clearance in the 1850s allowed tsetse flies to spread south from savanna lands to Freetown on the West African coast. Tsetse flies transmit a parasite that kills horses and causes sleeping sickness in people. Horses can no longer be kept in Freetown, where the racetrack was once a busy meeting place. A victim may not feel the tsetse fly sucking blood, as the fly injects a local anaesthetic as it feeds.

Larvae have a breathing tube to the surface.

Petroleum Fly

A cut-away view through a pool of crude oil.

◀ Swimming in oil

The larvae of Petroleum Flies in California live in pools of thick, crude oil eating insects trapped on the sticky surface. They swim quickly about with only the ends of their breathing tubes above the surface. Adult flies walk on tip-toe across the pools, but get stuck if their wings or bodies touch the oil.

Anti-freeze ▶

Arctic beetles and Alaskan flies survive temperatures of −60°C. Although they freeze, ice crystals form outside the cells, which are undamaged. Springtails living in moss and soil on islands near Antarctica withstand temperatures of −38°C by supercooling.

Glycerol and other substances in their body fluids act as "anti-freeze".

Below 10°C, they cannot move.

Springtail

Insect mysteries

Ichneumon wasp

The ovipositor, as long as her body, can be driven accurately more than 3 cm into wood in less than 20 minutes.

The 4 cm long ovipositor is held inside a sheath.

The ovipositor is braced by her legs.

Horntail larva tunnelling in wood.

◄ Precision drilling

A large ichneumon wasp, *Rhyssa persuasoria*, drills into wood with her ovipositor to lay an egg in or close to the wood-boring larva of a Horntail. How does she find the larva? Chemical clues probably help her.

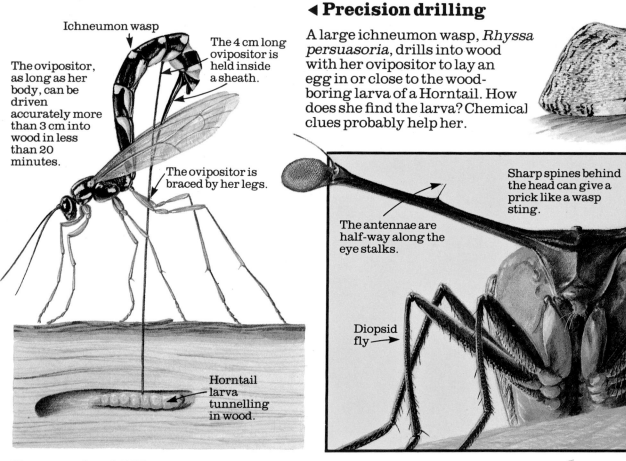

The antennae are half-way along the eye stalks.

Sharp spines behind the head can give a prick like a wasp sting.

Diopsid fly

Samson's riddle▼

In the story of Samson, in The Bible, Samson found a swarm of bees and honey in the body of a lion he had earlier killed. Could the bees have been drone flies – a type of hoverfly which mimics honeybees? Drone flies, unlike bees, sometimes breed in rotting carcasses.

Drone flies

"Out of the eater came something to eat and out of the strong came something sweet."

Unlike most weevils, this one has a short snout.

This weevil's scientific name is *Tribus attelabini*.

Lantern Bugs are harmless suckers of tree sap.

◀ Miniature monsters

The huge heads of Lantern Bugs were once thought to be luminous which is how they got their name. Why do they look so odd? Could a monkey mistake this 10 cm long bug for an alligator?

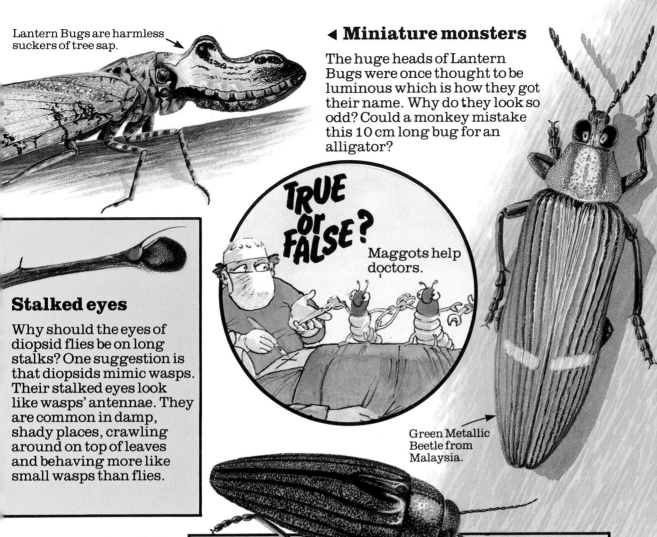

TRUE or FALSE?

Maggots help doctors.

Green Metallic Beetle from Malaysia.

Stalked eyes

Why should the eyes of diopsid flies be on long stalks? One suggestion is that diopsids mimic wasps. Their stalked eyes look like wasps' antennae. They are common in damp, shady places, crawling around on top of leaves and behaving more like small wasps than flies.

▼ Insect "giraffe"

This odd weevil from the island of Madagascar, off Africa, has a very long head, rather than a long, giraffe-like neck. No one is quite sure why it is this shape. When threatened, it drops down and plays dead.

A North American metallic wood-boring beetle.

Precious beetles

Amongst the most brilliantly coloured insects are metallic wood-boring beetles but the purpose of their colour is unclear. Their shining wing-cases have been used in jewellery and embroidery. Some people have even worn tethered beetles as brooches. Toasted larvae of the Green Metallic Beetle are a delicacy.

It is 2.5 cm long and the head takes up almost half this length.

Warning mimicry? ▶

On hearing a foot-step, worker termites foraging beneath dead leaves, vibrate their abdomens. When there are many of them, the rustling of leaves sounds like the hiss of a snake.

SSSSSS

Record breakers

Largest and smallest butterflies

Queen Alexandra's Birdwing from New Guinea has a wingspan of 28 cm; that of a blue butterfly from Africa is only 1.4 cm.

Loudest insect

Male cicadas produce the loudest insect sound, by vibrating ribbed plates in a pair of amplifying cavities at the base of the abdomen: this can be heard over 400 m away.

Population explosion

If all the offspring of a pair of fruit flies survived and bred, the 25th generation – one year later – would form a ball of flies that would reach nearly from the earth to the sun.

Killer bees

So-called killer bees are an African strain of honeybee, which tend to attack people and other animals. More than 70 deaths occurred in Venezuela recently in 3 years, the number of stings varying from 200 to over 2,000. In 1964, a Rhodesian survived 2,243 stings.

Fastest flight

The record has been claimed for a hawk moth flying at 53.6 km/h, but it probably had a following wind. A more reliable record is 28.57 km/h for a dragonfly *Anax parthenope*.

Fastest runner

Try to catch a cockroach and it seems very elusive. They are among the fastest runners, reaching 30 cm per second, but this is only 1.8 km/h.

Biggest group

The insect order Coleoptera (beetles) includes nearly 330,000 species, about a third of known insects. Roughly 40,000 are weevils.

Shortest life

An aphid may develop in 6 days and live another 4-5 days as an adult. Mayflies have the shortest adult life, many living only one day after emerging from the water.

Oldest group

The oldest fossils of winged insects, dating from more than 300 million years ago, include cockroach wings.

Biggest nest

The biggest termite mound, 6.1 m high and 31 m across at the base, was found in Australia. The tallest was a 12.8 m mound of an African species, but it was only 3 m across.

Most dangerous insect

Mosquitoes pass on the parasite causing malaria, which kills about a million people a year. They have probably been responsible for half the human deaths since the Stone Age.

Longest insect

Tropical stick insects are up to 33 cm from end to end, but are very slender and do not fly.

Smallest insect

The overall length of fairyflies, wasps that parasitize the eggs of insects, is as little as 0.21 mm.

Greatest wingspan

The largest recorded Great Owlet Moth *Thysania agrippina*, in tropical America, had a wingspan of 36 cm. The usual range of this species is 23-30 cm.

Longest life

Queens of some species of termites are reported to live for 50 years, although the average is nearer 15. Some metallic wood-boring beetles have a long larval life, emerging from timber after 30-40 years.

Sweetest insect

A hectare of vegetation may support 5,000 million aphids, which saturate the soil with 2 tonnes of sugar, in the form of honeydew, every day.

Fastest wing-beat

A tiny biting midge, or "no-see-um", *Forcipomyia*, beats its hairy wings 62,760 times a minute.

Heaviest insect

The massively armoured Goliath Beetle of Africa, which weighs about 100 gm, is almost certainly the heaviest flying insect.

Were they true or false?

page 101 Bumblebees have central heating.
TRUE. Bumblebees can maintain a temperature of 30-37°C when the air is near freezing. Heat is produced by a chemical process in the flight muscles.

page 103 Zebras have black and white fleas.
FALSE. A Zebra's fleas are not camouflaged.

page 105 In Africa there are man-eating flies.
TRUE. Maggots of the "tumbu" fly burrow into human skin causing painful open sores.

page 107 Ladybirds bite when annoyed.
FALSE. Blood oozes from their knee joints when they are molested, and this irritates sensitive skins.

page 109 Singing crickets attract more females.
TRUE. Males of a North American cricket attract females by "singing" in groups. Some males never sing but join the group and try to mate.

page 111 Butterflies live for only one day.
FALSE. Some live many months, hibernating in winter, or migrating long distances.

page 112 Bees make jellies.
PARTLY TRUE. The "brood food" produced by worker honeybees is called "royal jelly" because it is given only to future queens.

page 117 Crickets have thermometers.
PARTLY TRUE. The warmer it is, the faster they function. Add 40 to the number of chirps a Snowy Tree Cricket gives in 15 seconds, and you get the temperature in degrees Fahrenheit.

page 119 Springtail "jockeys" ride soldier termites.
TRUE. A West African springtail rides on a soldier's head and snatches its food.

page 121 Young beetles hitch lifts on bees.
TRUE. The larvae of some oil and blister beetles swarm over flowers and attach themselves to bees. Carried to a solitary bee's nest, they invade a brood cell and eat the egg and stored food.

page 122 Insects make long-distance phone calls
FALSE. However, termites frequently bore into underground telephone cables; moisture seeps in, insulation breaks down, and the cable no longer carries messages.

page 125 Maggots help doctors.
PARTLY TRUE. As a result of experience gained in the 1914-18 war, surgeons used maggots of Green-bottle Flies, reared in sterile conditions, to clean infected wounds.

Further reading

The Oxford Book of Insects, J. Burton (Oxford University Press)
The World of Insects, A. Zanetti (Sampson Low)
A Fieldguide to the Insects of Britain and Northern Europe, M. Chinery (Collins)
Larousse Encyclopedia of Animal Life, L. Bertin et al. (Hamlyn)
Insect Natural History, A. D. Imms (Collins)
Insect Life in the Tropics, T. W. Kirkpatrick (Longman)
An Introduction to the Study of Insects, D. J. Borror and D. M. DeLong (Holt, Rinehart and Winston)
Wildlife in House and Home, H. Mourier and O. Winding (Collins)
Towns and Gardens, D. F. Owen (Hodder and Stoughton)
The Natural History of the Garden, M. Chinery (Collins)
Fields and Lowlands, D. Boatman (Hodder and Stoughton)
Mountains and Moorlands, A. Darlington (Hodder and Stoughton)
Rivers, Lakes and Marshes, B. Whitton (Hodder and Stoughton)
The Pond, G. Thompson, J. Coldrey and G. Bernard (Collins)
Wildlife in Deserts, F. H. Wagner (Chanticleer)
Animal Ecology in Tropical Africa, D. F. Owen (Longman)
Animal Behavior, J. Alcock (Sinauer)
Animal Migration, O. von Frisch (Collins)
Feeding Strategy, J. Owen (Oxford University Press)
The Hunters, P. Whitfield and R. Orr (Hamlyn)
Camouflage and Mimicry, D. F. Owen (Oxford University Press)
Mimicry, W. Mickler (World University Library)
Defence in Animals, E. Edmunds (Longman)
Sexual Strategy, T. Halliday (Oxford University Press)
The Pollination of Flowers, M. Proctor and P. Yeo (Collins)
The Dictionary of Butterflies and Moths in Colour E. Laithwaite, A. Watson and P. E. S. Whalley (Michael Joseph)
Butterflies and Moths in Britain and Europe, D. Carter (British Museum (Natural History))
All Colour Book of Butterflies, R. Goodden (Octopus)
Social Insects, O. W. Richards (Harper)
The World of the Honeybee, C. G. Butler (Collins)
Bumblebee, J. B. Free and C. G. Butler (Collins)
Social Wasps, R. Edwards (Rentokil)

PART 5

MYSTERIES & MARVELS
OF THE
REPTILE
WORLD

Ian Spellerberg and Marit McKerchar

Designed by Linda Sandey

Illustrated by David Quinn,
Craig Austin (Garden Studios),
Ian Jackson and Sam Thompson

Cartoons by John Shackell

The Arboreal Pit Viper's strong prehensile tail helps it climb trees.

The Red Bellied Turtle forages for food at the edge of the lake.

Contents

Jackson's Chameleon has three horns which may help in defence against predators, such as birds.

By using its large food pouch, the Monitor Lizard often swallows prey, such as a Palm Squirrel, whole.

The Galapagos Tortoise lives on the Island's lowlands and wanders along paths, which have been beaten by generations, to the highlands for food and water.

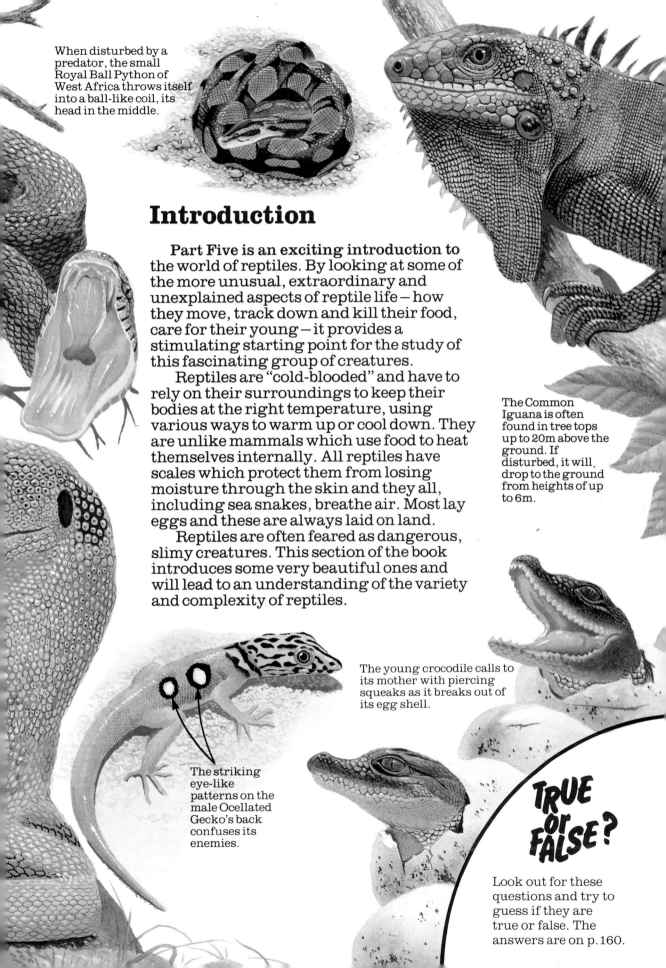

When disturbed by a predator, the small Royal Ball Python of West Africa throws itself into a ball-like coil, its head in the middle.

Introduction

Part Five is an exciting introduction to the world of reptiles. By looking at some of the more unusual, extraordinary and unexplained aspects of reptile life — how they move, track down and kill their food, care for their young — it provides a stimulating starting point for the study of this fascinating group of creatures.

Reptiles are "cold-blooded" and have to rely on their surroundings to keep their bodies at the right temperature, using various ways to warm up or cool down. They are unlike mammals which use food to heat themselves internally. All reptiles have scales which protect them from losing moisture through the skin and they all, including sea snakes, breathe air. Most lay eggs and these are always laid on land.

Reptiles are often feared as dangerous, slimy creatures. This section of the book introduces some very beautiful ones and will lead to an understanding of the variety and complexity of reptiles.

The Common Iguana is often found in tree tops up to 20m above the ground. If disturbed, it will drop to the ground from heights of up to 6m.

The young crocodile calls to its mother with piercing squeaks as it breaks out of its egg shell.

The striking eye-like patterns on the male Ocellated Gecko's back confuses its enemies.

TRUE or FALSE?

Look out for these questions and try to guess if they are true or false. The answers are on p.160.

Warming up and keeping cool

Reptiles are 'cold-blooded' and they have to rely on their surroundings to keep their bodies at a temperature of 30-35°C. 'Warm-blooded' animals keep their bodies warm by using food as fuel for their internal 'burners'. This difference explains why warm-blooded animals need fairly regular meals while reptiles, such as snakes, can survive on one very large meal every few weeks or even once a year. The behaviour of many reptiles is the result of this need to stay at a steady temperature.

Winter store

Some lizards hibernate in winter, going into a long, cool sleep. They do not eat during this time but use fat stored in their bodies. The large, stumpy tail of the South Australian Shingleback lizard is thought to be a winter store of fat.

Shingleback Lizard

Its tail, which looks very much like its head, may also confuse enemies as they may attack the wrong end.

Dwarf Puff Adder

◄Cool hiding place

The Dwarf Puff Adder hides its body from the hot sun by burying itself in the desert sand. Only its eyes show above the surface. As well as keeping cool, the snake lies motionless for hours and even days, waiting to ambush small rodents and lizards which come close enough to provide a meal.

Dancing Lizards▼

The Fringe-Toed Lizard of Southwestern Africa 'dances' to keep cool. It lifts each foot in turn off the hot desert sand and sometimes raises all four feet at once, resting on its stomach. Like many other lizards, this lizard buries itself when the sun is at its hottest. Flaps over its ears and nose keep out the sand when it is underground.

The long, fringed toes help the lizard to run very fast over soft, loose sand in the Namib Desert – one of the hottest places on earth.

Fringe-Toed Lizards

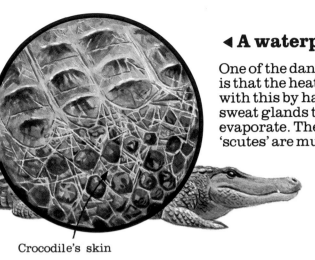

Crocodile's skin

◀ A waterproof skin

One of the dangers of warming up by basking in the sun is that the heat can also dry out the body. Reptiles cope with this by having almost watertight skins, with no sweat glands through which water in their bodies could evaporate. The scales of crocodiles and alligators, called 'scutes' are much larger on their backs, making the skin more waterproof. The scales underneath, shaded from the sun are smaller and more flexible.

▼ In and out of the sun

Each morning, before starting the days hunting for insects, spiders, worms and birds' eggs, the Jewelled Lizard lies in the sun to raise its temperature to 30-35°C. When warm, it is very active but soon becomes too hot. It then runs into the shade to cool down. For the rest of the day, it shuttles in and out of the sun to keep its body at the right temperature.

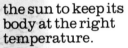

A Jewelled Lizard using the shade. Growing up to 75cm long, it can run very fast over sand and rocks.

Cool character ▲

The Tuatara is a unique reptile, being able to survive on the small cold islands off New Zealand. Most reptiles live in warm areas as it is easier for them to cool down by keeping out of the sun than to warm up if the air is cold. The Tuatara is active at body temperatures lower than those of any other reptile and keeps its body at about 12°C.

As its body is so cool, this lizard is very slow. When moving, it breathes about once every seven seconds but this slows down to about once an hour when it is still. It also grows slowly taking 20 years to reach a length of about 60cm.

Tuataras spend most of the day in their burrows but often lie in the sun in the morning and evening. They come out at night to hunt for insects and spiders but also eat worms and snails.

Super senses

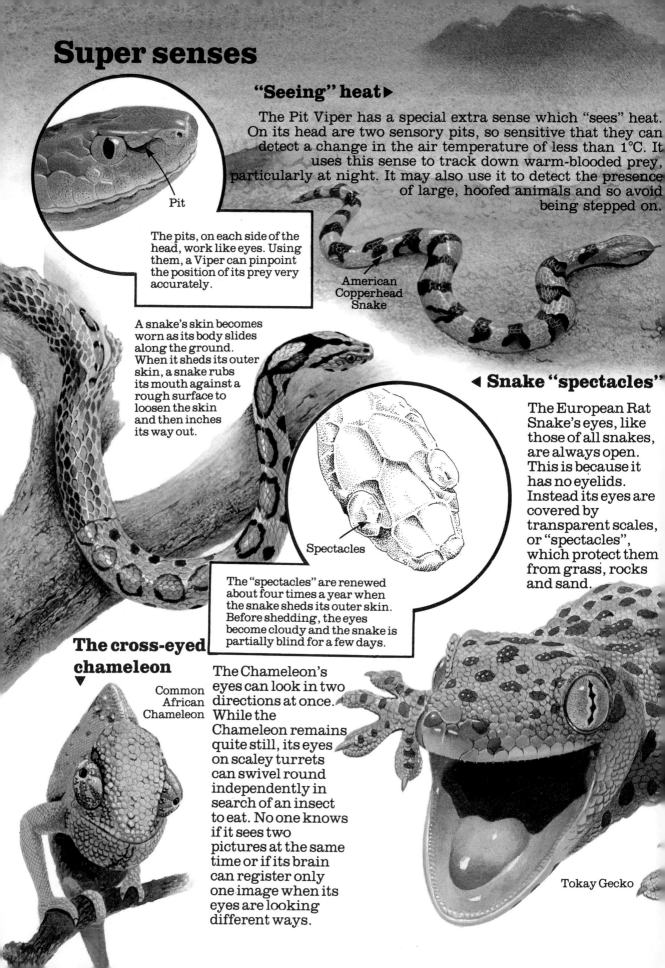

"Seeing" heat ▶

The Pit Viper has a special extra sense which "sees" heat. On its head are two sensory pits, so sensitive that they can detect a change in the air temperature of less than 1°C. It uses this sense to track down warm-blooded prey, particularly at night. It may also use it to detect the presence of large, hoofed animals and so avoid being stepped on.

Pit

The pits, on each side of the head, work like eyes. Using them, a Viper can pinpoint the position of its prey very accurately.

American Copperhead Snake

A snake's skin becomes worn as its body slides along the ground. When it sheds its outer skin, a snake rubs its mouth against a rough surface to loosen the skin and then inches its way out.

◀ Snake "spectacles"

The European Rat Snake's eyes, like those of all snakes, are always open. This is because it has no eyelids. Instead its eyes are covered by transparent scales, or "spectacles", which protect them from grass, rocks and sand.

Spectacles

The "spectacles" are renewed about four times a year when the snake sheds its outer skin. Before shedding, the eyes become cloudy and the snake is partially blind for a few days.

The cross-eyed chameleon ▼

Common African Chameleon

The Chameleon's eyes can look in two directions at once. While the Chameleon remains quite still, its eyes on scaley turrets can swivel round independently in search of an insect to eat. No one knows if it sees two pictures at the same time or if its brain can register only one image when its eyes are looking different ways.

Tokay Gecko

Kangaroo Rat

It follows the Rat down the dark tunnel of its burrow.

This Pit Viper, an American Copperhead, detects the heat given off by the body of a Kangaroo Rat about 50cm away.

When the Viper reaches the Rat, its pits detect the place and distance of its prey. The snake then strikes and kills with its poisonous fangs.

Jacobson's organ

In the mouths of snakes and lizards are two openings which lead to the Jacobson's organ. This extra sense organ detects and identifies the smell of a meal or a mate.

"Tasting" the air ▼

The forked tongues of snakes and lizards are not poisonous, as is often believed. They are harmless and are used to "taste" the air. The flicking tongue picks up smell particles from the air and ground and delivers them to the Jacobson's organ in the roof of the mouth.

The Nile Monitor uses its tongue to find its prey of small mammals, snakes and lizards. Growing to over 2m long, it also steals eggs from crocodiles' nests.

◄ Wide eyes

The common Tropical Gecko hunts at night and has huge eyes with very large pupils in order to see as much as possible in the dark. In daylight, the pupils close up, leaving four tiny pinholes, so only a small amount of light can enter the eyes. It uses its long tongue to clean its eyes which have no eyelids.

The Gecko does not see four pictures out of the pinholes but one sharp image.

TRUE or FALSE?

The Cobra dances to the music of the snake charmer's pipe.

Catching food

Catapult tongue ▼

During the day, the Chameleon moves slowly along the branches of trees in the forest hunting for insects and spiders to eat.

When near enough to its prey, it wraps its tail firmly round a twig, watching its target. Suddenly it shoots out its tongue, which stretches up to the length of its own body, with great accuracy. Then its tongue springs back into its mouth, bringing in the meal. The whole action takes less than a second.

Graceful Chameleon

The round end of the tongue acts like a suction pad and sticks to the prey. Back inside the mouth, the tongue is short and fat. It is like a sleeve of muscle round a long "launching bone" on the Chameleon's lower jaw.

Sticky suction pad

Launching bone

Causing a current

The Matamata Turtle lurks in the muddy rivers of Brazil. When small fish swim close, it opens its jaws so quickly that the fish are swept into its mouth by the current of water this makes.

Using its long neck, the turtle can hold its nostrils out of the water and breathe without moving and scaring the fish. Algae growing on the bumpy 40cm shell helps to camouflage the turtle.

Long tassels of skin look like weed and tempt passing fish to swim close.

False worm ▼

The Alligator Snapping Turtle's colours exactly match the muddy waters of the rivers in North America where it lives. It lies on the river bed with its mouth wide open, completely still except for its bright tongue which it wiggles to look like a worm. Hungry fish dart into its mouth after the "worm", the turtle snaps its jaws shut and swallows the fish. This turtle gets its name from its strong alligator-like tail and powerful jaws.

Weighing up to 100kg and 75cm long, this is the largest of the American fresh-water turtles.

Alligator Snapping Turtle.

Super swallowers ▼

The Boa Constrictor strikes its prey swiftly with its long, sharp teeth. The teeth slope backwards into the mouth so the more a victim struggles, the more firmly it is wedged on to them. The 2m Rainbow Boa suffocates its prey by squeezing it and then swallows it whole. A Boa, like all snakes, can swallow birds and other animals thicker than its own body because of its amazing jaw – the two halves move right apart at the hinge and are joined only by muscle.

Brazilian Rainbow Boa

The snake lies completely still while it waits for its prey to come close.

A snorkel-like windpipe allows the snake to breathe while it swallows a large meal. A 7.5m Python was seen to eat a pig weighing about 54kg and later it swallowed a 47kg goat.

Egg eater

The African egg-eating snake lives in trees where it searches birds' nests hoping to find a meal of eggs. It often swallows eggs which are more than twice the width of its own body.

The snake stretches its elasticated jaws wide apart to fit round the egg, which it grips with its blunt teeth.

In its throat 30 special "teeth", which are extensions of the snake's spine, break the shell as the egg is swallowed. The egg white and yolk flow into the snake's stomach but the shell remains outside and is regurgitated.

Living larder ▶

The Australian Blind Snake lives in its larder – a termites' nest, where it feeds on its termite hosts. Surprisingly, the soldier termites do not often attack the snake. This may be because the snake smells like the termites and so goes unnoticed in the dark tunnels of the mound.

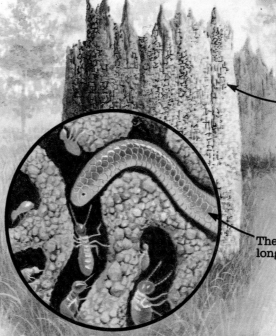

Compass Termites get their name from their mounds which they build in a north-south direction. The tower-like mounds are 3m high by 21m wide, but only 8-10cm thick. Their orientation helps reduce heat in summer but makes the most of winter sun.

The Blind Snake, about 40cm long, inside the termites' nest.

The snake's shiny skin acts like a smooth armour protecting it against bites from the termites' powerful jaws.

137

Fangs and poisons

Poisonous lizards

Of the 3,000 different kinds of lizards only two, the Gila Monster of North America and the Mexican Beaded Lizard, are poisonous. The Gila Monster does not have fangs to inject its poison. Instead, the venom flows from glands in its lower jaw on to grooves in its bottom teeth. When the Gila Monster bites its victim, venom washes around the teeth and is chewed into the wound. The potent venom acts on the victim's nerves and muscles causing internal bleeding and paralysis.

This "Monster" is only just over ½m long and weighs about 1½kg.

Gila Monster

Venomous vipers

The Viper's poison injecting fangs are so long that, when they are not being used, they hinge back against the roof of its mouth.

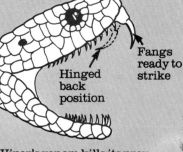

Hinged back position

Fangs ready to strike

The Viper's venom kills its prey by causing its blood to clot. This venom has been used in medicine to help cure blood diseases, such as haemophilia.

The Mongoose is one of the few animals which dares to confront a Cobra. It jumps close, before the Cobra strikes, and grabs the snake's head and jaw.

The Mongoose grips tightly with its teeth and can often win fights with small Cobras which have little chance of injecting their venom.

Spitting Cobra

The venom is squeezed out through holes at the tip of the fangs. It can spit about six times before the venom supply runs out, but this is replaced within a day.

The 2m long Spitting Cobra is found in many parts of Africa.

◀ The venom pistol

The Spitting Cobra squirts a fine stream of venom at its enemy's face, aiming for its eyes. The venom does not kill but it is painful and can make the victim blind. The venom can reach animals up to 3m away but the Cobra's shot is only accurate up to 2m. Using this "weapon" the Cobra can "warn off" its enemy from a safe distance.

King Cobra

Deadly babies

The long fangs of the Fer-de-Lance delivers very deadly venom. The young snakes are born alive in litters of 60-80 babies. Each baby is born complete with fangs and venom, making it dangerous from the start of life. They grow up to nearly 2m long.

The Fer-de-Lance was given its name because of its lance-shaped head and body. It lives in South America and the West Indies, where it is greatly feared because its search for rats and mice has brought it close to human homes.

Head of Fer-de-Lance

◄ The hooded cobra

The King Cobra is the largest poisonous snake, growing up to 5½m. Its tubular fangs stab directly into the victim when it strikes. They are connected to a venom gland which pumps poison through the fangs into the victim. When disturbed, the Cobra raises its body into the strike position, its neck stretched into a threatening hood. Its venom is lethal to most animals, and its fangs deliver more venom than any other snake – one bite can kill an elephant in four hours.

African Boomslang—about 1m long.

Boomslangs have the most deadly poison of any rear-fanged snake, but they rarely bite people as they are shy, hiding away in the trees.

A back-fanged killer ▶

Some snakes, such as the Boomslang, have fangs at the back of their mouths rather than at the front.

Chameleon

The short, fragile fangs are set well back in the upper jaw.

When the Boomslang attacks its prey it needs to hold on with its mouth and chew the victim's flesh in order to inject a large dose of venom. This way of poisoning is not as efficient as the speedy strike of front-fanged snakes, but the Boomslang's venom, when injected, is just as deadly.

TRUE or FALSE?

Snakes have been used as weapons of war.

Escape and defence

If cornered by an enemy, this Bearded lizard makes a threatening display. It stretches out the spiny pouch round its throat, making its head look twice its normal size. It expands its body, opens its mouth to show the bright colours inside and hisses, but it rarely bites.

Frilled Lizard

The lizard, which is over 60cm long, uses its long tail to balance when running fast on two legs.

A two-legged escape

The Frilled Lizard of Australia escapes from predators by running away on its hind legs. This is a mystery because it travels faster on all fours. It may be that, as running makes it very hot, it can keep cooler by holding its body upright in the air, above the hot ground.

A shell fortress ▶

The tortoise carries its shell fortress on its back. The shell is made of horny plates, strengthened underneath by bone so that the tortoise's body is enclosed in a box which can resist almost any attack. It can withdraw its head and legs into this box when danger threatens. Under its stomach is another plate of shell, called the plastron, which in some tortoises hinges in the middle. The Box Tortoise can draw up each end of this plate tightly against the top shell, called the carapace.

Radiated Tortoise of Madagascar

This defence is so effective that tortoises and turtles have survived, almost unchanged, for over 200 million years. Not all of them can withdraw into their shells — the Big-Headed Turtle's head, as its name suggests, can not be withdrawn, and the Snake-Necked Turtle bends its neck sideways, along its shell, to tuck it out of sight.

Stinkpot

The tiny, 10cm Stinkpot is North America's smallest water turtle. As well as its shell, it has a second line of defence against predators, such as crows. When disturbed it gives off a terrible smell from special musk glands. This turtle can climb well and the female usually lays her eggs in nests dug on land.

Musk Turtles spend most of their time in pools and sluggish streams. They feed on water insects, tadpoles, snails and fish and often also take fishermen's bait from the end of lines.

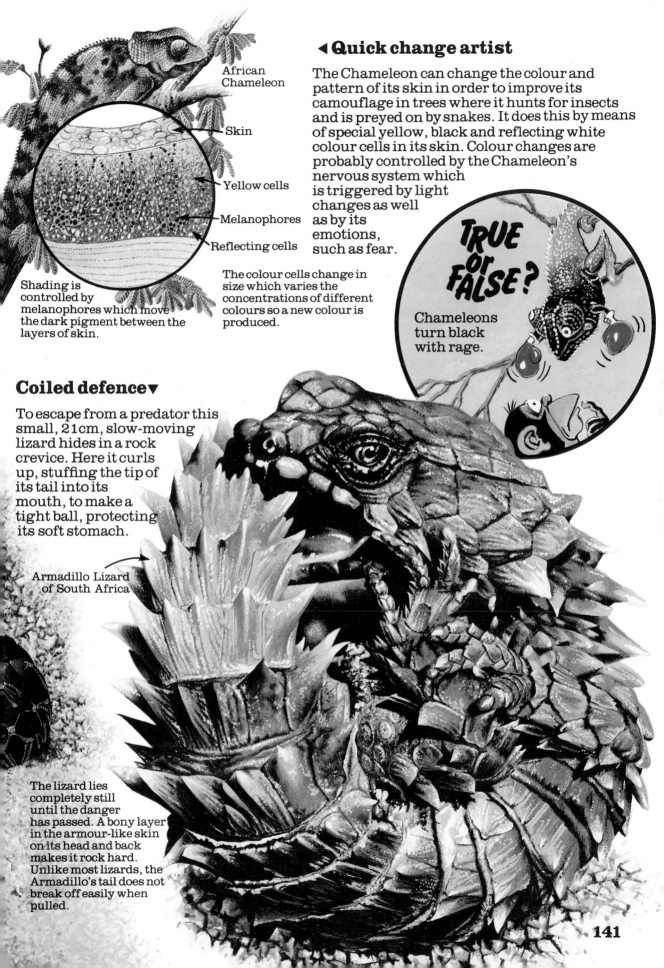

◀ Quick change artist

The Chameleon can change the colour and pattern of its skin in order to improve its camouflage in trees where it hunts for insects and is preyed on by snakes. It does this by means of special yellow, black and reflecting white colour cells in its skin. Colour changes are probably controlled by the Chameleon's nervous system which is triggered by light changes as well as by its emotions, such as fear.

The colour cells change in size which varies the concentrations of different colours so a new colour is produced.

African Chameleon

Skin

Yellow cells

Melanophores

Reflecting cells

Shading is controlled by melanophores which move the dark pigment between the layers of skin.

TRUE or FALSE?

Chameleons turn black with rage.

Coiled defence ▼

To escape from a predator this small, 21cm, slow-moving lizard hides in a rock crevice. Here it curls up, stuffing the tip of its tail into its mouth, to make a tight ball, protecting its soft stomach.

Armadillo Lizard of South Africa

The lizard lies completely still until the danger has passed. A bony layer in the armour-like skin on its head and back makes it rock hard. Unlike most lizards, the Armadillo's tail does not break off easily when pulled.

The art of bluff

Many reptiles defend themselves by deceiving their enemy in some unusual and curious ways.

American Hognosed Snake

The inside of the snake's mouth looks like rotting meat and the snake gives off a terrible smell which helps to convince its enemy that it is dead.

◄ Instant death

The Hognosed Snake imitates a Rattlesnake when it meets an enemy. It raises its head and rubs its tail against the side of its body to make a rattling sound. If this does not frighten off the enemy, the snake rolls on to its back and pretends to be dead, lying completely still with its mouth open. Surprisingly, a mammal or bird is usually taken in by this sham, although it saw that the snake was alive only a moment before. Most of them will not eat the flesh of long-dead animals as its tastes unpleasant and could be poisonous.

Snake look-alikes

The Milk Snake protects itself from attack by looking very like the poisonous Coral Snake. The brightly coloured bands on the Coral Snake's body alerts mammals of its poisonous nature. By copying this pattern, the Milk Snake is also thought to be poisonous even though it is quite harmless.

Coral Snake

Milk Snake

The model for the mimic is one of the less poisonous of the many Coral Snakes. Because mammals survive encounters with them, they remember and learn to avoid them in future. The Milk Snake can be told apart from the Coral Snake, as in the rhyme:

Red and black, friend of Jack,
Red and yellow, kill a fellow.

This lizard can hardly be seen against the pebbles – its markings, irregular shape and a line along its spine divide up its body and disguise its shape.

A sad tail ▶

When grabbed by a predator, a skink's tail breaks off without harming its body. The detached tail goes on wriggling for several minutes, attracting the predator's attention and giving the little lizard time to escape to safety. The bright blue of a young skink's tail would seem to make it an obvious target, but by deliberately drawing an enemy's attention away from its body, the lizard can survive an attack. As the skink grows older, its tail becomes a duller blue.

Badger

Horned Toad – a lizard with a toad-like face.

The blood squirter

The Horned Toad startles its enemies by squirting blood from its eyes. No one knows why the lizard does this. The blood spray may irritate its enemy's eyes, or it could fool the enemy into thinking that the lizard has been wounded. Some scientists think that the blood squirt is caused by parasites living in its eyes, and that it has nothing to do with defence. The blood comes from a special eyelid which swells up, and the little lizard – it only grows up to 13cm – can squirt blood up to 1m away.

Most lizards' tails can break off. They have a special crack in each of the tail bones, with muscles each side which separate easily. New tails grow again within a couple of seasons, but these are usually shorter than the first tail.

Sudanese skink

Scars on the gentle 60cm Boa's tail are proof of attacks it has survived by using this clever bluff.

Rubber Boa of Mexico and southwestern U.S.A.

Two-faced snake ▶

When the Rubber Boa is disturbed by an enemy, it coils into a tight ball and hides its head under its body. It raises instead its blunt head-like tail and waves it aggressively at its enemy. If the enemy attacks, it will go for what it thinks is the snake's head, while the real head remains safely hidden.

143

Frills and decorations

Disappearing act ▶

The Leaf-Tailed Gecko of Madagascar is almost impossible to spot, even when seen close to, against the bark of trees where it lives. Its unusual tail, dappled colours and the fringe of scales along its sides and legs give it perfect camouflage. It can curl its tail round to hold on to branches and its huge eyes are useful when hunting at night.

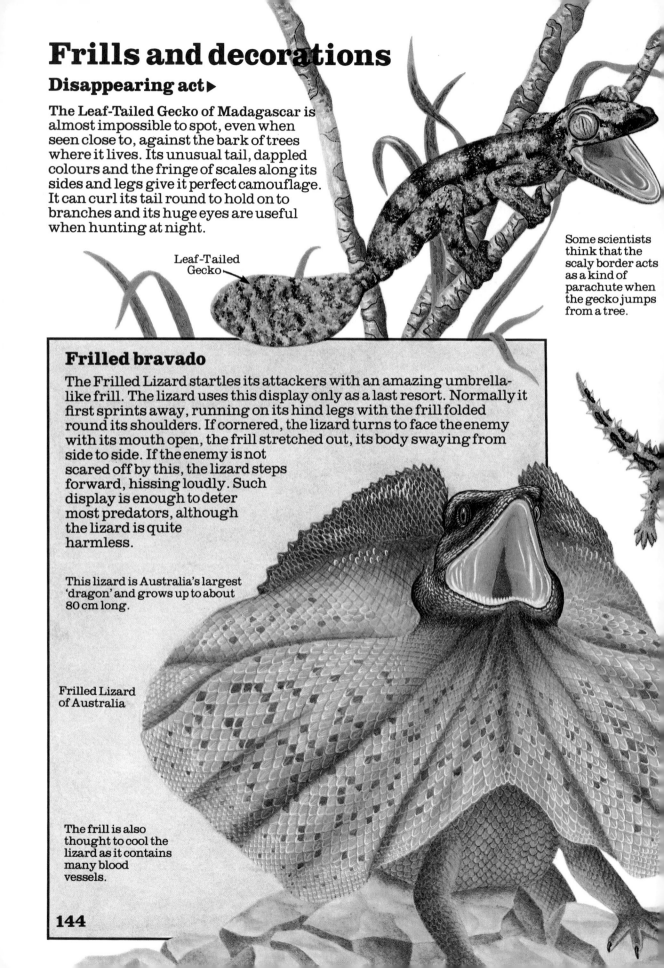

Leaf-Tailed Gecko

Some scientists think that the scaly border acts as a kind of parachute when the gecko jumps from a tree.

Frilled bravado

The Frilled Lizard startles its attackers with an amazing umbrella-like frill. The lizard uses this display only as a last resort. Normally it first sprints away, running on its hind legs with the frill folded round its shoulders. If cornered, the lizard turns to face the enemy with its mouth open, the frill stretched out, its body swaying from side to side. If the enemy is not scared off by this, the lizard steps forward, hissing loudly. Such display is enough to deter most predators, although the lizard is quite harmless.

This lizard is Australia's largest 'dragon' and grows up to about 80 cm long.

Frilled Lizard of Australia

The frill is also thought to cool the lizard as it contains many blood vessels.

Threatening throat ▶

The male Anole defends his territory against other males by extending his brilliant throat sac. A smaller lizard will retreat immediately but anoles of the same size may display to each other for several hours.

The two males sidle round each other with their bodies puffed up. Then one, followed by the other raises his body off the ground, stretches his throat sac and wags his tail up and down. After a few minutes, they both drop down before starting again. Usually they rarely fight and eventually lose interest in each other and walk away.

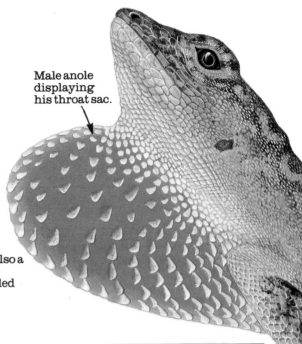

Male anole displaying his throat sac.

The display of the throat is also a sign of courtship to a female anole. The sac is usually folded against the anole's throat otherwise it would be easily spotted by hawks and other predators.

Thorny devil

The Moloch is a very prickly mouthful for a predator. Its body is covered with a mass of spikes as sharp as thorns. Apart from protecting this 15cm lizard, the spikes are very useful in the hot, dry desert as they collect water. Dew condenses on them and runs along tiny grooves in the Moloch's skin and into its mouth. This enables it to live for months without drinking.

Australian Moloch

Although it looks so fierce, the Moloch is quite harmless and eats only ants. It sits by an ant trail, flicking out its tongue and picking up 20 or 30 in a minute. One meal can consist of up to 1,500 ants which it crushes with its cheek teeth.

Rattle alarm ▶

The Rattlesnake warns intruders by sounding its alarm rattle. This gives an approaching animal time to escape and also saves the snake from being stepped on by large, hoofed animals. The rattle is made of loosely linked scaley sections which are the remains of the tail each time the snake sheds its skin. To sound the alarm, the snake vibrates its tail about 50 times a minute and the noise can be heard up to 30 metres away.

The snake sheds its skin three or four times a year, adding a new section to its tail each time. But the rattle cannot be used to tell the snake's age because the older ones start to wear off when there are about eight.

Rattle

Timber Rattlesnake of North America

Courtship

During the mating season, many male reptiles try to attract females with impressive displays. They also fight other males for mates and for territory.

Monitor wrestlers ▶

Male Monitor Lizards wrestle at the beginning of the mating season for female lizards. Surprisingly, neither male is hurt in these fights, although they are armed with sharp teeth and claws and strong tails. It seems that the wrestling is more a trial of strength than an attempt to kill each other — each lizard tries to push the other to the ground, and the first one to succeed wins the female.

The Two-Banded Monitor grows up to 3m long and is one of the largest lizards in the world. The gentlemanly mock battles only occur in the mating season. The Monitors do have very fierce fights over food which often result in bad injuries.

Two-Banded Monitor Lizard

Battering ram

The courtship of Greek Tortoises takes place in warm weather when they are able to move fairly quickly — up to 4.5km per hour, which is about the same speed as a man walking. The male chases his chosen female, and when he catches her he starts to butt her from behind, using his head like a battering ram. At the same time he bites her back legs quite fiercely. This onslaught makes the female draw her head and legs into the shell, and mating then takes place.

If the male cannot find a female during the breeding season, he has been known to butt anything in sight, from flower pots to people.

The male hisses while butting the female

Greek Tortoises — about 30cm long

TRUE or FALSE?

Boas tickle their mates

Cheek caressing ▶

In spring and early summer, the Painted Turtle male seeks out females and makes an attempt to court any one he comes across. He swims quickly after the female, overtakes, and turns to face her head on. She continues to swim on so the male is pushed backwards. In this face to face position, the male gently strokes the female's cheeks with his long foreclaws. If the female is receptive, she sinks to the bottom of the pond and allows the male to mate with her.

146

Common Night Adders of Africa grow 70-90cm long.

The female lays between 12 and 24 eggs which take up to 4 months to hatch.

◄ A love dance

Early in spring, Night Adders dance together as a prelude to mating. The male approaches the female from behind and rubs his chin and throat over her tail. He slowly jerks forward, moving himself along her body. After a while, the female slows down and throws her body in loops with the male following every move. He then wraps his tail around her body and twists, ready to mate.

Splashing out

Before courting starts, the male Nile Crocodile fights with other males to establish a breeding territory on the river bank. The male then patrols the patch of water close to the beach, bellowing at any rival male and fighting off intruders. When a female approaches, he gives off a strong smell of musk and roars. He claps his jaws and lashes his tail, sending clouds of spray all around. He swims in smaller and smaller circles round the female until he is close enough for them to mate.

The female choses a male with a territory which has good sunbathing and nest sites on the bank. She calls him with deep, husky noises.

Male Nile Crocodile

Female Painted Turtles grow to over 15cm long and are considerably larger than the 11cm males. Only males have long foreclaws.

Painted Turtles

Eggs and nurseries

Most reptiles lay eggs, although a few species do give birth to live young. All the ones that hatch from eggs have a special "tool" for breaking out of their shells; snakes and lizards have a sharp egg tooth, while tortoises and crocodiles have a horny knob on the end of their snouts.

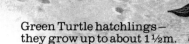

Green Tree Python of New Guinea

Green Turtle hatchlings —
they grow up to about 1½m.

The baby Pythons are born yellow or red and change to the rich green colour of the adult snakes when they are about 1m long. Adults grow up to about 2m.

Body warmers

Three to four months after mating, the female python lays up to 100 eggs. She gathers the eggs into a pile and coils her body around them for about three months until they hatch. By a special kind of shivering, the mother python can raise her body temperature by about 8°C while she incubates the eggs — an unusual ability in "cold-blooded" animals. She only leaves her eggs for occasional visits to the water and for rare meals.

Caring crocodiles ▶

Each year, the female Nile Crocodile lays up to 40 eggs in a nest dug in the sand above the waterline on the riverbank. She builds the nest in a shady place, about 20-30cm deep, so that the eggs keep at an even temperature — not varying more than 3°C. She covers the eggs with sand and both parents guard them during the 90 days incubation. Predators, such as the Nile Monitor, have a taste for crocodile eggs.

When it is ready to hatch, the young crocodile makes loud piping calls. Its mother scrapes away the sand covering the eggs, gently picks up each baby with her teeth, and carries them in a special pouch at the bottom of her mouth to a "nursery" pool area off the river. The young crocodiles follow their mother about like ducklings and crawl over her face and back.

The young crocodile stays in the "nursery" for about two months, guarded by its parents.

The first few steps of the Turtle's life are its most dangerous – it has to find its way to the sea past hungry crabs and Frigate Birds. The Turtles have more chance of reaching the sea if they make the dash together. Somehow the young Turtles know which direction to go when they leave their nests. They may follow the sound of the waves or head for the brighter light which is reflected off the sea.

Obstacle course ▲

The female Green Turtle lays her eggs in the sand dunes on the beaches of Ascension Island where they are incubated by the heat of the sun. She digs a nest with her hind flippers and, after laying about 100 eggs, covers them with sand and lumbers back to the sea. The male Turtle waits for her offshore, and they mate again and produce two or three more batches of eggs in the mating year. They usually return to the breeding grounds only once every three years.

On a limb

Most chameleons bury their parchment-like eggs underground and the babies then hatch about eight months later. The Dwarf Chameleon's eggs develop inside the mother's body and she gives birth to about 16 eggs which hatch almost immediately. The mother places each sticky egg carefully on a twig or leaf as they are laid. The young Chameleon then wriggles and twists its way out of the soft egg shell.

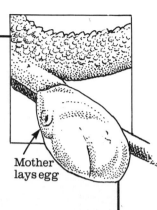

Mother lays egg

Egg sticks to twig

Chameleon twists out of the egg

The baby Dwarf Chameleon is only 3-4cm long, but it starts to hunt for insects within a few hours of being born. Adults grow up to 20cm.

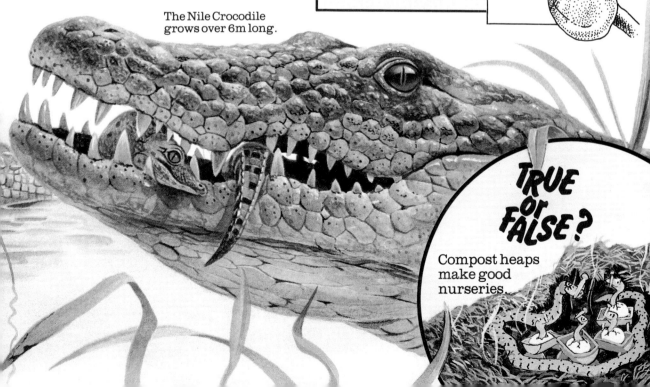

The Nile Crocodile grows over 6m long.

TRUE or FALSE?

Compost heaps make good nurseries.

On the move

Tree gecko

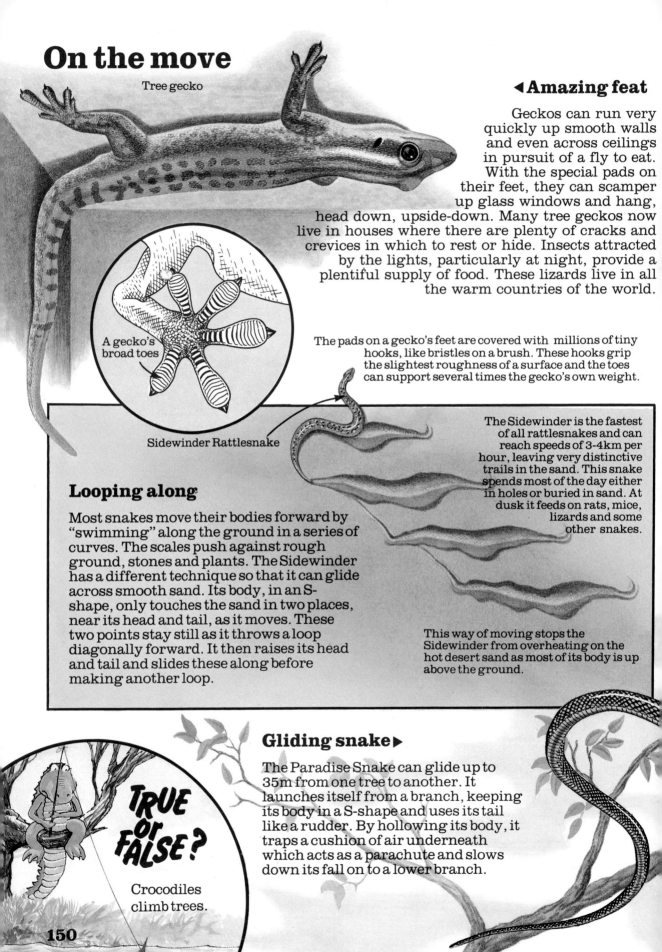

◄ Amazing feat

Geckos can run very quickly up smooth walls and even across ceilings in pursuit of a fly to eat. With the special pads on their feet, they can scamper up glass windows and hang, head down, upside-down. Many tree geckos now live in houses where there are plenty of cracks and crevices in which to rest or hide. Insects attracted by the lights, particularly at night, provide a plentiful supply of food. These lizards live in all the warm countries of the world.

A gecko's broad toes

The pads on a gecko's feet are covered with millions of tiny hooks, like bristles on a brush. These hooks grip the slightest roughness of a surface and the toes can support several times the gecko's own weight.

Sidewinder Rattlesnake

The Sidewinder is the fastest of all rattlesnakes and can reach speeds of 3-4km per hour, leaving very distinctive trails in the sand. This snake spends most of the day either in holes or buried in sand. At dusk it feeds on rats, mice, lizards and some other snakes.

Looping along

Most snakes move their bodies forward by "swimming" along the ground in a series of curves. The scales push against rough ground, stones and plants. The Sidewinder has a different technique so that it can glide across smooth sand. Its body, in an S-shape, only touches the sand in two places, near its head and tail, as it moves. These two points stay still as it throws a loop diagonally forward. It then raises its head and tail and slides these along before making another loop.

This way of moving stops the Sidewinder from overheating on the hot desert sand as most of its body is up above the ground.

Gliding snake ▶

The Paradise Snake can glide up to 35m from one tree to another. It launches itself from a branch, keeping its body in a S-shape and uses its tail like a rudder. By hollowing its body, it traps a cushion of air underneath which acts as a parachute and slows down its fall on to a lower branch.

TRUE or FALSE?

Crocodiles climb trees.

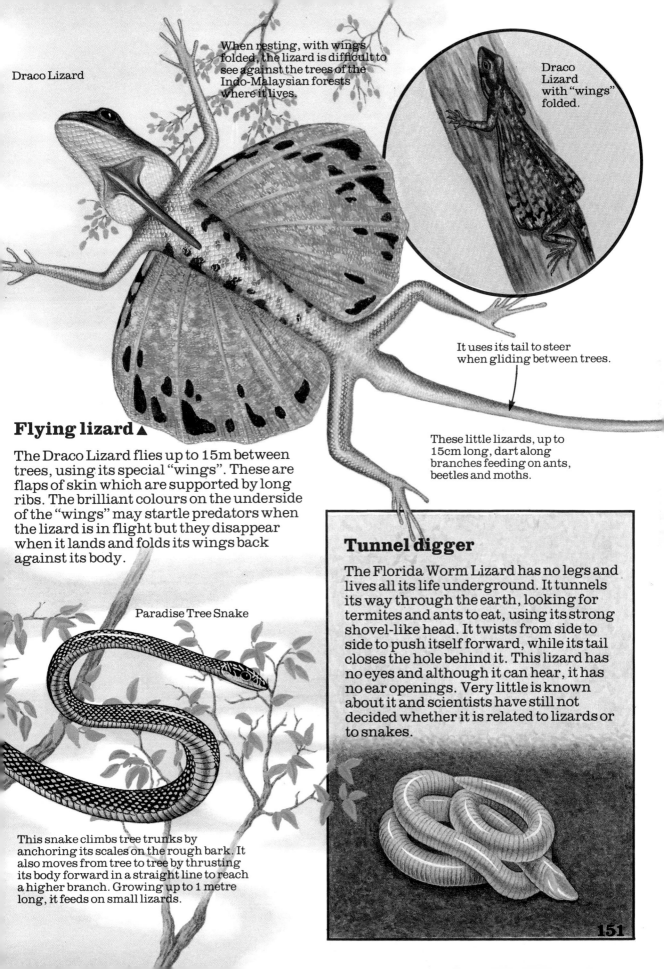

Draco Lizard

When resting, with wings folded, the lizard is difficult to see against the trees of the Indo-Malaysian forests where it lives.

Draco Lizard with "wings" folded.

It uses its tail to steer when gliding between trees.

Flying lizard ▲

The Draco Lizard flies up to 15m between trees, using its special "wings". These are flaps of skin which are supported by long ribs. The brilliant colours on the underside of the "wings" may startle predators when the lizard is in flight but they disappear when it lands and folds its wings back against its body.

These little lizards, up to 15cm long, dart along branches feeding on ants, beetles and moths.

Paradise Tree Snake

Tunnel digger

The Florida Worm Lizard has no legs and lives all its life underground. It tunnels its way through the earth, looking for termites and ants to eat, using its strong shovel-like head. It twists from side to side to push itself forward, while its tail closes the hole behind it. This lizard has no eyes and although it can hear, it has no ear openings. Very little is known about it and scientists have still not decided whether it is related to lizards or to snakes.

This snake climbs tree trunks by anchoring its scales on the rough bark. It also moves from tree to tree by thrusting its body forward in a straight line to reach a higher branch. Growing up to 1 metre long, it feeds on small lizards.

151

Taking to the water

Walking on the water ▶

The Basilisk Lizard escapes from its enemies by dropping on to the water from river-side trees or bushes. It then runs, at speeds up to 12kph, across the top of the water. It moves so fast on the long, fringed toes on its back legs that it does not have time to sink. If it does slow down, the lizard breaks through the surface of the water and swims, partly submerged, for the rest of its journey.

The Basilisk Lizard is called the Jésus Christo lizard in South America because it runs on water.

The Basilisk is named after the crested lizard which, according to the legend, hatched from an egg laid by a cockerel and could kill anything with just one glance. This iguanid lizard, which grows up to 60cm long, is quite harmless and feeds on plants and insects in tropical America.

The Anaconda can swim fast and often feeds on fish, turtles and even caimans.

◀ A swimming serpent

The Anaconda spends most of its day lying in the sluggish rivers or swamps of tropical South America, or sunbathing on low trees. At dusk it waits for its prey, usually birds and small mammals, to come down to the water to drink. Then it grabs its victim in its mouth and quickly loops its body round it. The snake slowly tightens its coils until its prey can no longer breathe and dies of suffocation, or drags it into the water to drown before eating it.

The snake eats its prey whole. A 7m Anaconda was reported to have swallowed a 2m caiman – a meal which would have lasted the snake for several weeks.

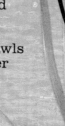

Submarine reptiles ▶

The Hawksbill Turtle, which lives in tropical seas around the world, has a light-weight shell and paddle-like legs. It uses its front legs to swim slowly through the water and its back legs to steer, like a rudder. The female Hawksbill crawls clumsily on land when she comes out to lay her eggs while the male rarely leaves the water.

Stone ballast ▼

The Gharial is a long, slender-snouted crocodile which lives in Indian rivers. It spends much of its time lying in the water with only its eyes and nostrils above the surface. Like all crocodiles, the Gharial swallows stones to help it stay under the water. Without this extra weight, young crocodiles become top heavy and would tip over. The Gharial can stay under the water for over an hour. It has special flaps which cover its nostrils and a valve which shuts off its windpipe so it can open its mouth to catch fish without swallowing lots of water.

TRUE or FALSE?

Crocodiles cry when eating their victims.

The lump on the end of some adults' snouts is a mystery. It may increase the noise of the mating call but no one really knows.

The Gharial's snout has over 100 sharp, even, teeth which it uses to catch fish.

The Hawksbill has always been hunted for its shell. Although plastics have largely replaced tortoise-shell, this turtle is still in danger of extinction.

The turtle eats water plants, sea urchins, fish and crabs. Its flesh is sometimes poisonous to human beings, perhaps because it also eats stinging jelly fish and Portuguese men-of-war.

Underwater grazing grounds

The Marine Iguana of the Galapagos Islands is the only lizard which is at home in the sea. There is little food on the barren volcanic shores and the lizard goes to sea for its meals of seaweed. When the tide goes out, exposing the reefs and algae-covered rocks, it plunges into the cool water. Clinging to the rocks with its sharp claws, it tears off the seaweed with its mouth. Some iguanas may swim out beyond the surf and dive down 5m to feed on the seabed, each dive lasting about 15 minutes.

Marine Iguanas on Hood Island.

Before diving into the cool sea, iguanas warm themselves in the sun. To avoid over-heating, they hold their bodies off the hot rocks or face the sun, so their heads provide shade for their bodies.

A place to live

Bird perch▼

Many snakes spend their lives in trees. The African Vine Snake lies along the branch of a tree with the front part of its 1.5m body held out stiffly in space. It stays motionless for hours, its long, slender body looking like a small branch to an unwary bird. It can move very fast through the trees, as well as on the ground, looking for meals of small birds and lizards.

Ruby-Topaz Hummingbird

The tiny Ruby-Topaz Hummingbird hovers near the snake, its wings beating 50-80 times a second.

The Vine Snake keeps its tongue quite still, instead of flicking it in and out like most snakes. It is thought that it may use its tongue as a bait to attract its prey.

African Vine Snake

Pine Snake

← Spiders live and weave webs at the entrance to the burrow.

Gopher mice eat seeds that they collect or fall in.

Gopher frogs eat insects that come or fall in.

Cave crickets feed on beetle dung.

Beetles feed on the tortoise's dung.

At home in the sea

The Olive Sea Snake spends its life in warm, tropical Asian seas. Here it eats, breeds and produces live young, never leaving the water to go ashore. The snake's body is flat and its tail acts like an oar, driving it through the water. The snake breathes air and with special lungs, almost the length of its body, it can stay underwater for up to two hours. Flaps cover its nostrils when it is submerged. It can also "breathe" in air from the sea through its skin in much the same way as a fish "breathes" through its gills.

Shared shelter▲

The Gopher Tortoise digs its own home, a long, cool tunnel, amongst the sand hills of southern parts of the United States. Here it can escape during the day from the heat of the sun and it shares the burrow with several other animals. They all live together quite happily, each with its own place and habits. The tortoise can defend its home against unwelcome visitors, such as a Pine Snake, by blocking the entrance with its shell.

TRUE or FALSE?

Alligators live in sewers

154

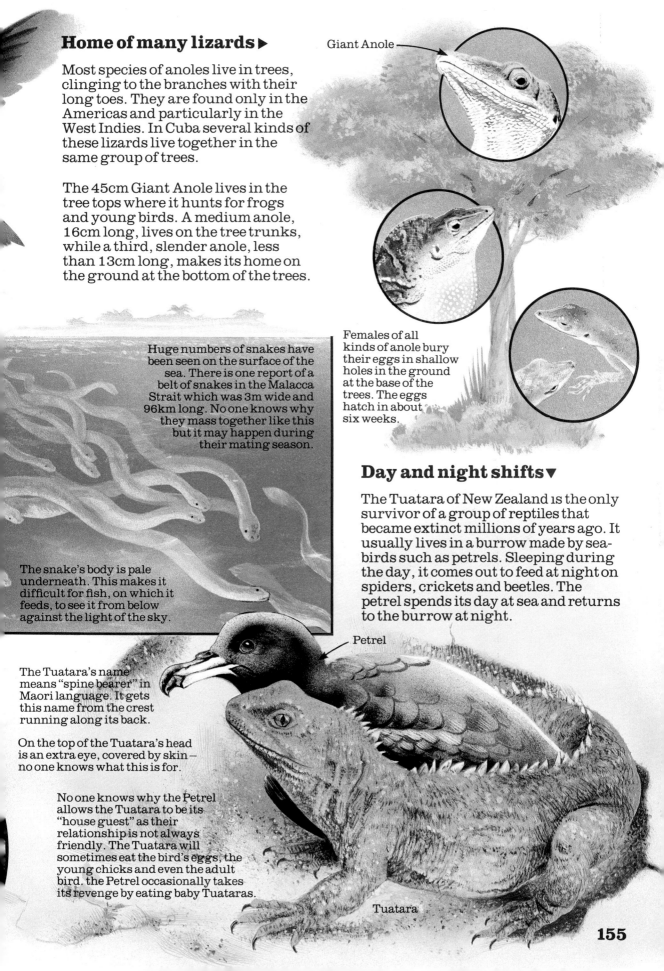

Home of many lizards ▶

Most species of anoles live in trees, clinging to the branches with their long toes. They are found only in the Americas and particularly in the West Indies. In Cuba several kinds of these lizards live together in the same group of trees.

The 45cm Giant Anole lives in the tree tops where it hunts for frogs and young birds. A medium anole, 16cm long, lives on the tree trunks, while a third, slender anole, less than 13cm long, makes its home on the ground at the bottom of the trees.

Giant Anole

Females of all kinds of anole bury their eggs in shallow holes in the ground at the base of the trees. The eggs hatch in about six weeks.

Huge numbers of snakes have been seen on the surface of the sea. There is one report of a belt of snakes in the Malacca Strait which was 3m wide and 96km long. No one knows why they mass together like this but it may happen during their mating season.

The snake's body is pale underneath. This makes it difficult for fish, on which it feeds, to see it from below against the light of the sky.

Day and night shifts ▼

The Tuatara of New Zealand is the only survivor of a group of reptiles that became extinct millions of years ago. It usually lives in a burrow made by sea-birds such as petrels. Sleeping during the day, it comes out to feed at night on spiders, crickets and beetles. The petrel spends its day at sea and returns to the burrow at night.

Petrel

The Tuatara's name means "spine bearer" in Maori language. It gets this name from the crest running along its back.

On the top of the Tuatara's head is an extra eye, covered by skin — no one knows what this is for.

No one knows why the Petrel allows the Tuatara to be its "house guest" as their relationship is not always friendly. The Tuatara will sometimes eat the bird's eggs, the young chicks and even the adult bird. the Petrel occasionally takes its revenge by eating baby Tuataras.

Tuatara

Curious events

Living toothbrush ▶

During the heat of the day, the crocodile lies on a muddy bank with its mouth wide open. Water evaporates from its mouth, cooling it down, rather like a dog panting when hot. Plovers land on its jaw to peck food from its teeth. They seem to be in no danger. This may be because they clean the crocodile's teeth, which it cannot do itself as its tongue is not moveable. The birds may also remove leeches and other irritating insects.

No one knows why the inside of its mouth is such a brilliant colour, but the crocodile may use it as a shock tactic – suddenly opening its mouth and freezing its prey with terror.

Spur-winged Plover.

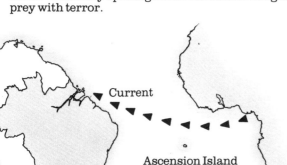

Current

Ascension Island

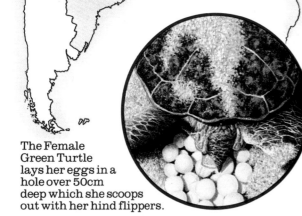

The Female Green Turtle lays her eggs in a hole over 50cm deep which she scoops out with her hind flippers.

◀ Long distance swimmers

Every three years, groups of Green Turtles gather together and swim 2,000km from their grazing grounds off the coast of Brazil to lay their eggs on Ascension Island. No one knows how the Turtles manage to find the small 13km by 9km island in the middle of the Atlantic. There is an ocean current running at just under 2km per hour from the African coast, past Ascension Island, to Brazil. To return to their grazing grounds the Turtles just have to drift with this. But as their swimming speed is only 2km per hour, they cannot go against the current on the outward journey and must find another route. Scientists think that they either follow smells given off by different parts of the sea, or navigate by means of the sun and stars. The round trip takes about three years.

Snake eats snake ▶

When a Rattlesnake comes across a King Snake it acts in a very unusual way. Instead of preparing to strike with its poison-injecting fangs, the rattler keeps its head as far as possible from the King Snake and uses the middle of its body to try to beat it off. The King Snake, not put off, grasps the rattler's neck in its teeth, wraps its body round the rattler and chokes it to death. The non-poisonous King Snake is successful in these battles because it is immune to the rattler's, usually lethal, poison.

The King Snake also attacks and eats other King Snakes.

A two-headed serpent ▶

Occasionally freak two-headed snakes are born. A two-headed King Snake which lived in San Diego Zoo was always in danger because of the King Snake's habit of eating other snakes. One night one of the heads tried to swallow the other. The attacked head was rescued in the morning by a keeper, but it later tried to take its revenge on the first head and this attack killed both heads and their one body.

The two-headed snake of San Diego Zoo also had two lungs, instead of one, and two hearts.

Rafts ▼

Scientists think that the reptiles on the Galapagos Islands reached there by means of natural rafts from the coast of Equador, 800-900km away. A tortoise, for example, would climb on to a piece of drift wood to rest, which then drifted out to sea.

Mammals are less able than reptiles to cope with the lack of food and water on rafts, and the Rice Rats are the only native land mammals which exist on the Galapagos Islands.

Stowaways ▶

Geckos living in ports quite often find their way on to ships while searching for insect meals. They have travelled to remote parts of the world on these ships as "stowaways" – the Turkish Gecko has migrated to most of the world's main tropical areas in this way.

California King Snake.

It swallows the Rattlesnake by "walking" its mouth and body over the dead snake.

TRUE or FALSE?

Snakes can jump a metre high.

Record breakers

The biggest meal

The biggest meal recorded was an Impala weighing nearly 60kg found in the stomach of a 4.87m African Rock Python.

The most deaths

In India, Indian Cobras kill about 7,500 people per year which is about 25% of all the snake bite deaths in India.

Fastest snake

The Black Mamba can reach speeds of 25km per hour in short bursts. It races along with its head and the front of its body raised, mouth open and tongue flicking.

The largest reptile

Salt-water Crocodiles are today's largest reptiles. They grow to an average of 4½m long, although there have been reports of larger beasts. A 8m Crocodile was killed in 1954 which was over 1.5m tall at the shoulder and would have weighed nearly 2 tons.

Fastest swimming snake

The Yellow-bellied Sea Snake of the Indo-Pacific region can swim at the rate of 1m per second. Sea Snakes can also dive 100m deep and stay under water for up to 5 hours.

Smallest snakes

Thread Snakes are only 1 to 1.3cm long and are so thin they could glide through the hole left in a normal pencil if the lead was removed.

Tiny but loud

The Least Geckos are the smallest reptiles at only 2½cm long. Some of these tiny lizards sing in loud chirrups, which can be heard up to 10km away and attract mates.

The longest starvation

The Okinawa Habu Snake of the West Pacific can survive for more than 3 years without food.

The longest fangs

The highly venomous Gaboon Viper of Tropical Africa has the longest fangs of any snake. One 1.2m snake had fangs nearly 3cm long. It will only bite if really provoked.

158

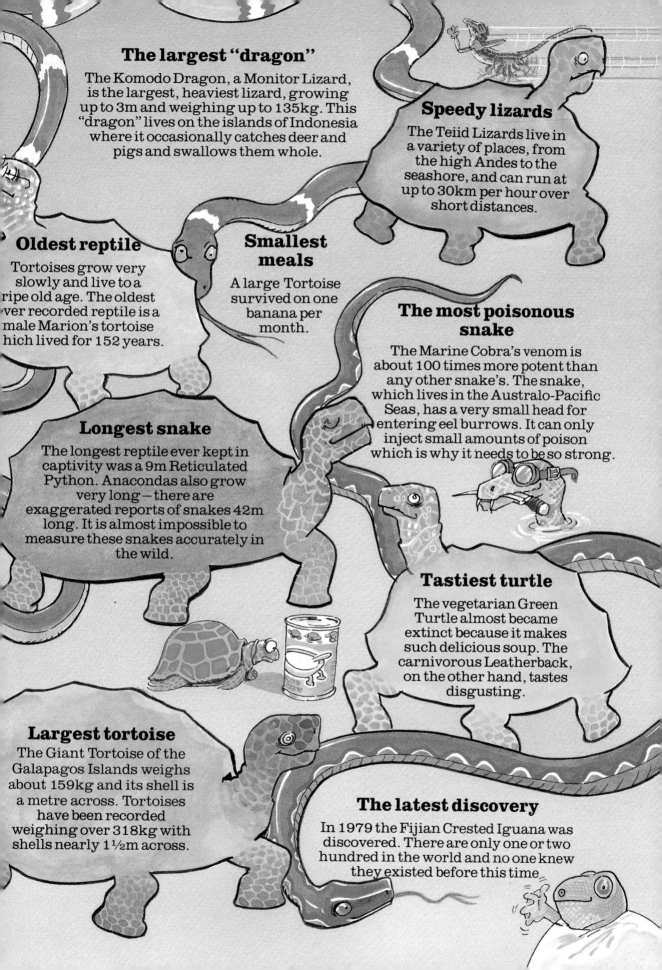

The largest "dragon"

The Komodo Dragon, a Monitor Lizard, is the largest, heaviest lizard, growing up to 3m and weighing up to 135kg. This "dragon" lives on the islands of Indonesia where it occasionally catches deer and pigs and swallows them whole.

Speedy lizards

The Teiid Lizards live in a variety of places, from the high Andes to the seashore, and can run at up to 30km per hour over short distances.

Oldest reptile

Tortoises grow very slowly and live to a ripe old age. The oldest ever recorded reptile is a male Marion's tortoise which lived for 152 years.

Smallest meals

A large Tortoise survived on one banana per month.

The most poisonous snake

The Marine Cobra's venom is about 100 times more potent than any other snake's. The snake, which lives in the Australo-Pacific Seas, has a very small head for entering eel burrows. It can only inject small amounts of poison which is why it needs to be so strong.

Longest snake

The longest reptile ever kept in captivity was a 9m Reticulated Python. Anacondas also grow very long — there are exaggerated reports of snakes 42m long. It is almost impossible to measure these snakes accurately in the wild.

Tastiest turtle

The vegetarian Green Turtle almost became extinct because it makes such delicious soup. The carnivorous Leatherback, on the other hand, tastes disgusting.

Largest tortoise

The Giant Tortoise of the Galapagos Islands weighs about 159kg and its shell is a metre across. Tortoises have been recorded weighing over 318kg with shells nearly 1½m across.

The latest discovery

In 1979 the Fijian Crested Iguana was discovered. There are only one or two hundred in the world and no one knew they existed before this time.

Were they true or false?

page 133 Skinks have antifreeze in their blood.
TRUE. The Water Skink of the Eastern Australian mountains emerges from its hibernation when there is still snow on the ground. Antifreeze in its blood keeps it active even when its body temperature is $-2°C$.

page 135 Cobras dance to the music of the snake charmer's pipe.
FALSE. The Cobra cannot hear the music. When its basket is opened, it rises in defence and then follows the movement of the pipe, ready to attack.

page 139 Snakes have been used as weapons of war.
TRUE. It is said that Hannibal had jars of live poisonous snakes thrown into his enemy's ships – a tactic which resulted in victory.

page 141 Chameleons turn black with rage.
PARTLY TRUE. Using its ability to change colour, the Chameleon may turn nearly black when faced by an enemy.

page 143 Crocodiles pretend to be logs to escape from enemies.
FALSE. The crocodile does look like a log but this is to stalk its prey.

page 146 Boas tickle their mates.
TRUE. Boas have spurs which are all that remain of back legs. The male uses his to scratch and tickle the female during courtship

page 149 Compost heaps make good nurseries.
TRUE. Grass Snakes seek warm, moist places to lay their eggs – a compost heap is ideal.

page 150 Crocodiles climb trees.
TRUE. Young crocodiles are good climbers and often rest on branches near water.

page 153 Crocodiles cry when eating their victims.
FALSE. Saltwater Crocodiles are often seen to cry on land, but this is to rid themselves of excess salt, not remorse.

page 154 Alligators live in sewers.
PARTLY TRUE. There are reports of alligators in the sewers beneath Manhattan Island, U.S.A These were probably pets, released into drains when their owners became bored with them.

page 157 Snakes can jump a metre high.
TRUE. A Viper of Central America can leap up to 1m to strike at its prey.

Further reading

Spotter's Guide to Dinosaurs & Other Prehistoric Animals, D. Norman (Usborne)
Spotter's Guide to Zoo Animals, R. Kidman Cox (Usborne)
Discovering Life on Earth, D. Attenborough (Collins)
Wild, Wild World of Animals: Reptiles and Amphibians, R. Oulahan (Time-Life)
Encyclopedia of Reptiles, Amphibians and Other Cold-blooded Animals (Octopus)
The Reptiles, A. Carr (Life Nature Library)
Grzimek's Animal Life Encyclopedia, Volume 6 Reptiles (Van Nostrand Reinhold)
Vanishing Species (Time Life Books)
Tortoises & Turtles, J. L. Cloudsley-Thompson (Bodley Head)
Crocodiles & Alligators, J. L. Cloudsley-Thompson (Bodley Head)
Snakes and Lizards, E. & C. Turner (Priory Press)
Strangest Creatures of the World, G. Kensinger (Ridge Press)
The Venomous Animals, R. Caras (Barre/Westover)
Venomous Animals, R. Burton (Colour Library International)
Colour for Survival, P. Ward (Orbis)
Keeping a Terrarium, S. Schmitz (Lutterworth Press)
Snakes – A Natural History, H.W. Parker & A.G.C. Grandison (British Museum)
The Hunters, P. Whitfield (Hamlyn)
The Fascination of Reptiles, M. Richardson (Andre Deutsch)
Biology of Reptiles, I. Spellerberg (Blackie)
Weird & Wonderful Wildlife, M. Marten et al (Secker & Warburg)
Poisonous Snakes, T. Phelps (Blandford Press)
Introducing Snakes, V.J. Stanek (Golden Pleasure Books)
Reptiles, A. Bellairs and J. Attridge (Hutchinson)
The World of Reptiles, A. Bellairs and R. Carrington (Chatto and Windus)

PART 6

MYSTERIES & MARVELS
OF
BIRD
LIFE

Ian Wallace, Rob Hume and Rick Morris

Edited by Rick Morris
with Marit McKerchar

Designed by Teresa Foster,
Anne Sharples, Sally Godfrey,
Lesley Davey and Polly Dawes

Illustrated by David Quinn,
Alan Harris, David Mead,
Wayne Ford and Ian Jackson

Cartoons by John Shackell

Contents

The Quetzal, from Central America, was worshipped by the Aztecs as "the god of the air".

To avoid damaging his long feather train, the male drops backwards off his perch before flying away. When he sits on the eggs the train pokes up to 30 cm out of the nest hole.

The colourful but balding King Vulture from the rainforests of Central and South America. It is probably one of the few birds to find its food by smell.

162

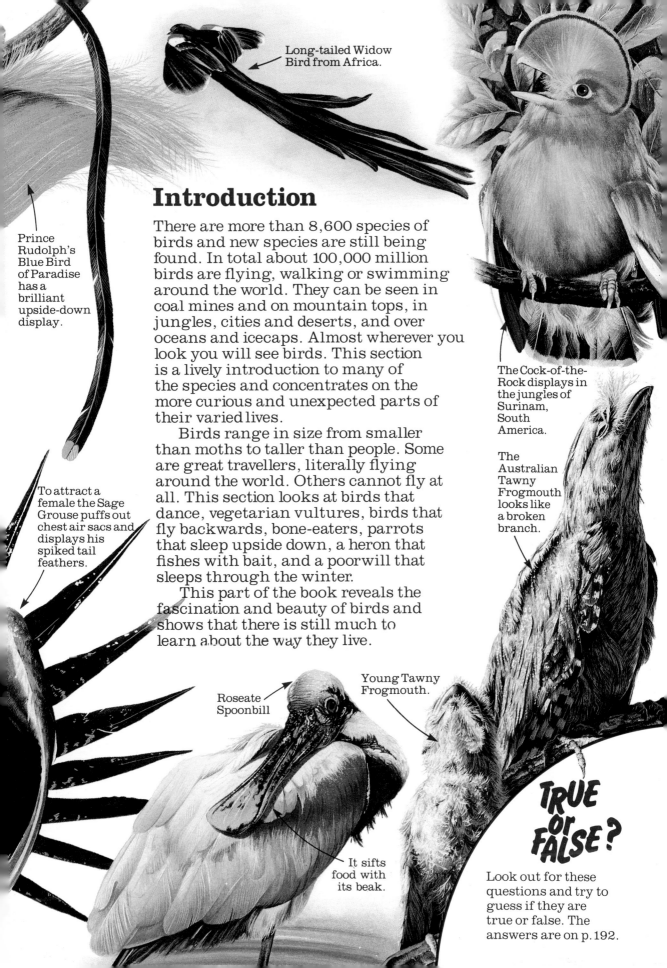

Long-tailed Widow Bird from Africa.

Prince Rudolph's Blue Bird of Paradise has a brilliant upside-down display.

Introduction

There are more than 8,600 species of birds and new species are still being found. In total about 100,000 million birds are flying, walking or swimming around the world. They can be seen in coal mines and on mountain tops, in jungles, cities and deserts, and over oceans and icecaps. Almost wherever you look you will see birds. This section is a lively introduction to many of the species and concentrates on the more curious and unexpected parts of their varied lives.

Birds range in size from smaller than moths to taller than people. Some are great travellers, literally flying around the world. Others cannot fly at all. This section looks at birds that dance, vegetarian vultures, birds that fly backwards, bone-eaters, parrots that sleep upside down, a heron that fishes with bait, and a poorwill that sleeps through the winter.

This part of the book reveals the fascination and beauty of birds and shows that there is still much to learn about the way they live.

The Cock-of-the-Rock displays in the jungles of Surinam, South America.

The Australian Tawny Frogmouth looks like a broken branch.

To attract a female the Sage Grouse puffs out chest air sacs and displays his spiked tail feathers.

Roseate Spoonbill

Young Tawny Frogmouth.

It sifts food with its beak.

TRUE or FALSE?

Look out for these questions and try to guess if they are true or false. The answers are on p.192.

Fabulous feathers

Birds are not the only animals which fly – bats and insects also do. But birds are the only animals with feathers. Feathers keep them warm and help them to stay up in the air. Their colours may be used in courtship or as camouflage.

Brown tip in autumn.

Worn feather in spring.

Autumn

Spring

Male Black Lark of Asia

Turning black ▶

The wear on feathers can change a bird's colours. In his new autumn plumage, the male Black Lark of Asia is mottled brown. As wear removes the feathers' pale brown tips, black patches appear. By the spring, he is totally jet black and ready to court a female.

African Snipe "drumming".

Long ones ▶

Many birds grow long feathers on their head, tail or wings.

Each plume is 60 cm long.

When displaying to females, the King of Saxony Bird of Paradise raises his two head plumes and bounces about on branches.

Male King of Saxony Bird of Paradise

◀ Musical feathers

The African Snipe dives steeply through the air when he displays over his breeding site. As he dives, he makes a bleating "hoo-oo-oo-oo-oo-oo-ooh" sound, known as "drumming". This noise is produced by the air passing through stiff tail feathers which are spread out on each side.

Ruby-throated Hummingbird

Feather facts

The Whistling Swan has over 25,000 feathers. The much smaller Pied-billed Grebe has far denser plumage, with 15,000 feathers. The tiny Ruby-throated Hummingbird has only 940 but still has more feathers per square centimetre than the swan.

Whistling Swan

Pied-billed Grebe

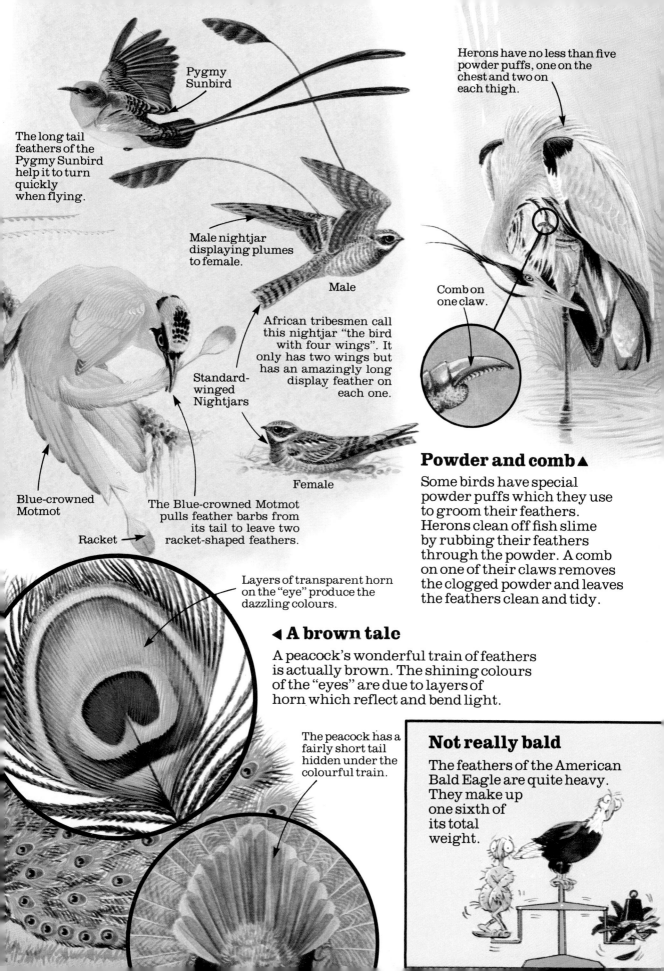

Pygmy Sunbird

The long tail feathers of the Pygmy Sunbird help it to turn quickly when flying.

Male nightjar displaying plumes to female.

Male

African tribesmen call this nightjar "the bird with four wings". It only has two wings but has an amazingly long display feather on each one.

Standard-winged Nightjars

Female

Blue-crowned Motmot

Racket →

The Blue-crowned Motmot pulls feather barbs from its tail to leave two racket-shaped feathers.

Herons have no less than five powder puffs, one on the chest and two on each thigh.

Comb on one claw.

Powder and comb ▲

Some birds have special powder puffs which they use to groom their feathers. Herons clean off fish slime by rubbing their feathers through the powder. A comb on one of their claws removes the clogged powder and leaves the feathers clean and tidy.

Layers of transparent horn on the "eye" produce the dazzling colours.

◄ A brown tale

A peacock's wonderful train of feathers is actually brown. The shining colours of the "eyes" are due to layers of horn which reflect and bend light.

The peacock has a fairly short tail hidden under the colourful train.

Not really bald

The feathers of the American Bald Eagle are quite heavy. They make up one sixth of its total weight.

Eating out

Birds have no hands, so they have to find their food with their beaks and feet.

Fishing bait ▶

Most herons wait patiently to catch fish but the Green Heron uses bait to attract them. It creeps to the water's edge with an insect caught for the purpose and drops it into the water. It then waits, completely still, for small fish to come to the bait. If the insect drifts away, the heron fetches it and puts it back in position.

Green Heron

Placing the insect . . .

. . . waiting . . .

. . . and a swift strike of the bill catches the fish.

The top of the bill is 5 cm long.

Chisel and spear ▶

A honeycreeper from Hawaii, the Akiapolaau, has a unique bill for finding food in the wood of dead trees. The top of the bill is long and curved, and the bird lifts this up while using the shorter, chisel-like bottom to pound into the tree. It spears the disturbed insects and larvae with the top of the bill.

The Limpkin even feeds snails to its young.

The Everglades Kite feeds only on snails.

Snail snacks

A water snail of the Florida swamps is the speciality of two birds. The Limpkin, with its long legs and bill, wades after snails, searching for them on underwater plants. The Everglades Kite — an odd bird of prey — must wait for the snails to come near the surface in the cool of the day. The kite snatches them up with its feet and flies to a branch. Its hooked beak prises the snail from the shell.

TRUE or FALSE?

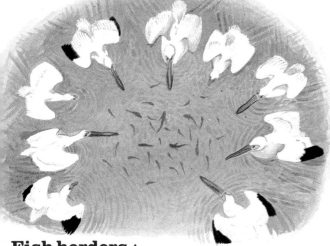

White
Pelicans

Fish herders▲

Up to 40 White Pelicans gather together in a
horseshoe formation to "herd" fish into
shallow water. Beating their wings and feet,
they drive the fish before them. Every 15-20
seconds, as though at a signal, they plunge
their bills into the centre of the arc and
scoop up the trapped fish. About one in every
five plunges is successful. Each pelican eats
roughly 1,200 grammes of fish a day.

The huge pouch
makes an excellent fishing net. It
shrinks to squeeze out the water before
the fish is swallowed.

A nutty larder▼

The Acorn Woodpecker lives in small flocks in
American oak woods. It harvests acorns and,
if available, almonds and walnuts as well. In
autumn it stores the nuts tightly in holes in
the trees – so tightly that squirrels cannot
pull them out. The woodpecker drills the
holes with its beak and will re-use them year
after year. The stored acorns are emergency
winter food for the little 20-24 cm woodpecker.

Teaspoon effect

Grey
Phalarope

To create whirlpools, the Grey
Phalarope swims in tight circles and
spins its body around. This has the same
effect as stirring coffee with a teaspoon.
Small animals in the water are probably
drawn into the centre of the whirlpool
where the phalarope can catch them.

Acorn
Woodpecker

The Harpy Eagle
eats monkeys for
breakfast.

Squirrel
trying
to steal
acorns.

The woodpeckers share
their acorns but
drive away birds
from other
flocks.

On mild days it
catches insects in
mid-air – most unusual
for a woodpecker.

Pirates and scavengers

Most birds find their own food but some have ways of stealing it from others. Birds are also good scavengers and are always on the lookout for an easy meal.

Arctic Tern

Arctic Skuas eat small mammals, birds, eggs and insects. Stolen fish is their main diet.

Arctic Skua

Sand Eel

Skuas catch the disgorged meal in mid-air.

The early bird . . .

Flocks of Lapwings and Golden Plovers feed together on worms they pull from the ground. Black-headed Gulls join these flocks and steal the worms if they can. Lapwings are the gulls' favourite targets because they take longer to pull out the worms and are less agile when chased.

The gulls may repay the plovers by warning them of predators.

Black-headed Gull

Golden Plover

Lapwing

Marine pirates ▲▼

The Arctic Skua is a graceful pirate which chases other seabirds to make them disgorge their catch of fish. The speed and agility of a pair of skuas when pursuing a gull or tern is amazing. In areas where the large Great Skua is common, the smaller Arctic Skua chases Arctic Terns, Kittiwakes and Puffins, while the Great Skua goes after Guillemots, Razorbills, Puffins and Gannets.

The Great Skua also pounces on seagulls, drowning them, and steals seabird chicks.

Truly Magnificent Frigatebird ▼

The Magnificent Frigatebird is a master of the air. It has huge, long wings and a long tail which it uses as a rudder and brake. It never settles on water and is clumsy on land but in the air it is a wonderful flier. Frigatebirds catch flying fish above the waves and feed on young turtles on beaches and fish disgorged by frightened boobies which they chase unmercifully. The way they chase these relatives of the Gannet was described in the log kept by Christopher Columbus.

Female

Male

Magnificent Frigatebird catching a flying fish.

Magnificent Frigatebird chasing a White Booby.

Arctic Skuas will fiercely attack people who come near the nest.

Lammergeier

Ant antics

As columns of army ants march through the forests of South America, they flush out insects, frogs and small mammals. The White-fronted Antbird follows the ant "armies", preying on the escaping creatures. The birds rarely eat the ants.

Bone breakers ▲

One vulture, the Lammergeier, has learnt to dispose of skeletons. It picks up a bone, flies very high with it and then drops it on to hard, flat rocks. The vulture eats the bone marrow from the broken pieces or, amazingly, swallows bits of bone. The White-necked Raven also drops bones but often gets its aim wrong and they fall on to grass.

Eye in the sky ▶

Eiders, Mergansers, Smews and other diving ducks are often watched by Herring Gulls. When they bring up fish and shell-fish, the gulls steal it if they can.

A patrolling Herring Gull, keeping an eye on the ducks.

Female

Male

Eiders diving for mussels. They can dive for over a minute to depths of 20 metres.

TRUE or FALSE?

After bathing, Starlings dry themselves on sheep.

Staking a claim

To breed successfully, birds need a safe place to build their nests, freedom from disturbance and a good supply of food. They may need to compete with other members of their own species for a suitable territory.

A reserved table ▼

Shelducks defend a breeding territory and the male also keeps a feeding territory nearby. The female feeds here unchallenged during the brief times she leaves the eggs. When the young hatch, they are led to this feeding area which is already free of other Shelducks who would compete for food.

As the sexes look alike, the male relies on song and display to get the right response from a female.

Robins' summer areas.

breeding territories

nest

Female with her ducklings.

The nest may be some way from the shore, in an old rabbit burrow.

Male Shelduck

◀Seeing red

The Robin's song can be heard clearly all around its territory. This saves it a lot of work patrolling the boundary. In spring, the male's song warns off other males but attracts females. The sight of a red breast on his territory sends the male into a fury. He attacks other males, or sometimes his own reflection or even a red rag hung in a tree.

winter

feeding

Robins' winter territories are smaller.

breeding territories

feeding

river

Shelduck territories defended by the male.

island

Non-defended feeding area

breeding areas

Australian Gannets

Gannets nest on cliffs and islands.

◀Sharing things

Gannets feed on fish in the sea. There is no point in having an individual feeding territory because they actually benefit from being in flocks, tiring out the fish by diving and chasing. Thousands of Gannets nest together and keep only a tiny territory – as far as a sitting bird can reach – around each nest.

TRUE or FALSE?

Bellbirds chime together.

Wedge-tailed
Eagles

The eagles fight
in mid-air and
on the ground.

▲ Fighting eagles

Eagles hunt over huge
areas and only defend a
small area around the nest
from other eagles. The
great Wedge-tailed Eagle
of Australia, however,
fights to keep strange
eagles out of its whole area.
Eagles may fall to the
ground and be locked in
battle for up to half an
hour. To help avoid such
fights, the eagle performs
territorial displays to
"warn off" the intruder.

The defending eagle soars through
the air performing aerobatics.

Male and
female
displaying.

Woodpeckers
know their mate's and
neighbour's drumming and
recognise intruders.

Pileated Woodpecker

Drumming accents▶

Woodpeckers do not
sing to mark their
territory, but they
drum their beaks against
a tree to produce a loud,
rapid rattle. The birds
can hear enough difference
in the speed and rhythm to
recognise each other.

The Great Grey Owl of northern
Europe and North America has
a wingspan of 150 cm.

Fearsome defender ▲

The Great Grey Owl defends its nest and
young fearlessly. It will attack
human intruders and can cause serious
wounds. Some skuas, eagles and
other owls also attack people in
defence of their nest.

Wooing a mate

All birds have a strong urge to breed. Finding a fit and loyal mate is all important. Generally the male advertises himself with a song, a loud call or bright plumage to attract a female.

Sunbittern showing hidden markings

Turning it on▶

These striking birds are males trying to impress females. Some, such as Temminck's Tragopan, grow special feathers or fleshy skin for the breeding season. Others reveal hidden markings in their wings.

Count Raggi's Bird of Paradise males.

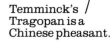

Horns

Temminck's Tragopan – the horns and wattle are colourful flesh which expands.

Wattle

◄ Brilliant display

Up to ten males of Count Raggi's Bird of Paradise display together in a tree. Each one clears away leaves that might block out the sun and defends his perch. Loud calls and bright, shimmering feathers attract a drab female. She chooses the male with the most dazzling plumage and most dramatic display. This top bird will mate with many females but the other males will probably not mate at all.

Temminck's Tragopan is a Chinese pheasant.

◄Come into my bower

In Australia and New Guinea, male bowerbirds build and decorate a bower to attract a female. Usually, the duller the bird, the more elaborate and decorative his bower. Some collect snail shells or whitened bones, or anything blue, such as flowers, feathers and berries. When the female arrives, the male dances. She inspects him and his bower and they mate. She then builds her nest and rears the chicks on her own.

The Satin Bowerbird paints the inside of his bower with the blue juices from berries, using bark as a paintbrush.

Over 500 bones and 300 snail shells were found on the dance floor of one bower.

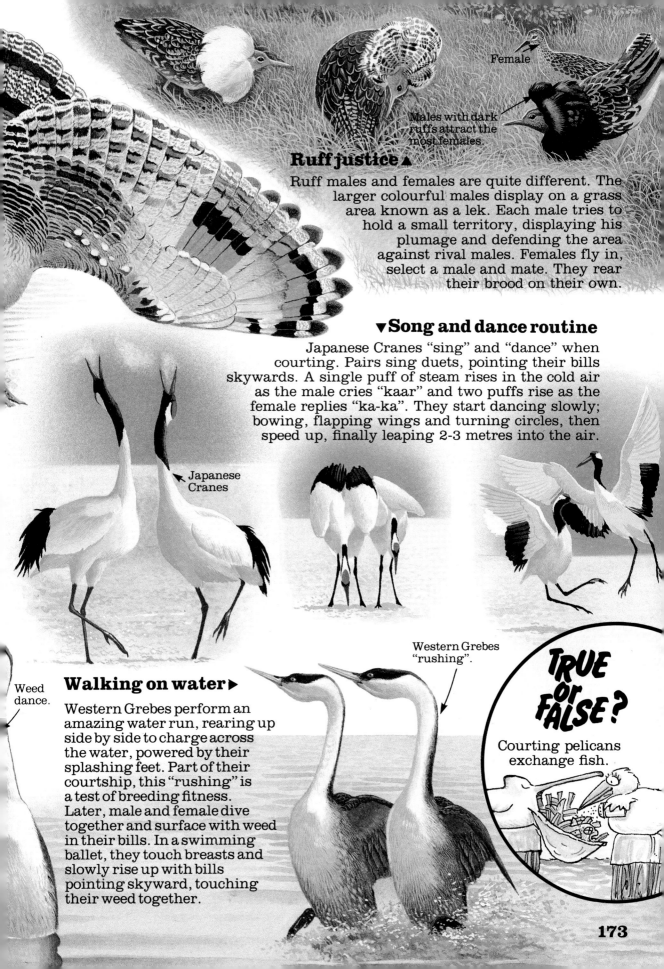

Female

Males with dark ruffs attract the most females.

Ruff justice ▲

Ruff males and females are quite different. The larger colourful males display on a grass area known as a lek. Each male tries to hold a small territory, displaying his plumage and defending the area against rival males. Females fly in, select a male and mate. They rear their brood on their own.

▼Song and dance routine

Japanese Cranes "sing" and "dance" when courting. Pairs sing duets, pointing their bills skywards. A single puff of steam rises in the cold air as the male cries "kaar" and two puffs rise as the female replies "ka-ka". They start dancing slowly; bowing, flapping wings and turning circles, then speed up, finally leaping 2-3 metres into the air.

Japanese Cranes

Weed dance.

Western Grebes "rushing".

Walking on water ▶

Western Grebes perform an amazing water run, rearing up side by side to charge across the water, powered by their splashing feet. Part of their courtship, this "rushing" is a test of breeding fitness. Later, male and female dive together and surface with weed in their bills. In a swimming ballet, they touch breasts and slowly rise up with bills pointing skyward, touching their weed together.

TRUE or FALSE?

Courting pelicans exchange fish.

Setting up home

Many animals – including mammals, insects and even fish – make some sort of nest. But birds make the most amazing and varied nests to hold their eggs and young.

Several thousand pairs of flamingos nest together.

▼ Dad's compost nest

The Mallee Fowl's nest is the largest made by any bird. The male builds a vast mound of soil and fills the egg chambers with damp, rotting plant material. The female lays her eggs inside these chambers and the male covers them over. Like a compost heap, the plant material rots and ferments, creating enough heat to incubate the eggs. The male opens up the chambers to reduce the heat and, at night, covers them with warm sand.

The young birds, which are almost fully feathered, break out of the mound on their own and may never see their parents.

The female sometimes lays 2 eggs.

Mallee Fowl

The male looks after the mound for 9 months.

← Mallee Fowl's nest. →

The nest is 1 metre deep. The mound over it can be 1 m high and 5 m across.

The male's beak is a "thermometer". It helps him keep the nest at a constant temperature of 33°C.

Egg cup ▼

The Greater Treeswift glues strips of bark together to make a tiny cup. The cup, on a high branch, is just large enough to hold one egg and is one of the smallest nests in the world.

Greater Treeswift

Nest →

TRUE or FALSE?

Parrots nest with termites.

Fairy Tern

No nest ▶

The Fairy Tern makes no nest at all. The female lays her one egg in a tiny hollow on a branch or in the fork of two branches. The chick has sharp claws for clinging to the swaying branch which is often high off the ground.

Sitting behind the egg, adults incubate it with their breast feathers.

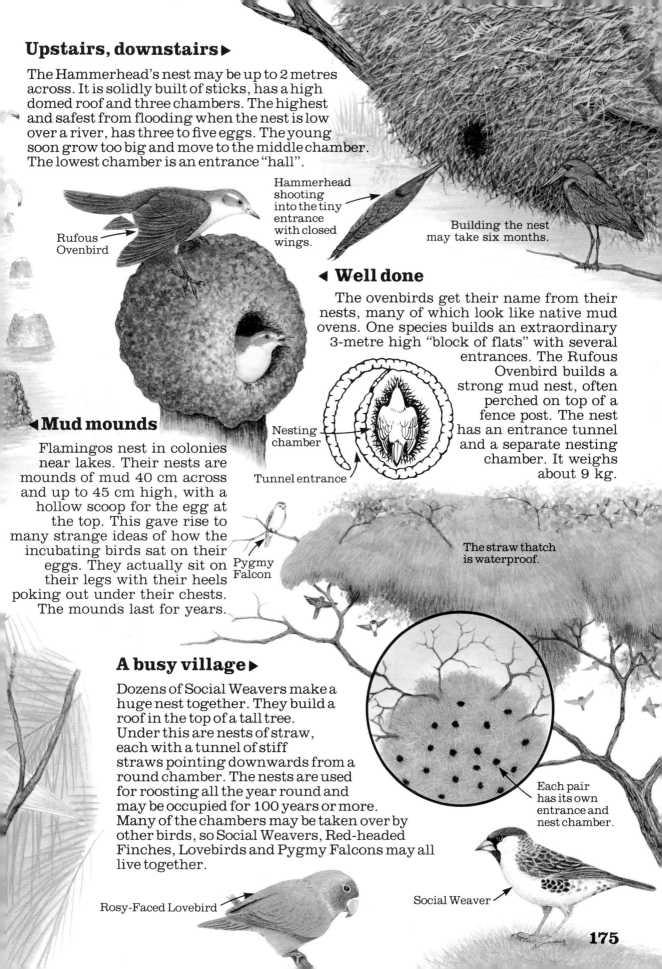

Upstairs, downstairs ▶

The Hammerhead's nest may be up to 2 metres across. It is solidly built of sticks, has a high domed roof and three chambers. The highest and safest from flooding when the nest is low over a river, has three to five eggs. The young soon grow too big and move to the middle chamber. The lowest chamber is an entrance "hall".

Rufous Ovenbird

Hammerhead shooting into the tiny entrance with closed wings.

Building the nest may take six months.

◀ Well done

The ovenbirds get their name from their nests, many of which look like native mud ovens. One species builds an extraordinary 3-metre high "block of flats" with several entrances. The Rufous Ovenbird builds a strong mud nest, often perched on top of a fence post. The nest has an entrance tunnel and a separate nesting chamber. It weighs about 9 kg.

Nesting chamber

Tunnel entrance

◀ Mud mounds

Flamingos nest in colonies near lakes. Their nests are mounds of mud 40 cm across and up to 45 cm high, with a hollow scoop for the egg at the top. This gave rise to many strange ideas of how the incubating birds sat on their eggs. They actually sit on their legs with their heels poking out under their chests. The mounds last for years.

Pygmy Falcon

The straw thatch is waterproof.

A busy village ▶

Dozens of Social Weavers make a huge nest together. They build a roof in the top of a tall tree. Under this are nests of straw, each with a tunnel of stiff straws pointing downwards from a round chamber. The nests are used for roosting all the year round and may be occupied for 100 years or more. Many of the chambers may be taken over by other birds, so Social Weavers, Red-headed Finches, Lovebirds and Pygmy Falcons may all live together.

Each pair has its own entrance and nest chamber.

Rosy-Faced Lovebird

Social Weaver

Eggs to adults

Inside the egg the nervous system and heart of the young bird develop first – then the limbs, body and head, swollen by enormous eyes. When the embryo is fully developed it starts to breathe from an air space inside the shell. To get out of the egg it grows an "egg-tooth" to crack the shell.

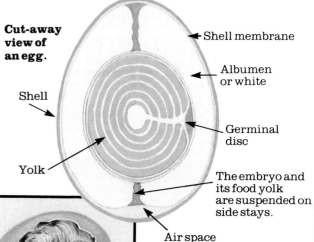

Cut-away view of an egg.

Shell membrane

Albumen or white

Shell

Germinal disc

Yolk

The embryo and its food yolk are suspended on side stays.

Air space

Chicken's egg

At 3 days the chick's heart already beats. It has blood vessels.

At 15 days the chick is recognisable as a bird.

At 20 days it is fully developed and will hatch next day.

The eggs must be turned regularly by the parents to help the chicks develop properly. This is not easy for the Black-winged Stilt, with its long legs and long beak.

Egg care ▶

Some birds have one large patch of bare skin (a brood patch) to cover their eggs, while others have separate patches for each egg. The sitting bird leaves the eggs from time to time to stop them getting too hot. Overheating is more of a risk than the cold.

Gamebirds, gulls and waders have separate brood patches.

The Oystercatcher has three brood patches.

▼ Hard-working parents

Great Tit with a caterpillar for the young.

All that nestlings want is food, warmth, shelter, and more food. A pair of Great Tits visited their brood with food 10,685 times in 14 days. A female Wren fed her young 1,217 times in 16 hours.

"Hello, mum" ▶

Several days before hatching, the chick makes peeping calls from inside the egg. The hen replies, so when the chick hatches it already knows its mother's voice. Chicks which leave the nest soon after hatching quickly learn to follow their mother – she becomes "imprinted" on the chick. If they do not see their mother first, something else may become imprinted on them as "mother". Greylag Goose chicks have become attached to people in this way and one even regarded a wheelbarrow as its mother.

TRUE or FALSE?

Hungry young eaglets eat their parents.

A row of owlets ▶

Owls start incubating when the first egg is laid. The later eggs may hatch several days after the first, and the chicks will be different sizes. If the parents cannot catch enough food, the oldest, biggest chicks dominate the others and take it all. That way, one or two chicks survive, which is better than all of them having an equal share of food, and all starving at the same time.

Long-eared Owl

When there is plenty of food all the chicks survive.

Female

Unlike most birds, each female mates with several males.

Each female lays 11-18 eggs.

Male

Too many eggs

An old male Rhea may attract up to eight hens to his nest. The hens, however, will lay eggs anywhere before the nest is ready and then they will overfill it with 30 or more eggs. The cock cannot cover them all, and the hen may lay more eggs out of his reach. Since the nesting and care of the eggs and young is left entirely to the male, many of the eggs are completely wasted.

One male may incubate as many as 80 eggs.

The scientist, Konrad Lorenz, has acted as "mother" to many geese while studying their behaviour.

Canada Geese and goslings.

Nursery group ▲

Several adult Canada Geese will often look after the young of other parents. They may be in charge of dozens of goslings. Some ducks also have nursery groups of up to 100.

177

Special relationships

To find food and survive, some birds have developed special relationships with other birds, with human beings and other animals. Sometimes this works to the benefit of both but often one takes advantage of the other.

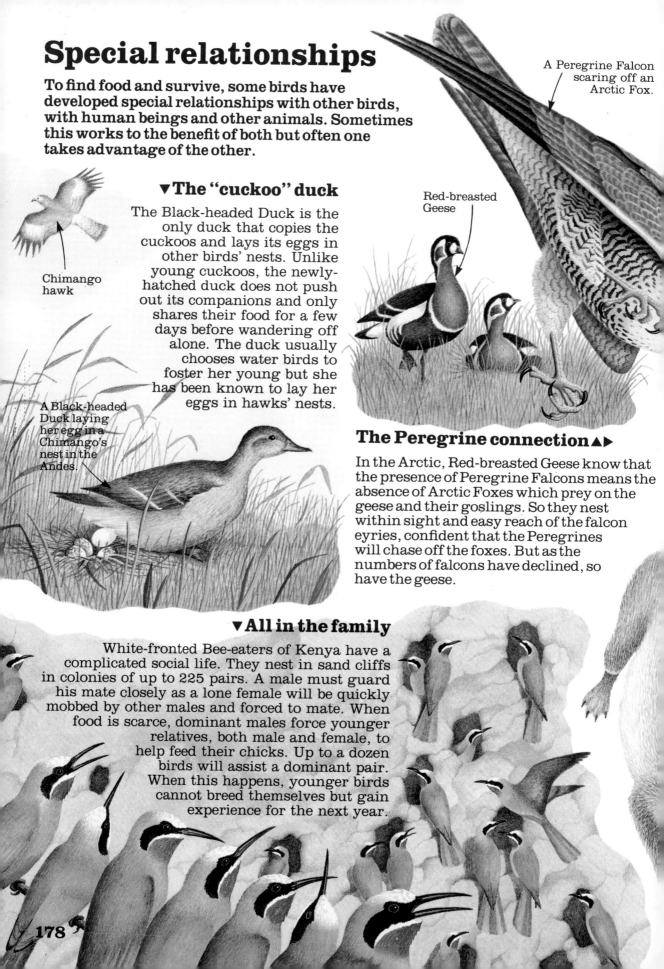

A Peregrine Falcon scaring off an Arctic Fox.

▼ The "cuckoo" duck

The Black-headed Duck is the only duck that copies the cuckoos and lays its eggs in other birds' nests. Unlike young cuckoos, the newly-hatched duck does not push out its companions and only shares their food for a few days before wandering off alone. The duck usually chooses water birds to foster her young but she has been known to lay her eggs in hawks' nests.

Chimango hawk

Red-breasted Geese

A Black-headed Duck laying her egg in a Chimango's nest in the Andes.

The Peregrine connection ▲▶

In the Arctic, Red-breasted Geese know that the presence of Peregrine Falcons means the absence of Arctic Foxes which prey on the geese and their goslings. So they nest within sight and easy reach of the falcon eyries, confident that the Peregrines will chase off the foxes. But as the numbers of falcons have declined, so have the geese.

▼ All in the family

White-fronted Bee-eaters of Kenya have a complicated social life. They nest in sand cliffs in colonies of up to 225 pairs. A male must guard his mate closely as a lone female will be quickly mobbed by other males and forced to mate. When food is scarce, dominant males force younger relatives, both male and female, to help feed their chicks. Up to a dozen birds will assist a dominant pair. When this happens, younger birds cannot breed themselves but gain experience for the next year.

Elder Sisters ▶

Sometimes young birds from a first brood will play "elder sister" to their parents' later broods. Young Moorhens often do this, looking after and feeding one or two broods of younger brothers and sisters. This probably makes them better parents.

A young Moorhen helping the adult with nest repairs.

Young Moorhen feeding a new chick.

Cattle Tyrant

◀▼ Easy Rider

Some birds hitch lifts on larger animals and wait for food to be provided by them. In Africa, the Carmine Bee-eater rides the huge Kori Bustard. In South America, the Cattle Tyrant sits on cows. Both watch for flying insects put up by their hosts and then capture them in the air.

Carmine Bee-eater riding on the back of a Kori Bustard.

TRUE or FALSE?

Blue Drongos help Chinese fishermen.

Where eagles dare ▼

Since the White-tailed Eagle has been protected, it has become less shy. Many eagles have learnt that fishermen will throw them fish scraps. Returning fishing boats are now followed by gulls, Fulmars and White-tailed Eagles.

White-tailed Eagle

Fulmar

Gulls

Arctic Fox

Colourful characters

Birds use colour in displays against rival males and to attract mates. Bright colours also attract predators, so some birds only show off their colours in display, and some are only coloured during the mating season. Females, who normally guard the eggs, are generally duller than the males, but this is not always so.

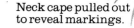

Neck cape pulled out to reveal markings.

Male Lady Amherst's Pheasant

Mating mask ▼

During the mating season, the Tufted Puffin's normally sober appearance undergoes a complete change. He wears coloured "spectacles", a brightly coloured bill, and golden head plumes like overgrown eyebrows. The Puffin uses its bill for "billing" in courtship — the male and female rub bills together.

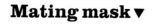

Tufted Puffins "billing".

The Tufted Puffin is much duller in winter.

Lady's man ▲▶

Male Lady Amherst's Pheasants have a glorious plumage, as do most cock pheasants. The female, though, is a dull mottled brown which gives her excellent camouflage amongst scrub, bamboo thickets and woods. During courtship the male prances around the female, spreading his feathers to show his brilliant colours to their best advantage.

▼ Snipe's stripes

The Jack Snipe uses the stripes which run along its body to give it perfect camouflage in the marshes where it lives. When it lands, it turns its body, so that the stripes go in the same direction as the surrounding vegetation.

Jack Snipe

The bird remains quite still when its body is in the correct position.

Male frigatebird

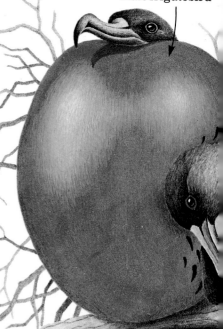

TRUE or FALSE?

The Booby's feet are blue with cold.

Toco Toucan

The beak is very light but strong. Serrated edges, like teeth, slice through its food.

The 23 cm beak is as long as its body.

Colour collection ▶

The Lesser Flamingo's delicate colour is thought to come from chemicals, called cartenoids, in its food. Flamingos in zoos may lose their colour if not fed on the right diet. The flamingo filters algae from the water through bristles in its bill.

Lesser Flamingo

Beautiful beaks ▲

The brilliant colours and size of the toucan's beak are a mystery. The toucan uses its beak to reach for fruit, duel with rival males and to scare small birds in order to eat their eggs, but there appears to be no reason for the beak to be quite so colourful.

▼ Fabulous females

For a long time, scientists thought that the male and female Red-lined Parrot were males of two separate species because they look so different. Both are very colourful but, surprisingly, the female is more striking than the male. In addition to the bright plumage, its noisy cries announce its presence in the jungle.

▼ Balloon bird

The male frigatebird attracts his mate with an amazing wobbly "balloon", which is an inflated throat sac. During the display he vibrates his wings and makes gobbling noises. The female shows her consent by nibbling his feathers and she rubs her head on the "balloon".

Frigatebirds nest in bushes and trees.

Male

Female

The Red-lined Parrot feeds on fruits, berries and nuts.

They live in Australia and New Guinea.

181

Migration marvels

Each spring, many birds fly from their winter grounds to summer breeding areas. Some species fly thousands of kilometres on this migration. After breeding they return to their winter areas where the food supply will be more plentiful.

Bar-headed Geese

Over the top

Bar-headed Geese fly from central Asia over the Himalayas – the world's highest mountain range – to reach their winter grounds in north India and Burma. The flight takes the birds up to an amazing height of 8,000 m – almost as high as cruising jet planes.

Moon and mud myths ▶

Before scientists discovered the facts of bird migration, people had some amazing ideas to explain where birds went in winter. Swallows were believed to dive into ponds and sleep in the mud at the bottom until spring. Some people thought birds went to the moon. Others thought small birds, like Goldcrests, hitched lifts on large birds such as storks.

Having left its breeding areas around the Bering Straits, there are few places to stop before the bird reaches the Hawaiian islands.

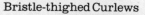

Bristle-thighed Curlews

Dots in the ocean ▶

The accuracy of some migrations is astonishing. For millions of years, Bristle-thighed Curlews from Alaska have wintered about 9,000 km away on tiny islands in the Pacific Ocean. To reach Hawaii or Tahiti they fly south on a bearing of 170°, continually altering course to allow for winds which drift them off target.

Migration mystery

House Martins are common summer breeders in Europe but where do they go in winter? They winter in Africa but no one is quite sure where. Many thousands have been ringed in the UK but so far only one has been recovered. In 1984 a ringed House Martin was found in Nigeria. Do all UK House Martins winter in Nigeria?

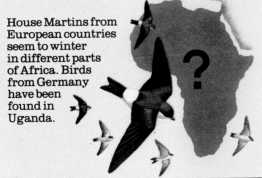

House Martins from European countries seem to winter in different parts of Africa. Birds from Germany have been found in Uganda.

Social seasons ▶

The Turtle Dove is common in the woods and farmlands of Europe in summer. In winter it travels to Africa and roosts in huge flocks. One roost was shared with 50 Tawny Eagles, 15 Fish Eagles and hundreds of Black Kites — strange company for a bird whose summer neighbours are Chaffinches and Blackbirds.

Fast flight ▲

A Knot ringed in England took only eight days to reach Liberia, 5,600 km away. Its average speed was 29 km/h.

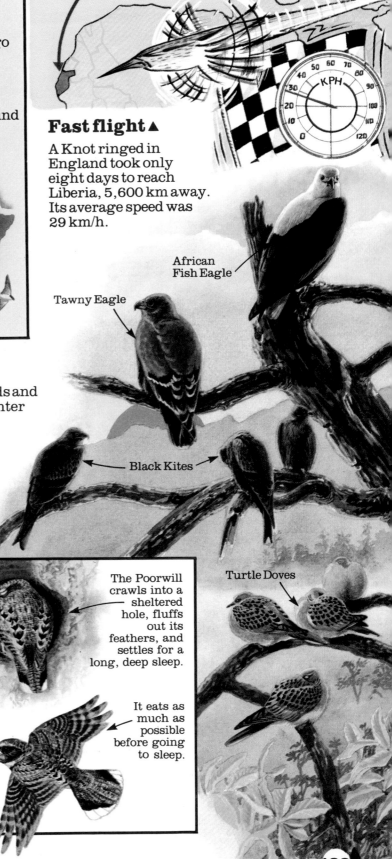

African Fish Eagle

Tawny Eagle

Black Kites

Turtle Doves

Deep sleep

Its temperature drops to 13°C and its heart beats very slowly.

The Poorwill crawls into a sheltered hole, fluffs out its feathers, and settles for a long, deep sleep.

The Poorwill of western North America stays put during the winter months. It copes with the hardest months, when food is scarce, by hibernating. (The Trilling Nighthawk is the only other bird found hibernating.) Before hibernating, it builds up a store of fat which it can live on. About 10 grams of fat is enough "fuel" for 100 days.

It eats as much as possible before going to sleep.

The ultimate fliers

Most birds fly and are great masters of the air. Their powers of flight are matched only by the finest of the insect fliers.

The 9 cm-long Ruby-throated Hummingbird migrates over 3,000 km. 800 km is over the Gulf of Mexico.

World's worst flier?

The tinamou flies off at breakneck speed but lacks control and may kill itself by crashing headlong into a tree. Speed soon exhausts it and, if flushed from its perch several times, it can become too tired to fly. Tinamous have been seen to dash half way across a river and then flutter down to the water, tired out. Fortunately, they swim quite well and so may reach the bank. Even when running, these birds sometimes stumble and fall.

The tiniest ◀ helicopter

Hummingbirds are not only quick and agile in forward flight, they can fly up, down, sideways, backwards and upside down. As well as this, they can hover perfectly, keeping their bills quite still as they suck nectar from flowers. Their narrow wings beat 20-50 times a second and one species has been recorded at 90 beats a second. The Bee Hummingbird (males are only 57mm long) is smaller and lighter than some hawk moths.

Hovering

Great Dusky Swift

Swift flowing▶

Great Dusky Swifts nest and roost on cliffs behind waterfalls and must fly through sheets of falling water. Occasionally they are swept away by a sudden torrent but usually manage to struggle free.

Swept-back wings and a torpedo-shaped body are a superb design for speed.

Flying backwards

Beginning to roll

Swifts fly in their sleep.

TRUE or FALSE?

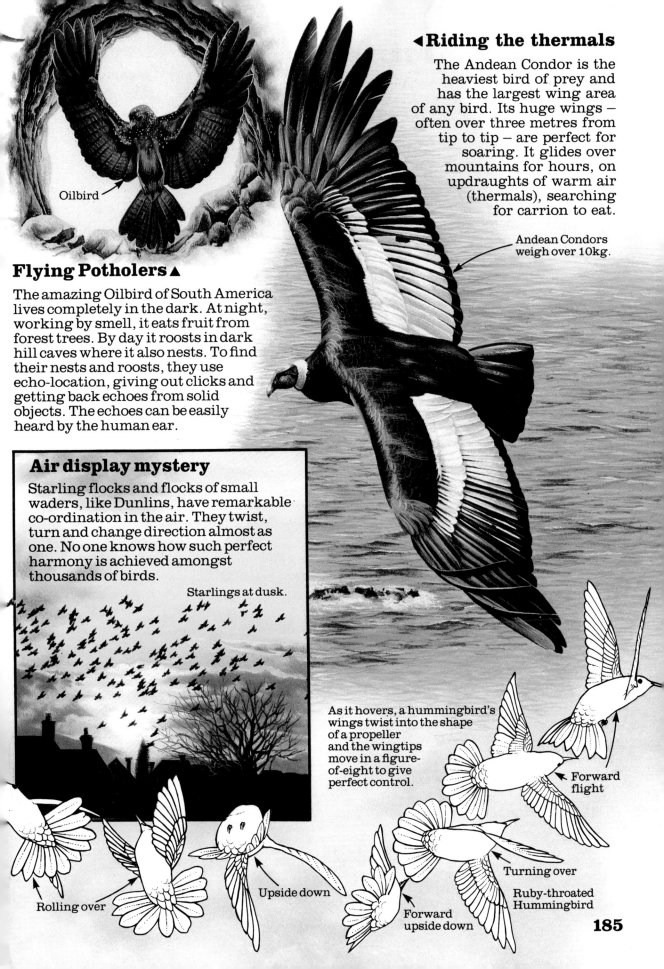

Flying Potholers ▲

Oilbird

The amazing Oilbird of South America lives completely in the dark. At night, working by smell, it eats fruit from forest trees. By day it roosts in dark hill caves where it also nests. To find their nests and roosts, they use echo-location, giving out clicks and getting back echoes from solid objects. The echoes can be easily heard by the human ear.

◄Riding the thermals

The Andean Condor is the heaviest bird of prey and has the largest wing area of any bird. Its huge wings – often over three metres from tip to tip – are perfect for soaring. It glides over mountains for hours, on updraughts of warm air (thermals), searching for carrion to eat.

Andean Condors weigh over 10kg.

Air display mystery

Starling flocks and flocks of small waders, like Dunlins, have remarkable co-ordination in the air. They twist, turn and change direction almost as one. No one knows how such perfect harmony is achieved amongst thousands of birds.

Starlings at dusk.

As it hovers, a hummingbird's wings twist into the shape of a propeller and the wingtips move in a figure-of-eight to give perfect control.

Forward flight

Turning over

Ruby-throated Hummingbird

Rolling over

Upside down

Forward upside down

185

Sprints and marathons

As well as flying, most birds walk, run or hop. Those which depend most on their legs and feet are the ones which have lost the power to fly. Feet are also a source of power for waterbirds.

Running on water ▶

No bird can actually walk on water but the African Jacana comes close. With toes and claws up to eight centimetres long, it can stalk or sprint over thinly scattered marsh plants with no risk of sinking. Its other name is Lily-trotter.

The African Jacana can fly, swim or dive if it has to.

Ostriches have been trained to herd sheep and to scare birds from crops.

Adelie Penguins

Greater Roadrunner

Running circles around a rattlesnake, the Roadrunner darts in and out, dodging the fangs and tiring out the snake.

At the right moment, it dashes in and hammers its bill against the snake's head to kill it.

◀ Beep, beep! ▼

The Roadrunner of North America is a member of the cuckoo family. It is a poor flier and is best on the ground, running long distances, sprinting, zigzagging and darting nimbly between obstacles. It reaches speeds of 40 km/h, and is faster than any Olympic athlete. A cunning hunter, it will sprint out of cover and catch swifts flying down to drink from desert pools.

The Roadrunner swallows the dead snake whole. It may be seen running around with the snake's tail hanging from its bill.

◄ Long legs

The flightless Ostrich can be up to 2.7 metres tall with legs over 1.2 metres long. These are the longest and most powerful legs of any bird. The Ostrich can easily run at 45 km/h for 15-20 minutes and sprint at more than 70 km/h. Ostriches are nomads, joining in the game migrations of Africa to graze hundreds of kilometres of grassland.

The Ostrich only has two toes.

An Ostrich's kick can kill a man.

Sanderling

◄ On its toes

All wading birds are nimble but the Sanderling moves so fast along the water's edge that it no longer grows a hind toe. It tilts forward and dashes about on its three front toes.

Impeyan Pheasant

Snow Leopard

◄ Penguin marathons

Penguins cannot fly. To reach their Antarctic breeding grounds, Adelie Penguins waddle for up to 320 kilometres over ice floes and snow-covered rocks. When the sun is out, they march steadily in the right direction, but when it is cloudy they seem to lose their way.

▲ Hill walker

All pheasants fly only short distances because they lack the normal ability of birds to quickly replace oxygen in their blood. To avoid a predator, the heavy Impeyan of the Himalayas takes off with a burst of wing beats and glides downhill. It then has to walk back up again.

Young auks →

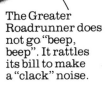

The Greater Roadrunner does not go "beep, beep". It rattles its bill to make a "clack" noise.

▲ Long-distance swimmers

Young auks, Fulmars and Gannets are too fat to fly. They crash dive into the sea from their cliff ledges and swim hundreds of kilometres towards their winter quarters. Constant paddling burns up their fat and, when they are light enough, they stagger into the air.

TRUE or FALSE?

The speedy Cassowary wears a crash helmet.

Odd birds

The Kea calls loudly as it soars on mountain winds.

Fish supper ▶

Many young birds have bright orange or yellow mouths which make obvious targets for their parents to push food into. One adult bird made a mistake, and fed goldfish! A male Cardinal in North Carolina, USA, flew to the edge of a garden pool, chirped, and waited for the gaping goldfish mouths to break the surface.

Male Cardinal

Meat-eating parrot ▲

The Kea is a fine parrot which lives near the snow line of New Zealand's mountains. It is still largely vegetarian like other parrots, but it has taken to eating carrion and is particularly fond of dead sheep. Because it has a strong, hooked beak, it was thought to be a sheep-killer and was almost wiped out by farmers. Only recent studies of its true behaviour have saved it.

The Hoatzin is also called "Stinkbird" because the contents of its crop – balls of leaves – smell awful.

◀A nutty vulture

The Palmnut Vulture – also called the Vulturine Fish Eagle – looks like normal vultures, but actually eats fruit rather than meat. Its main diet is the fleshy outsides of the African oil nut. It is the only vegetarian bird of prey.

It also eats shellfish and hunts for small fish.

◀Puzzling bird▶

The very odd Hoatzin of South America is probably related to cuckoos but its behaviour and body structure are more like a reptile than a bird in several ways. The newly-hatched Hoatzin is naked. If threatened, the young bird will jump into water to escape. It climbs up branches back to the nest, using its beak, feet and unique claws on its wrists. The claws soon disappear. The bird then grows a huge gullet (crop) to store food. Like a large reptile, the Hoatzin gorges itself with food, then has to have a long rest.

Nestlings open their mouths wide and cry for food.

Blue-crowned Hanging Parrots roosting.

Upside down ▶

Hanging parrots go to sleep hanging upside down. In this position they look like a bunch of leaves and must be very difficult for predators to spot. They sometimes hang upside down during the day and even feed upside down.

House Sparrows eating dead flies.

Flies become stuck to the radiator as the car moves along.

◀ Meals on wheels

The House Sparrow is very common in cities where it takes advantage of city life. Some House Sparrows have learnt to hop inside the engines of parked cars – they are taking flies off the radiator.

Marbled Murrelet – the small 25 cm seabird is common on the sea.

Nesting mystery ▼▶

Although millions of Marbled Murrelets can be seen on the sea off Siberia and North America, almost nothing is known about their nesting habits. They are often seen flying inland with food but only three nests have been found since the first was discovered in 1931. Two nests were on rocky slopes, one in a felled tree and another, astonishingly, was 40 metres up in a fir tree. The Marbled Murrelet is probably the only auk to nest in trees. Before they can fly, the young of other auks leap from their sea-cliff nests into the sea and swim off. How young Marbled Murrelets reach the sea is a mystery.

The Hoatzin is a poor flier.

Young Hoatzin climbing out of the water, using the unusual claws on its wings.

189

Record breakers

Flying giant

The Kori Bustard is probably the heaviest bird, weighing about 13-14kg and sometimes over 18kg. There have been reports of a Great Bustard even heavier than this which probably could not get off the ground.

Years in the air

The young Swift dives out of its nest in Britain for the first time and flies off to Africa. It returns to a nest site 2 or 3 years later, having covered about 72,000km – probably without ever stopping. The Sooty Tern takes off over the vast oceans and continues to fly for 3 or 4 years without ever settling on water or land.

Great birds of prey

The heaviest bird of prey is the Andean Condor, weighing up to 12kg. The Black Vulture is also very heavy. One female was reported at 12.5kg although they normally weigh less than the Condor.

Greatest span

The Wandering Albatross has the greatest wingspan of up to 3.7m from wingtip to wingtip. A Marabou was reported with an even greater wingspan of 4m, although most have a span of 2.5m.

Lighter than a moth

The tiniest birds in the world are some of the hummingbirds. The Bee Hummingbird of Cuba is only about 57mm long, half of which is beak and tail, and weighs only just over 1.5g.

Deep-sea diver

Emperor Penguins can dive down to depths of 265m, surfacing quickly again, before decompression becomes a problem.

Toughest egg

Eggs are very strong – a chicken's egg survived a 183m drop from a helicopter. An Ostrich egg will withstand the weight of an 115kg man.

Great migrations

The Arctic Tern flies 40,000km in its migration from its nesting site and back each year. The Lesser Golden Plover covers 24-27,000km in just over 6 months and flies from the Aleutians to Hawaii non-stop – 3,300km in about 1½ days with over 250,000 wingbeats.

Most ferocious bird

The most savage and efficient predators are hawks and falcons. They fly fast and when they spot their prey, swoop down and hit it hard with their outstretched talons.

Largest breeding colony

Up to 10 million Boobies and Cormorants breed together on the islands in the fish-rich currents of Peru.

Rarest bird

The Kauai e'e of Hawaii, was reduced to one pair in the world by 1980. In America, the Ivory-billed Woodpecker is nearly extinct, if not already gone for ever.

Senior citizens

A captive Andean Condor, one of the world's largest birds, lived for 72 years. In the wild, a Laysan Albatross marked with a ring, was seen alive and well at 53 years old.

Speed merchants

The Peregrine may reach speeds of about 250km per hour in long steep dives and, at this speed, a diving Golden Eagle could almost catch it. In level flight their maximum speed is 100km per hour, unless there is a following wind, and they would both be beaten by the White-throated Spinetail Swift which flies at about 171km/h.

Blurred wings

The Horned Sungem, a hummingbird, beats its wings at 90 beats per second — much faster than most hummingbirds and any other species.

The biggest swimmer

The Emperor Penguin is the biggest swimming bird, standing up to 1.2m, with a chest measurement of about 1.3m and weighing up to 42.6kg — more than twice the weight of any flying bird. The Emu is taller at nearly 2m and it swims well although it is a land bird. (Ostriches can also swim.)

Millions of birds

Of the approximately 100,000 million birds in the world, about 3,000 million are domestic chickens. The most numerous wild bird is the Red-billed Quelea of Africa — there are about 10,000 million birds.

Largest bird

The world's largest bird is the Ostrich, growing up to about 2.4m tall. Some reach 2.7m and weigh about 156kg.

The quietest bird

The Treecreeper's notes are so high and hiss-like that they can hardly be heard.

Dizzy heights

The Alpine Chough has been recorded on Everest at 8,200m and the Lammergeier at 7,620m — both high enough to fly over the top. An airline pilot reported Whooper Swans at 8,230m, which had risen from sea level to hitch a ride from the jetstream winds.

Largest egg

The Ostrich lays the largest egg — 13.5cm long, weighing 1.65kg. It is equivalent to about 18 chickens' eggs and takes about 40 minutes to soft boil!

Loudest bird

The Indian Peacock has the loudest, most far-carrying calls which echo for kilometres.

Were they true or false?

page 167 The Harpy Eagle eats monkeys for breakfast.
TRUE. The Harpy Eagle is the king of predators in South American forests. On its short, broad wings it slips easily between the trees and probably feeds largely on monkeys.

page 169 After bathing, Starlings dry themselves on sheep.
TRUE. Starlings normally dry themselves by vigorous fluttering and preening but a Starling in Shetland was seen to use the fleece of a sheep as a towel.

page 170 Bellbirds chime together.
FALSE. The Bearded Bellbird does chime like a bell but not in unison with others. It has one of the loudest calls of any bird and its metallic peal carries up to a kilometre through the South American forests.

page 173 Courting pelicans exchange fish.
FALSE. Males of many species do bring food to the female during courtship but pelicans have not been seen doing this.

page 174 Parrots nest with termites.
TRUE. Both the Hooded Parrot and the Golden-shouldered Parrot of Australia burrow into termite mounds to make their nests. They seem to live in harmony with the termites.

page 176 Hungry young eaglets eat their parents.
FALSE. Adult eagles are too strong to allow this. The oldest eaglet, however, often kills the younger eaglets and sometimes eats them.

page 179 Blue Drongos help Chinese fishermen.
FALSE. There are several drongos but not a blue one. Some Chinese fishermen use a cormorant on a lead to catch fish for them.

page 180 The Booby's feet are blue with cold.
FALSE. No one quite knows why the Blue-footed Booby's feet are blue, but it is not because of the temperature.

page 184 Swifts fly in their sleep.
TRUE. They rise high into the sky at dusk and sleep on the wing, flying down again at dawn.

page 187 The speedy Cassowary wears a crash helmet.
TRUE. The flattened horny crown on top of the head seems to act as a crash helmet as the Cassowary dashes through undergrowth in the rain forests of Australia and Papua New Guinea.

Further reading

Gone Birding, W. E. Oddie (Eyre Methuen)
Bill Oddie's Little Black Bird Book, W. E. Oddie (Eyre Methuen)
Discover Birds, D. I. M. Wallace (Whizzard Press/Andre Deutsch)
Bird Families of the World, C. J. O. Harrison (Abrams)
The Dictionary of Birds in Colour, B. Campbell (Michael Joseph/Peerage Books)
Watching Birds, D. I. M. Wallace (Usborne)
Where to Watch Birds, J. Gooders (Andre Deutsch)
Birdwatcher's Yearbook (published annually), J. E. Pemberton (Buckingham Press)
Usborne Guide to Birds of Britain and Europe, R. A. Hume (Usborne)
The Mitchell Beazley Birdwatcher's Pocket Guide, P. Hayman (Mitchell Beazley)
A Field Guide to the Birds of Britain and Europe, R. Peterson, G. Mountfort and P. A. D. Hollom (Collins)
The Birds of Britain and Europe with North Africa and the Middle East, H. Heinzel, R. Fitter and J. Parslow (Collins)
The Atlas of Breeding Birds in Britain and Ireland, J. T. R. Sharrock (T. & A. D. Poyser)
Threatened Birds of Europe, R. Hudson (Macmillan)
Birds – An Illustrated Survey of the Bird Families of the World, J. Gooders (Hamlyn)
The World Atlas of Birds, M. Bramwell (Mitchell Beazley)
Bird Life, J. Nicolai (Thames & Hudson)
The Audubon Society Field Guide to North American Birds, J. Bull and J. Farrand (Knopf)
Birds of North America – A Personal Selection, E. Porter (A & W Visual Library)
Birds and their World, J. Andrews (Hamlyn)
Every Australian Bird Illustrated, P. Wade (Rigby)
The Pictorial Encyclopedia of Birds, J. Hanzak (Hamlyn)
The Illustrated Encyclopedia of Birds, J. Hanzak and J. Formanek (Octopus)
Birds of Britain and Europe, N. Hammond and M. Everett (Pan)
A Field Guide to Australian Birds, P. Slater (Rigby)

Index

193